SOME ASSURED

SOME ASSURED

Nicholas Rhea

severn House

This first world edition published in Great Britain 2004 by
SEVERN HOUSE PUBLISHERS LTD of
9–15 High Street, Sutton, Surrey SM1 1DF.
This first world edition published in the USA 2004 by
SEVERN HOUSE PUBLISHERS INC of
595 Madison Avenue, New York, N.Y. 10022.

British Library Cataloguing in Publication Data

Rhea, Nicholas, 1936-
    Some assured
    1. Insurance agents - England - Yorkshire - Fiction
    2. Yorkshire (England) - Social life and customs - Fiction
    I. Title
    823.9'14 [F]

    ISBN 0-7278-6167-0

Typeset by Palimpsest Book Production Ltd.,
Polmont, Stirlingshire, Scotland.
Printed and bound in Great Britain by
MPG Books Ltd., Bodmin, Cornwall.

One

*'My car was parked legally when
it backed into a bus'*
From a claim form

'Hadn't you better be going?'

Evelyn, my wife, busily feeding two-year-old Paul in his high chair, seemed keen for me to leave the house to start my new job; after all, she'd given her full support when I'd considered changing my work to something that was likely to bring in more money, and I didn't want to be late on my very first day. The fact that I was making these preparations at all was really something quite extraordinary in my rather modest life.

I'd been serving at the counter in the butcher's shop where I was employed, thinking there must be something better I could do with the rest of my life, when an inspector from the Premier happened to come in to buy some meat. He and his wife were spending a few days on holiday in a cottage at Micklesfield, and he was doing the shopping.

At the time I had no idea who he was as I discussed the merits of various cuts and joints, giving my earnest advice about the best piece to purchase or which was likely to be the most tasty or the easiest to carve. He seemed very interested in what I was telling him. When I'd finished, he'd said, 'If you can sell meat like that, young man, you could sell insurance. We're looking for a lively new agent for the Delverdale agency, someone who knows the area well, and can relate to the local people. Would you be interested?'

1

Delverdale was the valley in which I lived. It comprised a collection of tiny moorland villages, including my home village of Micklesfield. Some villages clung to the edges of the moors, others reclined on the exposed and weather-beaten heights and yet more clustered round the banks of the River Delver. That beautiful river joins the upper reaches of the Esk long before it enters the North Sea at Whitby.

When I expressed a modest interest in his proposal, my new friend painted wonderful images of an increased income coupled with happiness, success and security – in fact, I thought he'd have made a good meat salesman. If what he said was true, it did seem to me that with some hard work and enterprise, I might eventually be able to buy a house, afford a car, and even have the telephone installed. One benefit was that I could earn some very good commission in my new job. The harder I worked, the more money I would earn. That would be a wonderful addition to my basic salary and, most certainly, I was not afraid of hard work and long hours. After all, I worked long hours in the butcher's shop for very little reward – although I did get a weekly meat allowance: a joint of beef, lamb or pork, a pound of sausages, a pound of bacon, a pound of black puddings or liver and even a dozen eggs. I could buy other things at a good discount, too, and I was aware that if I took the Premier job I would lose those benefits. Nonetheless, that chance to better myself seemed to outweigh the merits of free meat and eggs. Furthermore, the opportunity for change was both timely and sensible – and something of a challenge.

I'd be working from home, too, and I would get a small allowance to help run my office.

There wasn't really room for an office in my cottage, but I could make use of a corner of one of the downstairs rooms. And, of course, I would go to work in a suit! I wondered if that would make me posh . . . The more I thought about it, the more I began to realize that such a job, with all its flexibility, would be far better than climbing out of bed at dawn to work in a chilly and bloodstained butcher's slaughter house.

No longer would I be standing at the counter all day dealing with customers or delivering joints of meat from the tray of a large black bicycle. Ever since leaving school, that had been my work, other than a wartime spell in the army. I realized, of course, that working for a village butcher was a steady job and moderately secure, but it did lack any opportunity for progression. My apprenticeship had been with George Wade, our local meat purveyor, as his shop sign said. He was a first-class butcher and a good businessman. I had qualified and worked in his tiny shop and slaughterhouse; it was regular employment and quite hard at times but I could see no prospects, especially as George had a son and heir. It meant I'd always be an employee. I'd never be the boss, and, as I was in my late twenties at this point, a lifetime standing at a meat counter or slaughtering animals held little appeal.

Perhaps my army service had unsettled me. The war had interrupted that work – even before I had qualified as a butcher I was called up, to find myself in khaki as a private in the Green Howards. With impeccable military logic, they made me – a trainee butcher – into a motor mechanic and sent me on a course to learn about things like thread clearances, hydraulic brakes, masked inlet valves and fuel pumps. Although I could service military vehicles such as machine gun carriers, jeeps and personnel vehicles, I found myself specializing in motorcycles – the course taught me, among other things, how to strip the gear boxes of BSAs, Royal Enfields and Nortons, how to cope with their electrical bits and how to achieve perfect timing. After the war, I returned to my former trade, which was how I managed to qualify as a time-served butcher; but my war service was very useful, especially if, in my new profession, my trusty Coventry Eagle should ever let me down. Although it did seem to run without any kind of regular maintenance, and a good kick in the right place usually worked wonders if there were problems.

Before the man from the Premier recruited me, I had considered working in a garage, where I could use my army experience and qualifications. I thought my knowledge of motorbikes would appeal to any garage owner, but there were no vacancies for mechanics locally, no full-time openings for motorcycle specialists and not many machine-gun carriers, jeeps or personnel vehicles to maintain in civvy street.

So, having accepted the Premier's challenge, I had successfully applied for the post and attended a three-day induction course. I wondered whether my change of direction had been thrust upon me – certainly things had happened very quickly and I'd had very little time to think about it – but here I was, embarking on my very first day in my brand new job.

My first call was to be at Lexingthorpe, a remote moorland village some ten miles from my home in high dale territory that was somewhat unfamiliar to me. I'd been to Lexingthorpe, but only to pass through it on the train.

I was nervous – anyone would be – but I tried to conceal my anxiety by repeatedly examining my briefcase and its packed contents, making sure I had a map of my rugged North Riding of Yorkshire moorland agency and my list of clients – and potential clients, whose names had been given to me by my predecessor, Jim Villiers, now retired. I was constantly peering into my haversack to check I'd got my sandwiches and flask of tea, and I kept examining my watch.

'Are you sure you've got everything?' Evelyn, her thick brown hair held in place by a hairnet, was hovering like a mother hen. I could see she was excited at my new position in life; her brown eyes were shining, her cheeks pink with happiness. She'd always wanted me to better myself, always saying I was capable of more than serving behind the counter in someone else's shop. Baby Paul, on the other hand, was sitting quietly in his high chair, smothering his face with lashing of porridge from the end of a spoon.

'Yes, yes, I think I've got everything,' I murmured,

opening the briefcase for yet another check of the contents. 'Proposal forms, claim forms, collecting book, list of clients with their addresses, renewal dates for existing clients, business cards, publicity leaflets, plenty of small change, fountain pen full of ink, blotting paper, copying ink pencils . . .'

'Oh, for heaven's sake, Matthew!' she laughed. 'You've gone through all that a hundred times. Just get on your bike and go.'

'Suppose somebody asks me a question I can't answer . . .'

'You can always tell them you don't know, but then it's important that you say you'll find out. You must do that. Find out, I mean. You must find out, you mustn't leave customers without a response. Always be sure to answer their questions even if it takes time, and be honest with them. We were told that at training college – a good teacher will always find an answer for an enquiring pupil. The same principle applies in business as well. Remember that. Don't pretend to know when you don't!'

'Right, I'll remember that, thanks. Well, I must be off. I'm going to Beckside Farm in Lexingthorpe,' I told her. 'Featherstone's place.'

'Yes, you've told me that umpteen times, and then you're going collecting in the rest of Lexingthorpe and you'll be home for tea. You've told me all that, Matthew.'

'Well, I'll be off then, back at five o'clock or thereabouts.'

'I'll be here, and I'll make sure your ham and eggs are ready . . .'

And so, with a deep breath to steady my nerves, I kissed her and Paul goodbye, skilfully avoiding the porridge on his face and the tip of his waving spoon. I did not want porridge all over my suit just before I set off! I struggled into my motorcycle outfit, fastened all the buttons I could find and left the house. I kept my old Coventry Eagle under a lean-to in the garden of our rented cottage; that modest shelter kept the saddle dry in winter and meant

5

the electrical bits didn't get wet. If they did, the bike would not start.

If the wind was coming from the wrong direction, however, the electrical bits could sometimes get wet, which meant drying them and sometimes removing the plug and putting it in the fireside oven to dry and warm up. Most mornings, however, the bike fired after a few sharp kicks on the starter. Even my mechanical skills would not prevent delays and problems in the really severe weather and there were times I was convinced the bike had a mind of its own. I had modified it slightly, fitting a pair of leg shields to ward off the dirt and wet, and adding a couple of panniers over the rear wheel to accommodate my briefcase. While the bike carried its own load, I could cope with my ruck-sack of flask and sandwiches and anything else I required – by carrying it on my back.

Motorbikes were wonderful in fine weather and on dry roads, but in winter they were cold, very wet and dirty, but it was all I could afford. As there was limited public trans-port through Micklesfield – only a modest train service and an even more modest local bus, which did not visit all the villages – I had to provide my own. Trains ran four times a day, two up and two down the dale, but they didn't reach the majority of the moorland villages that formed my agency. Many of the villages did not have a bus service due to the very steep hills and narrow lanes. No bus oper-ator would trust the brakes or gears of their buses – or even their drivers – on those testing roads. Sometimes it was possible to catch a train to one of the villages that was also served by a bus service and complete the rest of the journey by bus, but that took for ever and a day. There was no way I could do my job by relying on trains and buses.

I needed some kind of mechanically propelled vehicle if I was to travel swiftly round my agency, parts of which were very remote. Due to petrol rationing, a motorbike was the answer – it would cover a lot of miles on a tank full of petrol. I had been fortunate to find it in a local sale at rather short notice. A pedal cycle was too slow, too sweat-

6

producing and a guarantee of untidinesss for the rider, hardly the right transport if I was to get round those hilly moorland villages with any degree of dignity in my smart suit. Besides, I couldn't afford a car . . . not yet, anyway. But all that was academic – at this moment the motorbike was all I possessed, albeit with buses and trains to help should I ever have to economize with my petrol coupons.

When I began that first tour, I was clad in my winter motor cycling gear: a thick, heavy army greatcoat, a pair of woollen balaclavas because the wind could penetrate a single one, and wellington boots padded with two pairs of socks. Also, I had a pair of thick leather gauntlets with woollen gloves inside and a pair of goggles of the kind used by pilots in open-topped aeroplanes. That ungainly outfit was designed to keep me fairly warm and dry in the worst of the winter and was ideal for this chilly November morning. Underneath, I was wearing my ill-fitting demob suit, now with a few years of service behind it, but porridge free. It was my only suit, which, until now, I had kept for best, which meant it was really for funerals and weddings. I knew that, round the farms and cottages in which my clients lived, I could park the bike in some convenient place, remove my dirty and cumbersome greatcoat and arrive looking reasonably smart, complete with my briefcase.

I could even leave the bike somewhere in a village as I completed my rounds on foot. I felt rather like the adverts featuring 'The Man From the Premier'. However, I did not wear a smart trilby hat like their model, nor a smart double-breasted suit with a white handkerchief in the breast pocket, nor did I carry a document wallet tucked under my arm.

It is hardly true to say I walked out to my bike. Owing to my solid mass of thick clothing, I waddled with my arms sticking out of the unforgiving layers as I carried my briefcase and gauntlets like a scarecrow holding a pair of turnips; my haversack was on my back and I guessed I must have looked like Scott of the Antarctic or someone from an Arctic whaling boat. Happily, once I had packed things in the panniers the Coventry Eagle fired immediately and soon I was sitting aboard, chugging down the garden path, out of the gate and up through Micklesfield for my first professional call. There was ice about, I noted; some of the puddles were frozen and I knew I must ride with extreme care. But I was fairly young, my reactions were swift and I was a very capable motorcyclist – icy roads held no terrors for me. We were accustomed to such conditions on our moors.

As I was passing the butcher's shop, however, I noticed a small crowd outside, and when they heard my bike approaching one of the bystanders – Tony Wade – waved me to a halt. Puzzled, I braked and sat astride the bike, engine running, as Tony ran towards me.

'It is you in there, isn't it, Matt? Under all that armour plating?' he peered into my face, so I lifted the goggles and rested them on my forehead.

'Good morning, Tony,' I greeted him. 'Yes, it's me. A bit on the chilly side today, isn't it?'

'Watch the roads,' he said. 'Seriously, they're treacherous. I stopped you because Dad's had a nasty fall this morning . . . on the ice . . . he's broken his leg . . .'

My heart sank at the news. 'I can't help you out, Tony, I've got a new job you know. I'm on my way to see a client, my very first, in fact.'

'It's not that. I'm not asking you to come back to us.' he smiled. 'We'll cope, we'll have to, but it's our day for delivering in Freyerthorpe and when I saw you going up the street, I wondered if you're heading that way . . .'

'I am, yes, I'm going through Freyerthorpe, but I've no room for a vanload of meat, my panniers are nearly full.'

'I'm not asking you to deliver for us,' he said. 'I just wondered if you could call on Miss Gibbons at Hartside. She's our first call. Tell her Dad's broken his leg so she'll have to do without her bacon, sausages and liver, at least for the time being. It's a bit of an emergency but we should get someone to do his rounds very soon, later today with a bit of luck, once we get ourselves organized.'

'That should be no problem, I'll be going right past her front door.'

'Good. Make sure to tell her we haven't forgotten her and ask her to pass the word around her village. We should be back in action later today, and by tomorrow we should be back to normal.'

'Oh, right, yes, I'll pass the word on,' I assured him, for most of the moorfolk did not have telephones. Word of mouth was a very efficient means of communication in the moorland villages. 'No problem. I'm sorry about your dad!'

'We could do with you here, Matt, I don't mind admitting that, but we've got a new lad to take your place, an apprentice. He's just out of school and needs careful training, he can't work unsupervised just yet. The snag is he can't ride even the bike with a full load of meat in the tray . . . wobbles all over, he does, the local dogs have a wonderful time picking up all the sausages and liver he loses overboard.'

'He'll learn, I had to. Anyway, give my best wishes to your dad,' I said, adding quickly, 'And tell him he should be insured . . . you can get a good policy, you know, to cover things like having to take time off work due to injuries!'

'He'll not spend money on insurance, Matt, he's a Yorkshireman, remember!'

'Maybe, but while he's off work he'll have time to think about it afresh. It makes a lot of sense, you know. I could pop in sometime and maybe do a bit of business with him.'

Tony laughed and slapped me on the back. 'You can try, we've been nagging him for years. Maybe this broken leg'll convince him . . .' and he turned away to rejoin the little group outside the shop.

I slipped my goggles back over my eyes, revved up the bike and then realized I could actually carry Miss Gibbons' order. I was sure there was enough room in my rucksack.

'Tony!' I called after him, and he halted before returning to the shop.

'Yes?'

9

'If there's only Miss Gibbons' order, I could take it. If I'm calling on her anyway, it's no problem, there's room for her order in my rucksack.'

'No, it doesn't matter. We've got three deliveries in Freyerthorpe today . . . one joint of beef at Mrs Blenkin's, six pork chops and a pound of mince for Miss Newton, and Miss Gibbons' order. We'll get someone to take the stuff once we get ourselves sorted out.'

'Well, if it'll help you, I'm sure I could fit all those orders into my rucksack . . . I wouldn't want such good customers of yours to go without their dinners.'

'Well, if it's no trouble, it would help us out of a pickle.'

And so I found my rucksack being stuffed with pieces of wrapped meat, all labelled with the customers' names and with the prices shown. Tony thanked me profusely, saying I'd got him out of a mess, because Miss Gibbons was not the easiest of customers, especially when she felt she'd been let down or ignored. And so it was that I swept away, pleased to do something to help my former boss in his hour of need. And, of course, when, in the fullness of time, I approached him with a view to taking out some kind of personal insurance, he might be sympathetic.

First call, therefore, would now be at Miss Gibbons in Freyerthorpe followed by the others, so it would be some time before I got to the Featherstones' farm in Lexingthorpe. Fortunately, I had not made an appointment – I was going on spec.

When I arrived at Miss Gibbons' little terrace cottage, my fingers were frozen and my cheeks felt as if they were blocks of marble rather than human flesh, but I hoisted the bike on to its rest, unpacked her order and waddled in my cumbersome motorcycle gear towards her smart back door. People seldom went to the front door of these moorland homes; almost the only time they were used was during important events such as weddings or funerals, or visits by important people and strangers. Miss Gibbons had a front garden the size of a postage stamp and a little Jack Russell terrier that barked at the window as it spotted what must have looked like a man from outer space ambling along the path to the rear of the house. I rapped on the door then lifted my goggles and waited. A fussy little seventy-ish woman with grey hair and a flowered apron opened the door and stared at me as her dog barked.

'Go away, I don't want anything today, go away or I'll call the police,' and she prepared to slam the door.

I was tempted to prevent her with a well-timed and carefully placed foot in the door, but decided it wasn't a good idea, so, as the door was being closed, I almost shouted that I had brought her meat from Wade's.

In spite of that, there was questioning hostility in her eyes, but the door remained open. 'You're not Mr Wade. What's happened to Mr Wade? He always brings my order, not one of his underlings. In a van, too, I might add, much more hygenic.' And she glared at my motorbike on its stand.

I explained that George had broken his leg on the ice this morning and that he was doing his best to find a relief driver so that he could accommodate all his customers. As I was speaking, I removed my rucksack from my back and extracted the package bearing her name. I passed it to her.

She looked at it with a frown on her face, accepted it and opened it while I stood there.

'There's no kidney, young man. This isn't my order.'

'Well, it's got your name on and it was handed to me by the shop, I don't work there, so I can't help.'

'This is no good, young man, this kind of sloppy treatment of customers. Why is my kidney missing? Tell me that! And, more important, what are you going to do about it?'

She was treating me like a junior member of George Wade's staff and I decided I was not going to tolerate this. I was doing a favour for both George and Miss Gibbons, so I took two steps back, well beyond the reach of the meat if she decided to thrust it back into my hands. Somewhat angrily, I explained that I had to visit a client higher up the dale, that I was not working for Wade's any longer and that

11

George would do his best to attend to her requirements as soon as he could.

'How do you think I'm going to manage until he finds somebody? And how long will it be? I have no telephone to make my orders, not without walking to the kiosk in the village, and then there's the question of getting the meat here – with a kidney I might add – and then paying for it. I don't want folks to think I don't pay my way . . .'

'I'm sure Mr Wade will organize something. His accident only happened this morning, so he's hardly had time to make arrangements . . .' I got the impression she wasn't really listening.

'So who are you then?' she asked eventually.

'Matthew Taylor from Micklesfield. I used to work for Wade's, before the war and until just recently. Now I'm with Premier Assurance—'

'Well, so long as you don't try to sell me any insurance, you can fetch my meat for me, and remember next time I want a kidney as well, and once a month I get a big joint of beef . . .'

'I don't expect to be delivering meat—'

'Well, somebody will have to, I can't get to the shops. In the meantime here's the money.' And she dug into her apron pocket to find the necessary one and ninepence. 'Give that to Wade's and tell them I want the same next week, with a kidney. Remember that, with a kidney. I insist on a kidney.'

'Yes but—'

'No buts. And I don't want insurance at my age, I'm in a funeral club, which will see to things when I go. Goodbye, Mr Taylor.'

With no more ado, she closed the door and I was left standing on the doorstep with her money in my hand. I had little alternative but to take it and hand it over to Wade's when I returned this evening, but I must make sure I did not get it mixed up with my own business cash, or my personal pocket money. I placed it in the gigantic pocket of my greatcoat and made a mental note not to forget it.

12

Then I prepared to resume my journey. I had just kicked the Coventry Eagle into life when I became aware of a young woman running along the lane towards me.

Dressed in men's overalls and black wellingtons, she looked distraught, her blond hair flying as she ran towards me. Her arms were waving as she shouted something. I couldn't hear what she was saying so I turned off the engine. She would be about fifteen or sixteen, I estimated, and was very pretty, with a good figure beneath her unflattering clothes. I did not know her but waited to see how I could help.

'You must . . . come . . .' She could hardly gasp out the words. 'Somebody must . . . come quickly . . . please . . . please say you'll come . . .'

I was still astride the bike when she reached me.

'What's wrong?'

She was now standing at my side, panting heavily, and I waited for her to regain her breath. 'It's . . . Milly,' she gasped, standing with a stoop as she rested her hands on her knees while taking huge gasps of breath. 'Please come . . . somebody must help me . . . I was going to ask Miss Gibbons but you might help me . . . please say you will.'

'Yes, I will, but what's the problem?'

By this stage Miss Gibbons had reappeared at her doorway and was standing watching the little drama unfolding almost on her doorstep. It never occurred to me that she might think this was some kind of personal domestic drama that I'd brought with me, but soon the girl had regained her breath and she could speak coherently.

'Milly . . . the foal's coming . . . there's only me . . . please help me . . .'

'Foal?' I cried. 'Coming when?'

'Now, it's stuck. Milly's in agony. It won't come . . . I need help, I can't get it out . . . and Milly's so tired . . .'

'If it's stuck, it'll be the head, so you'll have to bring it round and you might need a rope to help the final push!' Miss Gibbons' eavesdropping had now given her an idea of what was happening and she began to give advice from the doorstep. Clearly she knew something about foals and horses, but she was an old lady and the girl was in a desperate hurry . . . And I had the motorbike. I could take her there, wherever 'there' was. Miss Gibbons began to shout at me, telling me to hurry and to remember to use a rope. I heard her say something about freeing the foal's head and using the rope to help the mare. I must admit it all meant very little at that moment.

Trying to absorb Miss Gibbons' advice, I told the girl to jump on to the pillion and direct me to her house. I had no idea what I would do when I arrived, but within seconds we were tearing along the lane and after a few hundred yards she guided me through a gate and into a stable yard, which was part of a large farm complex. As I halted she jumped off and ran towards an open door shouting, 'In here, in here.'

I parked the bike but had no time to remove my cumbersome overcoat, although I did cast away my twin balaclava helmets and gauntlets during my ungainly gallop into the stable. Inside it was rather gloomy, but I could literally hear the deep sighs and groans from the mare. Then I saw her standing in her stall, head down, sweating profusely, her flanks heaving from what I was later to learn had been hours of effort.

She was a beautiful Cleveland bay, a fine chestnut colour, and I could see a pair of small hoofed feet protruding from beneath her tail as she pressed and thrust with her tired and aching muscles. The new foal was not moving; it seemed to be stuck solid.

During my butchering days I'd heard about foals' heads getting twisted and jammed inside the birth canal, about people turning them into the normal birth position and then using ropes to help ease them out. At this point I realized that Miss Gibbons had provided me with sound advice. Fearful that the mare might lash out with her hind legs and kick me, I approached very cautiously with the girl, watching every move. First, I took hold of both tiny hooves and tugged them gently as the horse whimpered

14

and shivered. The foal was completely stuck, and I realized Miss Gibbons had been absolutely right: its head must be fast somewhere. From my butchering experience, I knew that this was a fairly common condition, so I reached inside the mare, pressing my arm in deep, and found the foal's head. I could feel it, and it was twisted. I knew that if we forced out the foal it would be strangled and would die and so, with the poor horse groaning and sweating, I began to turn the head gently, very gently to be sure I was presenting it in the right position. Then, suddenly, it moved and slid between the tops of the foal's outstretched front legs, still inside the mother. It felt right and so I withdrew my hand. The head was resting between the legs now, streamlining the operation like a skilled diver heading into the water. I took hold of the little ankles above the hooves but they were covered with slime of some kind, and when I tugged my hands simply slid off.

I could not maintain a grip and there was nothing else to seize.

'We need a rope,' I said, recalling Miss Gibbons' advice, and the girl found one hanging from a hook.

In seconds I had fashioned it into a pair of loops but decided its roughness might damage the tender skin of this newborn foal, so I asked the girl to find a rag, a piece of blanket or sheet, which I wrapped tightly round the foal's ankles before lashing the rope over it. Thus I had a primitive but effective noose cushioned round both legs.

Then, sweating profusely in my heavy coat, I said, 'I've realigned the head. It should come now with a bit of a push from the mare. If you can take the weight of the foal as it comes out, I'll haul on this rope . . . I've got to be careful, though, that I don't damage the foal, its skin will be very tender . . . Ready?'

The girl indicated she was ready and said she understood, and then she spoke to the mare, who whinnied pitifully. Clearly the animal was in pain and distress, and she stood there showing no sign of wishing to continue this difficult and painful birth.

'Come on, Milly, come on, one last push . . .'

As the girl called those words, I put my weight on the rope, gently at first, and when the mare felt the tension it encouraged her to try just once more. Now that the head was in the right position for birth, the foal began to move. I felt the movement, just a very small one at first, but it was definitely there.

I maintained my pressure on the rope, but now it was all down to that brave mare, who turned to look at me with her large dark eyes. Her flanks began to heave as she groaned loudly, as if realizing this was the final effort.

'It's coming, it's coming,' I called to the girl. 'Help it if you can, try to make the mare understand it's happening. If it comes out take the weight . . . it's easier now . . .'

'Look, the head's showing . . . look, oh, wonderful . . . come on Milly . . .'

I saw the head appear, tucked between the front legs like a diver's head between the arms, and once the head had cleared the narrow part of the birth canal, the rest was comparatively easy. Within minutes, a wet, slimy and slightly smelly brown foal with two white forelegs was lying on the straw, with the mother licking it and the girl attempting to clean it with handfuls of straw.

'Oh thank you, thank you . . .' Instantly, she became absorbed in her task, and my presence faded in her new world.

'Will you be all right now?' I asked, wondering how the girl had come to be left on her own at this time.

'Oh, yes, but isn't he lovely . . . Yes, thank you, and thank you for coming . . . I'm so relieved you were there, I didn't know what to do. Dad had to take mum to hospital in a rush, and I was left on my own.'

'I'm pleased to help,' I wondered who owned this farm; it was large, spacious and very clean, and, clearly, it was a horse-loving family.

'Milly wasn't due until tomorrow; we didn't expect this just now and there's no one around . . . You were very kind . . .'

16

I could see the girl did not wish to leave the foal, but I had to ask if I could wash my hands, and she directed me into the scullery. When I peered into the stable, the mare was still snuffling and prodding the foal with her nose and licking it as the girl sat beside it on the straw, cleaning it, stroking it and talking to Milly. I bade my farewell but I don't think she heard me. As I mounted my motorbike, I realized I didn't even know the girl's name, although as I left the premises I did see the name on the gate: Hollin Farm.

My next two deliveries were straightforward – they were pieces of meat, not foals, and I even got a very welcome cup of coffee at one of the houses. Then, somewhat later than I'd intended, I made for the Featherstones' farm. I had to check the location on my map because I was not familiar with this part of the higher dale, but Beckside Farm was clearly marked. Soon I was chugging down the rough unsurfaced track and as I carefully descended the steep hill, taking care not to skid on the loose surface or any lurking patches of ice, I could see the complex of buildings far below me. From here I enjoyed an elevated view of the dale.

This was tough country; the farm nestled in a deep cleft in the hills, while on the horizon above were the bleak heather-clad moors with craggy outcrops and acres of gorse bushes but no trees. Typical Delverdale country. Rivulets of fast-moving water divided the hillsides into patches of boulder-strewn land with sheep grazing on them and with dry stone walls clinging to the slopes almost as if by magic.

As the name indicated, Beckside Farm stood close to the River Delver, at this point little more than a fast-flowing moorland stream.

As it flowed down Delverdale, it broadened considerably before joining the River Esk and ultimately the North Sea, and, like the Esk, was noted for its trout and salmon. Many riverside properties had their own fishing rights, although some stretches of water belonged to angling clubs and there were other areas where the public could fish.

Beckside was a large farm, I realized, considerably bigger than most of the hill farms of this region, and, as I grew closer, I could see several people moving between the buildings. There was a number of farm vehicles in the yard, too. There appeared to be some kind of gathering and I began to wonder whether I should intrude, particularly as I had not made an appointment. Clearly something was happening, and I did not wish to gatecrash a family celebration or interrupt a demonstration of agricultural machinery or whatever it might be; then I realized a man was pointing at me. At this stage a handful of men gathered to observe my final approach – my precarious and nerve-racking descent over a rough, boulder-strewn track, which at times, I knew, would become a torrent of running water and which, this morning, had patches of ice in places the sun had not touched. Then I entered the farmyard, where I rode past a bare creel and an empty scalding tub, both indications of a pig-killing session. Now I realized what the purpose was of this gathering. It was a pig-killing day.

I chugged towards a concreted patch where I could safely park the bike on its stand and, having safely achieved this, I dismounted and was lifting up my goggles and unbuttoning my gigantic coat when one of the men appeared at my side.

He was very large and wore a thick sweater, corduroy jacket, corduroy trousers and brown leather boots with leggings. In his late forties, he had the red face of an outdoor worker, and a bristling ginger moustache, which complemented his thinning hair.

'What time's thoo call this?' he barked at me.

Several more men had arrived by this time, and were surrounding me, all looking far from pleased. All stood round me with angry faces, and I thought they looked like a lynching party. Certainly they were very threatening in appearance and I began to wonder about my personal safety.

'Time?' with an effort I hauled up my thick sleeves to check my watch. 'Ten past eleven,' I said.

'Ten past eleven, 'e says!' bellowed the ginger-haired one. 'Ten past bloody eleven! And what time did thoo tell us thoo'd git 'ere?'

'Time? I didn't give a time . . . I just came on spec . . .'

'Thoo did not come on spec! Thoo gave us a time. Eight o'clock, thoo said. Eight o'clock . . . and what time is it now? Gone eleven. Us chaps 'ave been waiting 'ere like charlies for three hours when we should 'ave bin deeaing other things.'

'There must have been some mistake,' I spluttered. 'I did not make any appointment . . . and I've no idea why you should all be here . . . waiting like this . . .'

'Well thoo made the bloody arrangements, or thy boss did, we were told thoo'd be 'ere tiday and thoo'd see ti ivverything.'

'Look, are you Mr Featherstone?' I tried to gain some kind of ascendancy.

'That's me, wheear else wad Ah be?'

'My predecessor, Jim Villiers from the Premier Assurance Association, suggested I call here today. I'm the new agent—'

'Thoo's nut t' butcher then, 'ere to kill oor pigs?' His questioning statement was followed by a long silence and a gradual dawning upon their hard faces.

'No, I am not the butcher!' I was beginning to think I would never rid myself of my former profession. 'I came here to discuss possible insurance cover, life insurance for you with All Risks policies for your farm and out-buildings . . . So which butcher are you expecting?'

'George Wade from Micklesfield, or rather 'is lad. George said he wad send 'is lad oot tiv us tiday. There were some deliveries in Freyersthorpe and 'e reckoned 'e could fit us in at eight . . . all on us. Seven pigs. If Ah'd got a telephone Ah'd 'ave bin ringing up and playing hell.'

'George has broken his leg,' I told them. By this stage, having rid myself of my overcoat, balaclavas and goggles, I was now standing before them in my smart suit, albeit

19

with wellingtons on my feet. 'He won't be coming and I'll bet Tony has forgotten all about you amid this morning's panic.'

'God Almighty, this would happen! We've customers waiting, we've got all t' gear 'ere, 'ired or borrowed for t'day, us chaps here with our pigs, copper full of boiling watter all ready an' waiting, women keen ti git rendering . . . Thoo can't just reorganize things at t'drop of an 'at, thoo knaws, it all taks planning and time.'

'I'll do it,' I said. 'I'll kill your pigs.'

'Thoo'll deea it? Did thoo 'ear that, lads? This smart-suited young feller says 'e'll kill oor pigs. Ah'll bet thoo disn't knaw a hock frev a ham, or its swathe side frev its backside!'

'I qualified with George Wade,' I told him. 'I'm time-served, a fully qualified butcher, and I'll bet I've killed more pigs than you've had hot dinners. Now I see the creel and scalding tub are ready, so if you want those pigs killed today, Mr Featherstone, you'd better find me a pair of over-alls, some proper knives and scrapers, all sharpened like cut-throat razors, a humane killer, and get somebody to bring that copper back to the boil . . .'

It took a long time but, with the willing assistance of those men and their wives, I killed all seven pigs and left the women to make the scrappings and brawn and to dispense the traditional pig-cheer. Mrs Featherstone – Ada – provided a superb dinner – dinner being the midday meal – and before I left, Mr Featherstone said, 'Ah deearn't rightly knaw 'ow ti thank thoo, Mr Taylor, but there'll be t' butchering fee, and my missus'll mak sure thoo gits some scrappings and a bowl o' brawn.'

'How about taking out an insurance policy?' I laughed, reminding myself of Jim Villiers' warning that a Yorkshire farmer sticks to his money like muck to a blanket. He did warn me I'd have difficulty persuading these chaps to spend money on something invisible.

'Ah'm a bit busy right noo,' Featherstone said. 'But 'ow

about next week? And if Ah was thoo, I'd drop in ti see them mates o' mine. We all owe you summat, you see, all on us.'

I heard myself launch into my untested sales patter about the merits of life assurance, endowment policies, mortgage protection, specialist livestock insurance, house and buildings insurance with combined burglary and fire risks, and personal insurance in case of injury or accident, not only for the breadwinner but all family members. I went on to tell them all about the special rates that might be effective if all the vehicles, both those on the farm and those used for domestic purposes, were included, along with agricultural machinery. Insurance of livestock was a specialist area, I had to explain, although we might consider insuring, say, a prize bull or ram, or a horse such as a stallion, mare or hunter. Specialist insurers or perhaps an agricultural mutual society might consider insuring flocks of sheep or herds of cattle, and there were policies against ramblers leaving gates open and lightning striking barns or even animals. My chat was, I suppose, a resumé of the three-day induction course I'd attended before starting work.

'As Ah said, Mr Taylor, we're all a bit thrang reet now, but call on thi rounds next time you're up this way. We'll nut forgit what thoo did for us. Thoo gat us oot of a spot, thoo did, mak neear mistak.'

Upon leaving Beckside Farm (without securing any business) I checked my collecting book to see which clients lived nearby, and called on them; the insurance man was expected, I realized, and from those who were not at home I found ready money on window-ledges, in outside toilets, under plant pots – places all mentioned by my other clients. They were most helpful, giving me advice such as, 'You're new, but Mr Villiers allus called on Mrs Parkinson before dinner, but if she's out the money'll be under that stone near the trough at the back door . . .'

* * *

And so I concluded my first day's work. As I rode home, I realized I'd experienced two of life's ineluctable aspects – birth and death – and somehow those events presaged the rest of my career. I would not be creating life or death, but each would figure large in my new profession. I found that very interesting and thought-provoking, but when I arrived home Evelyn brought me back to earth by asking, 'Well, did you get any new business? Earn any commission?'

'No, but I got a lot of promises and did some collecting – and I helped a mare give birth to a foal, I killed seven pigs and delivered some meat . . .'

'Killed pigs? And foaled a mare?' I could see she did not believe me, but after I'd changed out of my suit, had a wash and settled down to my tea, I told her about my day.

'So you've been butchering all day and haven't earned any commission for the new job you're supposed to be doing?' she said pointedly.

'No, but George Wade did give me a shilling for delivering those orders, and he insisted on giving me thirty bob for my pig killing, and all those farmers said I must contact them again to discuss their insurance . . .'

Before going to bed that night, though, I made a note in my diary to call on Farmer Featherstone in the future, and I must just drop in at Hollin Farm to see how the foal was progressing. One way or another, Yorkshiremen or not, I would do my best to persuade Featherstone and his pals to take out some policies – as someone once said, 'There are more ways of killing a pig . . .' I must admit I wondered if there was a policy to cover butchers who failed to turn up on pig-killing days? Or insurance men who might get kicked when foaling horses?

A week or so after the foaling event, I received a letter from Mrs Hebron at Hollin Farm, who thanked me for helping her daughter, Sandra, with the birth. She'd obtained my name and address from Miss Gibbons and said mother and foal were doing very well indeed. She suggested that I call soon because she wanted to insure the new arrival.

'He's a fine stallion,' she added in her note. 'He's going to be valuable asset to our stable and, for your part in saving his life, we're going to call him Matthew.'

Two

*'I thought my window was down but when I put
my head through it, I realized it wasn't'*
From a claim form

As I was working from home, I needed space for a desk,
some shelves and perhaps a filing cabinet, but in our
two-up two-down rented terrace cottage there was scarcely
anywhere suitable. The small back bedroom upstairs was
Paul's, and I could not use that, particularly if clients were
liable to visit me at all hours; the same applied to the
bedroom I shared with Evelyn. We did not want strangers
in there! There was no bathroom and no upstairs toilet, our
bath being a zinc coffin-shaped tub, which we filled with
hot water when required and bathed in in front of the kitchen
fire. The bath-tub hung from a nail in the outside washhouse when not in use, and we made sure the curtains were
shut and doors locked when it was!

None of the outbuildings was suitable as an office – I
kept my motorbike under a shelter outside, and the other
main outbuilding was the washhouse, which contained the
copper and mangle. We also kept things like the poss tub,
zinc bath, logs and other assorted necessities in there.

Downstairs there was a back kitchen with an open fire
in its black-leaded grate, an oven next to that, and a hot
water back boiler. There was also an electric cooker with
a grill, and we lived and ate in that cosy room. Adjoining
it was a tiny scullery, which was used for washing up, and
an even smaller pantry with a cold shelf made of concrete.

The front room, sometimes called the best room and

24

sometimes the sitting room, opened on to the small front garden. It was light and airy in summer, and in winter, with the fire glowing, it was cosy and comfortable. We only used it on special occasions such as Christmas Day or Sundays in winter if we had visitors. As a wedding present, our respective parents had helped us furnish it, and I did not like to sully it with something as unattractive as a desk and filing cabinet, but there was no alternative. It was the only possible room to which we could invite my clients, and the only one not in daily use.

'I'll agree on condition it's only temporary.' Evelyn was adamant. 'We need a bigger house, Matthew. You need somewhere for an office, and as Paul gets older he'll need more space, and we mustn't forget he might have a little brother or sister one day.'

'Hang on, we're nowhere near that stage yet . . .'

'I know we're being careful, but you must look ahead, Matthew, plan for the future. Isn't that why you took the insurance job? To earn more? To better yourself?'

'Yes but—'

'No buts, Matthew. So while you're out on your rounds, keep your ears and eyes open for a bigger house. I'll ask around the village when I'm out and about, too. Didn't you say the Premier will help you buy one? Don't they offer staff mortgages or some kind of help? Paying rent means we'll never own a house. It's like throwing money down the drain with nothing at the end of it. I would love a place of our own, really I would.'

She was right, of course. In her big Catholic family, Evelyn, along with her seven brothers and sisters, had been brought up in a spacious house that her parents owned. It was the Unicorn Inn, one of the local pubs in Micklesfield. Owing to their hard work, it was a thriving establishment with bedroom accommodation for guests, many of whom were anglers who came to fish the Esk and the Delver for the famous salmon and trout. It was known for its good food, fine ales, comfortable rooms and annual autumn sheep sale.

25

On the cobbles outside the Unicorn was a fruit and vegetable market. It was held every Wednesday and had been ever since the reign of Edward III – more than 500 years, in spite of wars and weather. The inn was also a working farm. It had been in Evelyn's family for generations, the idea being that the woman of the household looked after the bar and the accommodation while the men ran the farm. A country inn was rarely viable on its own; it could not support a man and his family, especially one as large as the Meads. In fact, many of the local inns were also farms. In every respect, it was a busy life, and Evelyn's parents were both hard working and generous. They were much better off than mine – my dad was the gardener at The Grange in Micklesfield, and lived in a small tied bungalow with my mother, who was a domestic help in the same house.

During these discussions I remembered that Evelyn's dad, Derek Mead, had lots of empty outbuildings. I began to wonder if he'd allow me to use one as an office. Conversion would not be all that difficult as most of the farm outbuildings were well built, dry and spacious.

It was just a passing thought, perhaps born out of desperation – but for the time being I would have to settle for a corner in our sitting room.

My work quickly fell into a regular routine. There were two main tasks: collecting and canvassing. On collecting days, I had to travel around the twenty or so small village communities within my Delverdale agency to collect premiums, almost invariably in cash; on canvassing days I called on potential customers in an attempt to persuade them to take out new or additional insurance. On many days I combined the two aspects of my work, although, from time to time, my bosses liked me to concentrate entirely upon generating new business, hence the need for occasional dedicated canvassing days. Often they would have specific targets in mind, say small businesses – such as builders and plumbers – householders, farmers, livestock breeders, vehicle operators, churches and chapels, and so forth. It is fair to say that motor vehicle policies provided a hefty slice of my regular turnover plus a secondary income from the commission I earned even if the premiums were paid annually. Most weeks several motor insurances were due for renewal or transfer to other vehicles, and, likewise, if a house was insured the policy had to be renewed annually. That kind of ongoing business kept me fairly busy throughout the year.

Collecting days were very routine, even mundane, particularly as most of my clients knew when I was due. Most of this work involved small domestic policies that covered things like funeral expenses, illness or injury at work, or perhaps a modest home fire insurance. These cost only a few pence per week. Some were as low as one penny per week.

Although I tried to collect such small premiums once a year or perhaps once a month, there were some I had to collect weekly because the policyholders had extremely modest incomes. Finding money to settle even small accounts each month was difficult for them, especially as they hated the idea of getting into debt, however small. For this reason I made lots of weekly calls to collect only very tiny amounts. In spite of their poverty, most of these policyholders had the money ready and waiting on the anticipated day of my visit. The poorer the policy holder, the more likely they were to have their money ready, while those with bigger incomes, who spent more on living expenses, would sometimes hide behind locked doors or make a point of being out. The residents of one village, Crossrigg, were particularly noted for that tendency.

My agency was wholly rural, although it might be said that Crossrigg was a small island of industry within an expansive, picturesque and unspoilt moorland setting. Some local people, who had not travelled far during their lives, thought it was a town, because it had a Co-Op store, a railway junction and a brickworks in addition to the usual shop, post office, churches and pubs. Because substantial clay deposits discovered nearby were ideal for manufacturing household bricks, tiles and drainpipes, this village had developed into a miniature industrial complex, something of a blot on the landscape, with its smoking chimneys, rows of brick kilns and masses of railway lines with trucks and little smoking engines.

Being pseudo-industrial, the people who worked there – around 150 (most of the men in the village) – did not behave like other country people. Their behaviour and outlook on life was rather more like that of labouring townies. Although their wages were higher than the country folk and other farm workers who inhabited the moors, they did not leave their premiums on window-ledges or in the outside toilets. The reasons I received for this were (a) because the money might get stolen and (b) because Crossrigg wage earners had more important things to do with their money, such as spending it in the pubs or betting on the horses. One valuable piece of advice left by my predecessor, Jim Villiers was, 'When you go collecting in Crossrigg, always go on a Monday. The men get paid on Saturday mornings, they can't spend it all on Saturday nights or Sundays, although some have a damned good try, but with a bit of luck they'll hand over some housekeeping to their wives so there'll be enough left for you on Monday. And be sure to go collecting there *every* Monday. Never wait until later in the week – and remember, people such as debt collectors, money lenders, local tradesmen and others are all trying to get their share of that same money! Make sure you get there first!'

His advice was cherished because every Wednesday before 1.00 p.m. I had to visit the post office in Micklesfield to pay in the monies I had collected, and for that my books had to balance. The Premier Assurance Association held an account there, which meant that each Wednesday morning was spent checking the columns in my cash books and taking my weekly salary and commission out of my collected monies along with any expenses for postage, phone calls from the kiosk or petrol.

Clearly, it looked better on paper if I collected enough

28

each week to cover my own wages, plus a little profit for the Premier – although if there was a shortfall then I could draw money from the company's account. Over the course of a year, things balanced out with a hefty profit for the Premier because some weekly collections produced considerable sums.

One Wednesday I made my usual visit to the post office in Micklesfield High Street with my bags of cash and found a curious sight at the high wooden counter. It was an elderly and very hairy man in a long black overcoat with a basket of crockery balanced on his head. It was like watching those wonderfully elegant African ladies who can carry almost the entire contents of their home upon their heads, except, of course, this fellow was by no means elegant. I knew this scruffy man. It was Crocky Morris from Crossrigg, who was renowned locally both for his amazing balancing skills and for his equally amazing capacity for copious quantities of beer. Immediately, I became concerned, because Crocky was swaying from side to side and backwards and forwards, somehow achieving all this at the same time, still with the basket in place. It was almost like watching one of those circus performers who can balance a plate on a stick and keep it there by twirling the stick even when lying on their backs or stomachs on the floor, kneeling down or performing somersaults.

As I stood behind him, Crocky was twirling and swaying, and I was almost hypnotized by the ever-moving basket of plates, cups and saucers, waiting for the inevitable crash of broken china. It never came, though.

Crocky never let the basket fall from his head, and this had made him into something of a legend in Delverdale. Today, he was tipsy – very tipsy in fact, certainly more than just slightly drunk. I think he had been to the Unicorn, because it was open all day on market day – and I guessed he would return before the day was out. He had probably left the bar only temporarily so he could sell a few pieces of crockery to raise some cash for more drinks. Being tipsy was a normal state of affairs for Crocky. His speech was almost always slurred and on this occasion he was trying to produce a serious conversation with the postmistress as he swayed from side to side like a blade of grass blowing in a brisk breeze. I didn't know whether to vacate the rather cramped premises in case I unwittingly caused him to over-balance his basket, or whether I should halt the proceedings by offering to lift the basket down from its precarious perch. It transpired, however, that neither was necessary, because soon after I entered he lifted the basket off his head and placed it carefully on the floor, then took out a cup and saucer, handed it to the postmistress and accepted her payment for them. He slipped the money into his pocket, wobbled alarmingly as he struggled to maintain his balance, then, with one swift and very smooth movement, lifted the basket back on to his head and made for the door. With the basket only just avoiding the edges of the doorway as the door stood open to allow his exit, and somehow balancing it even though he'd removed some of the items, the apparition vanished. I saw him pass the window as he turned down the High Street, and wondered how far his travels would take him that day.

Crocky was a familiar figure in all the Delverdale villages, travelling out to them from Crossrigg by train with his basket on his head. He made sure to visit all the local pubs, and Wednesday was his day in Micklesfield, owing to the market-day extension of the pub's liquor licence.

Local legend said he'd never dropped his basket, although there was one unconfirmed rumour that he'd once inad-vertently left it behind in a pub whereupon the locals had filled all his teapots with the dregs from pint pots of ale. Crocky had walked out with the basket on his head, managing to keep it safely balanced, even with the ale sloshing about above him.

'That basket's going to come a cropper one of these days!' I smiled at the postmistress, Jenny Blenkiron. She was a lady in her late sixties with a mass of thick curly grey hair and very florid cheeks; towering to more than six feet in height, she ran the post office most efficiently and was known for her ability to count pound notes and ten shilling notes with just two fingers of her left hand.

'Crocky's always like that, Matthew, and the more he drinks the more he seems capable of keeping that basket aloft. And I've no idea how he keeps the basket balanced when he takes things out . . . you'd think the whole lot would come crashing down if he took a full set of tea cups and saucers out – but it doesn't.'

Even at that early stage of making my acquaintance with Crocky, it was apparent he was something of a liability both to himself and to others.

Not surprisingly, I began to wonder if he ought to be insured, not necessarily for the loss or breakage of his precious basket of pots, but for what he might unwittingly cause to happen to others. I decided I would try to have a word with him, not that day but on some future occasion when he was not quite so affected by drink.

As we chatted, Jenny accepted my bag of pound notes, ten shilling notes and loose silver and copper, with just the occasional cheque, checking the contents with her usual efficiency and marking them off against the form I'd completed. She was familiar with this work: each week I paid in lots of notes and coins because so few people hereabouts had bank accounts. When her calculations corresponded with my figures she endorsed my forms with the post office rubber stamp and I was relieved, once again, of a very weighty bag of money.

'I'll be away next week,' she told me. 'I'm going to see my sister in the Lake District, but my niece will look after things. I'll tell her about your regular visits, Matthew, it shouldn't present any problems.'

I thanked her and left, deciding to use the afternoon for a spot of combined collecting and canvassing in Gaitingsby, a small village some two miles away. One great advantage of my job was that I could make my own hours and be as flexible as I wished, provided my commitments were fulfilled. Inevitably, there was some evening work, when a potential client could see me only after finishing his or her

31

own daily job, and there were a few weekend duties for the same reason, but, in the main, I could work a leisurely day between nine and five.

Because Wednesday mornings were accounted for with my bookkeeping, Wednesday afternoons meant I often tried to select a nearby village for a spot of canvassing and some collecting. On this occasion, I decided to visit Wilf Burgess, the joiner in Gaitingsby; I was fascinated by his workshop with its all-pervading scent of freshly planed wood, the piles of shavings, the tools he had arrayed along his walls and the variety of objects he created. He seemed to make everything from cart wheels to wardrobes via tables and chairs, chests of drawers and even children's toys. He kept these in what had once been a cowshed but was now a spacious storeroom adjoining his workshop. I must admit that, on this occasion, my call was prompted by something other than a sales pitch. I'd heard from local gossip that Wilf wanted to sell a lathe, one he'd used for years to turn table and chair legs, wooden fruit bowls, handles for brooms, spades and hoes, and other articles such as wooden spoons. The story was that he'd decided to buy a more modern one, which would produce finer work in a shorter time, and, as I'd aways fancied wood turning as a hobby, the idea of obtaining a good second-hand lathe held some appeal.

'Noo then, young Taylor's lad,' he said as I tapped on his stable-style door. 'Thoo'll be here on business?'

'I heard you've got a lathe for sale.' I came straight to the point for he was working on a chest of drawers, restoring it by making good the joints; I could smell the cauldron of glue that was heating over a coke fire and I sensed he did not wish to be unduly delayed by anyone.

'Ovver there,' and he pointed to a corner. 'Buyer takes away. It's a heavy bit o' stuff, young Taylor.'

'Is it in good working order?' I wandered across to the dark corner to try and examine this contraption.

'Yon lathe's been in good fettle for t' last fifty years that Ah know of.' He chuckled. 'There's nowt to go wrang wiv it onny road.'

'So why are you selling it?'

'It's treadle operated, my new 'un's electric.'

It was not even a relatively modern treadle; judging by the appearance of this lathe, Wilf had made it himself: there was a long and solid base standing on two thick wooden legs, and a home-made lathe rested upon it, at about waist height. Beneath was a primitive wooden treadle, little more than a piece of wood hinged on a strong piece of timber fixed at floor level. From the treadle there rose a kind of leather belt, which was wound around a chair leg, or whatever was being turned, and secured to a strong spring in the roof. By pressing the treadle, the leather belt turned the wood, which allowed the operator to use both hands to control the chisels and gouges while producing the desired effect. It meant standing before it and using one foot to press the treadle – I could imagine unbalancing myself and inadvertently cutting massive chunks out of the things I was hoping to produce. This was not for me, I decided; in fact, I thought it was more of a museum piece than a functional piece of machinery.

'Deearn't just stand leeaking at it, press it . . . You etti stand up and use one leg . . . and thoo'll see t'left end is adjustable.'

'It's a very primitive lathe,' I had to say. 'I don't think it's what I want, Wilf, I was looking for something more modern, probably powered by electricity and even with a treadle of the sort you get on sewing machines.'

'Please yourself,' he said. 'It's nivver let me down in all t' years Ah've used it and it costs nowt to run and nowt to maintain.'

I was now faced with the dilemma of whether or not to approach him about some kind of insurance for his work-shop and contents. I was thinking of the risk of fire, or perhaps some injury that would prevent him working and halt his income. It was clear, though, that he was anxious to complete his current task. And then his son walked in. I knew Billy; he was a couple of years older than me and over the years we'd encountered each other in local cricket matches.

'And where's thoo been?' snapped Wilf. 'Ah was expecting thoo back an hour since.'

'Ah've had an accident, Dad, in t' car, t' front end's all bashed in, mudguards and bonnet, and t' headlights are smashed . . . sidelights an' all . . .'

Wilf halted his activities at this news, and dashed outside with me and Billy on his heels. There was a dark blue Austin 16 parked next to my motorbike in the yard outside, the family car, it transpired, and I could see the damage. It was probably all superficial, well within the capabilities of a good car bodyworker to repair, but it looked quite severe.

It was more cosmetic than dangerous, I felt, and the fact the car had been driven here meant it was serviceable.

'What the 'ell was thoo doing?'

'It was awd Crocky,' said Billy. 'He tottered out in front of me, just outside Micklesfield. There was nowt Ah could do, Dad, it was either run into him or take to t' fields, so Ah took to t' fields and did this on that hedge along Highwood Lane.'

'Ah'll bet thoo was going like bat out of hell.'

'Ah wasn't, Dad, honest, Ah was driving real careful.'

'Are you hurt.' I decided to establish that vital matter, for it seemed Wilf was not concerned with the plight of his son.

'Not a scratch, Matthew.'

'And Crocky? What about him?'

''E gave me a fair bit o' lip but Ah never touched 'im, 'e just wobbled about with 'is basket on 'is 'ead and shouted summat filthy about my parentage then staggered doon t' middle of t' road. 'E never stopped to help me out o' that hedge bottom either.'

'What happened to that basket on his head?' I laughed.

'Oh, that never fell off, it never does, does it? 'E staggered about under it for a while, but 'e kept it up there and off 'e went . . . Leaving me with a garage bill.'

'Are you insured?' I asked both of them.

'Aye,' said Wilf. 'Not with your lot, though.'

34

'Only for third party, fire and theft,' added Billy. 'It's too expensive going comprehensive.'

'Well, if Crocky's not injured, it's a damage-only accident, and the damage is to your vehicle, so if you've not got comprehensive cover then you'll have to foot this bill yourself, Wilf.'

'So if we 'ad fully comprehensive with thoo, we could git this fettled on t' insurance?'

'Basically, yes, although there's always the question of liability,' I said, wondering who might be considered at fault in this case. 'But it seems to me you've good grounds for making a claim, and if the insurers think it was Crocky's fault, they could claim costs from him or his insurance, if he has any.'

'Crocky insured? I doubt 'e's enough to pay for 'is basket full o' stuff, let alone insure it.' Wilf's brow was now creased as he pondered something. 'So if we took a policy out with your lot, Matthew, we could git this repair done on t' insurance?'

'Not this particular damage, we can't back-date policies or car insurance cover notes, Wilf. But if you like I could fill in a proposal form for you, for your car. I would recommend comprehensive cover if you want to consider all risks, but I should add that, in my opinion, you should take out some kind of cover for your buildings, if you've not already done so.'

'Buildings? They've stood there for centuries, Matthew, they'll not tumble down and if it's a case of fixing t' roof or mending a window, well, Ah can do that.'

'I was thinking more of fire risk,' I said. 'You've that open coke fire surrounded by lots of wood and shavings and such, then you're going to have an electrically powered lathe. Electricity can short and cause sparks to set fire to things, and just think of all those items you've got stored in that cowshed, if they all went up in smoke, who'd pay for them . . .?'

'Is thoo trying to scare me?' He glowered.

'No, but I wouldn't want all your hard work to go up in

smoke and you be left destitute. That's what insurance is for, to cover risks like that.'

''E's right, Dad, we've a thriving business here. It's for me as well as thoo, I'll tak ovver yar day,' chipped in Billy. 'And there's lots o' valuable things in store here, tools, furniture and such, and suppose Ah'd crippled Crocky or smashed all his pots . . .'

'But it might nivver 'appen, it's like gambling, Matthew. You get blokes like me to pay for years on end with nowt at t' end of it . . . Ah might pay you for years and years and nivver git owt back from you.'

'That's what it's all about,' I had to tell him. 'That's the risk you take, but there are no-claims bonuses on lots of policies, that's a good saving. And if I did arrange for full cover for your business, your car and even your house, my company could arrange special rates, and any outgoings could be set against your business expenses.'

'Ah can't decide now, Matthew, there's a lot to think about, to say nowt about the cost of it all. Come and see me again one evening when Ah've finished for t'day. Ah'll give it a good thinking.'

To cut short a long story, Wilf, no doubt with some prompting from his son, did switch his insurance to me and I secured him very favourable business rates for all his enterprises, the car included – and I made sure it was insured for business use too.

And at my suggestion, he presented his old lathe to a local museum.

The following Wednesday, before 1.00 p.m., I presented myself at the post office as usual to discover Jenny Blenkiron's place had been taken by a young, pale-faced woman whose black hair was tied back in a severe and very tight bun. She must be the niece Jenny had mentioned. In her early thirties with dark eyes and an unsmiling expression, she wore a purple dress that came up to her neck, but, as she was on the other side of the counter, I could not see the rest of her. Our post office was, I suppose, unique

36

because it occupied two rooms of a private house – the owners served from one room while the customers occupied the other, and the connecting opening was a square hole through the separating wall, rather like a serving hatch – it is quite possible it had been a serving hatch in some bygone era. On the customer side there was a high polished counter and a couple of high stools, but little else.

When I entered, the girl slid back the glass window that filled the hatch and I stated my business before plonking the bag of notes, coins and forms before her. She seemed to have been well briefed by her aunt, because, with impressive speed, she counted the money.

She divided it into neat stacks of pound notes and ten shilling notes along with little piles of half crowns, florins, shillings, sixpences, threepenny bits, pennies, ha'pennies and even farthings, plus a handful of cheques and postal orders. After a flurry of banging away almost angrily with the rubber stamp, I was soon leaving the building with all my documentation complete, but wondering where this young woman had come from and what her past was. She offered nothing by way of revealing her name nor did she confirm her link with Jenny. She was not at all chatty or communicative, although I must admit I was impressed by her efficiency. I felt she must have worked in a bank or post office as she seemed to have that kind of flair.

Later that particular Wednesday afternoon I had to visit a haulier in Micklesfield. His name was Louis Bernard Russell and he traded very successfully as L. B. Russell Hauliers; the insurance for all his fleet of fourteen lorries was due for renewal and I had a prior arrangment to call at his company office that afternoon. This was a very good client to have on my rather modest books, and I had the relevant certificates with me – all I needed was his cheque after completion of the renewal form. His was one of the few cheques I received. Naturally, I wondered whether he represented scope for further insurance – his premises, perhaps? Contents of his office? It was something we could discuss.

As my gallant little Coventry Eagle motored along The Carrs towards his office, I was aware of a fire appliance hurtling towards me with bells ringing; our local fire brigade was based at Baysthorpe, a village within my agency, and it was staffed by volunteers.

It was something like a fifteen minute race from Baysthorpe to Micklesfield, the narrow lanes and steep hills preventing very high speeds, but this bright red appliance was hurtling along The Carrs into my village in full regalia and with firemen on board. My first instinct was that this would be a chip pan fire – they were a common problem around this time of day, when the children were due home from school, and my next concern was whether the victim was one of my clients. If so, there'd be a claim that would require my attention. Right now, though, I had an important appointment, and could not indulge in the excitement of chasing the fire engine.

What I had just witnessed provided me with a wonderful means of introducing the topic of fire insurance to Russell Hauliers, and, with the cheque for his vehicle fleet safely in my pocket, I lost no time in making overtures about the wisdom of insuring his spacious premises for all risks, particularly fire. He listened and agreed; could I obtain a quote from my Head Office? I assured him I would see to it immediately, stressing there may be need for an official and independent valuation of the premises, an assessment of the risks due to the activities, such as servicing and repairs, which were conducted within them, and consideration of terms bearing in mind that we already insured his fleet.

In all, that call occupied me for about an hour and as I left, feeling delighted at the prospect of securing a large policy, I decided I should try to ascertain the location of the fire. I popped into the shop and was told, much to my horror and shock, that the fire had been in the post office.

My first concern was the safety of that unsmiling young woman, and then I wondered if my earlier cash deposit had been affected – if so, my District Office would have to be told. I lost no time driving up the village, and found the fire tender still outside the premises along with half a dozen firemen, a policeman in uniform and several bystanders. Smoke was coming from a pile of burning materials in the garden behind the building, and I asked the bystanders what had happened. I discovered the fire had started on the domestic side of the post office building; smoke emerging from the ground floor windows had alerted a villager who'd called the brigade and they'd arrived in time to save the building.

The woman had been inside and she'd been rescued from the smoke and was under the care of a policewoman in a nearby house. As things had got under control, the firemen had managed to get most of the burning material outside. There was a smouldering carpet, curtains and mattress, which combined to produce lots of smoke but little danger, but I could not elicit any positive information about the cause or the precise damage. I decided to talk to PC Clifford, our local constable.

'Now then, Matthew,' he said. 'A rum do, eh? Is this one of yours, then?'

'No, the post office has its own insurance,' I told him. 'But I do need some information, for my District Office.'

'And why would you want that?' he asked solemnly.

'I'd just paid my week's takings in, just before one o'clock. My bosses will want to know what's happened to it.'

'I can tell you what's happened, Matthew, it's gone up in smoke.'

'I mean my money, not the stuff inside the house.'

'I'm talking about your money. Everyone's money. She set fire to all the pound notes and ten bob notes, cheques and postal orders that had been paid in today. She piled everything in the middle of the floor, curtains and furnishings as well, poured paraffin over it and put a match to it. She's as queer as a nine bob note, Matthew, she's got a thing about setting fire to money and belongings. She's been inside for it, she's under arrest now, we're waiting for Division to send a car out for her.'

'I wonder if Jenny knew about this?' I asked.

'I doubt it. The lass told her she'd been away working, not that she'd been locked up for setting fire to things. And the post office seemed happy for her to take over. No real harm done, though, and your money will be insured, I would hope! How much are we talking about, Matthew?'

'I paid just over £60 in, some coins but most of it in notes.'

'All I can suggest is that you contact your bosses and tell them what's happened – they'll be able to claim from the post office. There'll be an official report in due course. Tell your head office to write to our force headquarters at Northallerton for an abstract of the fire report. That will confirm everything.'

Even though the money had been destroyed in the custody of the post office, which meant that it was no longer my concern, I would have to write to my District Office tonight, just to make sure they knew I hadn't gone on a spending spree with their money. Of course, I'd already extracted my own wages and expenses.

'So how was your day?' smiled Evelyn as we settled down to our tea. 'Did you get some good business done?'

As she was feeding Paul in his high chair, I told her about my adventures, with due emphasis on the bizarre events at the post office, not forgetting Crocky and his basket of pots, and how I had secured some good policies, which would provide us with commission. She smiled her understanding and then, as we came towards the end of the meal, with baby Paul happily playing with his building bricks on the floor, she said with just a hint of mystery, 'I've got some news for you, Matthew.'

I thought she was going to announce she was pregnant and, for a moment, did not know how to react.

'News?' I gurgled.

'I got a letter this morning, after you'd gone. From the Education Department.'

'And?'

After leaving grammar school, Evelyn had attended a two-year teacher training course with the intention of working in infant schools within the county. On completion of her course, she had obtained a post in Whitby, but, after we married, she became pregnant with Paul. The pregnancy meant she had to give up work, but the North Riding County Council's Education Department had asked if she was willing to be placed on the supply list for infant schools. Being on the supply list meant she could be called upon, sometimes at very short notice, to work in an infant school for a temporary period, perhaps as little as a single morning, or perhaps a whole day or even longer. Short-term duties invariably arose at rather short notice, such as when a teacher fell ill, was injured or had to attend a sick or dying relative, whereas longer periods with more notice might arise, say, when a teacher was undergoing hospital treatment or one teacher retired and a replacement was awaited. There may be a need for a supply teacher to cover those gaps for perhaps a week or two, but however long or short the engagement Evelyn would get paid. For a woman with a young family it was a wonderful means of earning a few extra pounds. It was also a useful means for Evelyn to maintain contact with the Education Department should she ever decide to return to full-time teaching. Having had the system explained to her, Evelyn had agreed to be placed on the supply list, specifying that the schools she could attend would be those within the boundaries of my agency.

This was perfectly acceptable because supply teachers were always given a choice of possible locations. For us it meant that I could adapt my daily routine to accommodate her requirements, because, having no transport of her own and not being a driver, she would need to be transported to the school where she worked. However, not every train or bus ran from Micklesfield to all the villages in Delverdale at suitable times.

'They want me to cover at Graindale Bridge for a week,' she said. 'There's a gap between Miss Read's retirement and the new teacher being appointed.'

'Starting when?'

'Monday,' she told me.

'So what about Paul?'

'Maureen will look after him, so long as we can get him there. Then I can catch the school train down from here, and also back again. The times are just right.'

'I could rearrange my days to give you a lift,' I offered.

'On that dirty old bike of yours? No thank you, Matthew. I need to arrive looking clean and dry, not like something dragged through a hedge backwards. The trains will be fine, they are run especially to cater for the schoolchildren from the entire dale right down to Whitby. All I might need from you will be some help with Paul.'

'I can take him to Maureen's if you find yourself late.'

Maureen was one of Evelyn's sisters. Two years older than Evelyn, she lived in Micklesfield and was married to John Corner; they had three children ranging in age from three to ten. Paul enjoyed playing with his cousins and Maureen liked having him because he helped to keep her own youngest child occupied. And Graindale Bridge school was an ideal choice for Evelyn. Graindale Bridge was a small village only two miles from Micklesfield, and the busy school was a Catholic one; in fact, it was where Evelyn and her siblings had been taught – as had her parents.

As it was a short walk from our house to Maureen's, I knew I could help deliver Paul each morning before heading off to my own part of the dale for the day, and I might also arrange my plans so that I could do a little babysitting of my own. I could look after him while doing my books at home, for example.

This was not the first time Evelyn had been asked to undertake supply work, but on the previous occasions she'd always said she could not leave Paul because he was so young. Now, though, he was two and accustomed to spending time with his aunts and cousins. That, and the fact that I worked from home while making my own hours, meant she could accept her first supply post. I realized that, like me, she was about to embark on her new career.

42

'Have you accepted?' I asked.

'No, I thought I ought to ask you first. I can ring them tomorrow from the kiosk with my answer and confirm it by letter. So what do you think?'

'Well,' I said, with that dream house of our own in mind, 'if Paul can be looked after and you can get to work each day without risking life and limb on my motorbike, tell them you'll do it. I can always help out at short notice if necessary, my plans are usually fairly fluid.'

'Thanks, darling, I just hope I'm not too rusty!' She threw her arms round me and kissed me. When Paul saw her do that, he started to bawl.

Three

*'The man panicked and didn't know which way
to run, so I ran over him'*
From a claim form

Head office in London decided to campaign for increased awareness of fire risks. They wanted to target private individuals and commercial organizations, large and small, with the objective of persuading their target audience to take out new policies with fire risks in mind, or have their existing ones reviewed. The message was simple – even though the war had been over for nearly a decade, homes and businesses were still at risk, especially from fire. This was of increasing concern owing to the amount of electrical apparatus now being bought and installed in private houses and business premises. There had been a sudden and rapid increase in the use of electrically driven machinery and tools along with domestic equipment in kitchens and living areas, with a corresponding increase in lighting, with lots of very hot bulbs.

This initiative filtered down to me via our District Office and I received masses of leaflets, explanatory letters and proposal forms with which to impress and educate my clients and so, fired (if that is the right word) with enthusiasm, I embarked upon my quest in the remote villages within the moors.

Although most people knew that a naked flame could set fire to things like curtains or straw, the concept of a filament encased in glass did not suggest the same lethal consequences to many householders, farmers and businessmen.

To highlight the risk of fire from new sources was therefore a matter of education.

This was a factor on both commercial and private premises. This social development had created what was, in the minds of insurance companies, a massive increase in the range and number of fire risks from electrical malfunction, or shorts as they became known – a fact I found odd because many of the houses in my part of the world continued to have open fires both for cooking and heating, and oil lamps and candles for lighting. My personal view was that open fires, paraffin lamps and candles were far more likely to cause accidental blazes, but one cannot argue with officialdom.

It must be said that lots of fires were caused by domestic carelessness, such as chip pans overheating and flat irons being left face down on sheets and shirts, but on frequent occasions unattended or carelessly placed naked flames were the cause: hot coal spilling on to the hearth rug, ancient beams catching fire in chimneys, thatched roofs blazing in some moorland villages, clothing being dried too close to the fire, burning candles igniting bedspreads when people fell asleep, horses kicking over oil lanterns and even fires caused by rubbish being burned in the garden. When unattended bonfires were fanned by sudden gusts of wind, lines of washing and garden fences were the victims, although on one occasion a pigeon loft was set alight. Happily, the pigeons were out racing, but it meant they had no welcoming place to accommodate their homing instincts. There were farm fires, too, with haystacks igniting through spontaneous combustion, and moor fires where careless visitors dropped cigarette ends or lit fires among the heather to cook meals, then left the dying embers to God, providence and moorland breezes.

Even the open moors belong to someone, not to mention any structures placed there for the comfort of beast, bird or person.

It is not surprising we were advised to be circumspect in our approach to new clients – people known or even

45

suspected of deliberately setting fire to things had to be avoided, particularly those who were liable to burn down their properties in order to claim the insurance money to settle debts. In spite of the calm appearance and friendly nature of moorfolk, there were some dodgy people in my part of the world. In a small community like ours, such characters were generally known to all, even if they had never been convicted of arson.

One debt-ridden garage owner produced a magnificent blaze that burned his premises to the ground, but his surreptitious role in causing the fire was discovered through careful investigative work by the fire brigade, police and insurance assessors. Others made lesser claims – it was amazing how many fireside rugs were accidentally singed just as the Christmas bills were coming in or how many items of clothing got scorched when flames shot out of the domestic fireplace due to some abnormal wind activity. Such stories were all good fiction, and had been tried many times, with many scurrilous attempts being identified as bogus before the payouts were made.

I decided to launch my local campaign while going about my routine visits, identifying possible places of risk as I was out and about in the villages and moorland farms within my agency, so I made sure I had an adequate supply of forms in my panniers.

Because I had to take Paul to his Aunt Maureen's to allow Evelyn to catch the school train to Graindale Bridge, I decided to start my campaign in that village, as I had a household policy renewal to arrange in nearby Graindale, which was on the moors above its sister community. Graindale and Graindale Bridge were two quite distinct villages, separated by a mile-long very steep hill, but their proximity and part-shared name did tend to cause some confusion, albeit not among the locals. Having dropped off Paul at his aunt's with a promise that Evelyn would collect him on her way home from school, I drove across the moors to Graindale. It was while en route to my client's house that I spotted the perfect candidate for my campaign: smoke

46

was pouring from the premises, someone was coughing loudly and a horse was whinnying.

But this was no unexpected drama; it was the local farrier and blacksmith's, complete with a huge and very hot coke fire. The smithy was a single-storey building of local moorland stone, which was a dark grey colour, each piece being marked with the traditional herringbone design, and the roof was blue slate. Small windows permitted some daylight to enter, but most of the interior was lit by opening the huge double doors, large enough to permit entry by a stage coach – indeed, these had once been repaired and even constructed on these premises.

Outside there was a cobbled yard and a small paddock area, ideal for horses waiting to be shod or awaiting collection.

A couple of full horse troughs were in evidence, too, as were several iron rims for cart wheels and various other pieces of agricultural machinery, some awaiting repair and some rusting away because they were of no further use.

The smithy was owned and run by the Codlings, a father-and-son team, both called George, although this complexity did not cause undue confusion because everyone who patronized them knew the pair very well indeed. When I arrived, both men were outside, shoeing a huge, handsome and very elegant shire horse. With its chestnut coat and four white-socked hooves, wearing only a collar, the mare stood patiently on three legs as young George held her head and old George nailed a shoe to her left forefoot. This sight, still quite common on the moors, never failed to impress me; I was always amazed that such powerful and huge animals would allow humans to nail iron shoes to their feet.

It was almost as if the horses knew it was for their benefit that their hooves were re-shod at regular intervals, not to mention the spot of necessary manicuring that was effected with massive files. There is no doubt those gentle giants had total confidence in their human friends.

'Now then, Matthew,' greeted old George, not breaking from his work.

'Now then, Matthew,' echoed young George.

'Now then,' I responded. 'Not a bad morning.'

'Not bad at all,' said old George.

'Not bad at all,' agreed young George.

There was a long pause as old George attended to a tricky part of the shoeing process, checking that he was locating the shoe in exactly the right place; when he seemed satisfied, he carefully tapped home each nail and then released the horse's foot. She placed it on the ground, nodded her head as if in approval, and then young George walked her across to the paddock.

'Awd Dolly's as good as gold,' said old George. 'She'll be collected soon. So what can Ah do for you, Matthew?'

By this stage, young George was too far away to echo his father's words and I guessed the old man thought I was wanting him to fabricate some kind of metalwork for me – a garden gate perhaps, or some kind of garden tool, made to my design and requirements. In addition to their farrier work, the Georges also undertook a wide range of general blacksmith's work and both were known for their skills and efficiency.

'You know I'm now the Premier insurance agent?'

'Aye, word has got around, Matthew,' and he waited for me to say my next piece.

'I wondered if you were interested in fire insurance, George, for the smithy.' There was still a lot of smoke about, ample evidence of the open coke fire that burned constantly within.

'We're covered already,' he said, pointing to the wall high above the door.

'Covered? Oh, well, sorry I bothered you . . .' and I looked in the direction he had indicated.

Bolted to the wall was a metal plaque painted dark green and purple, which bore the image of a blackfaced sheep with white wool; along the top was the word 'MOOR-LAND' in capital letters, and along the bottom the figure 226.

'With yon sign up there, Matthew, we'll never catch

fire. Besides, there's allus plenty of watter in them troughs.'

'How do you mean, you'll never catch fire?' I recognized the plaque as an ancient firemark. From around the seventeenth century, until the time that formal fire brigades were established, insurance companies organized their own fire services and they insisted that their customers identified their properties by placing distinctive signs on the outer walls. These were often made of lead and had colourful emblems on them, readily identifiable from a distance. They were known as firemarks. With so few houses bearing names or street numbers, the galloping horse-drawn brigades required a simple but effective means of identifying their own customers' premises. The number each one bore was the number of the relevant insurance policy. There are stories that when a fire engine raced to a fire and saw the opposition's firemark on the wall, its crew would ignore the blaze. These colourful old signs became superfluous with the founding of the county fire services in the middle of the nineteenth century, and so became collectors' items.

George frowned as he considered my question, then said, 'Well, that sign protects me against fire.'

'Like those horseshoes bring you luck, you mean?' I smiled, indicating several that were secured to the smithy wall.

'Nay, lad, it's nowt like that!' he studied me seriously now. 'It's like when thoo puts t'burned bit o' t' yule log under t' bed. That stops t' house catching fire, just like a bread loaf does if it's baked on Good Friday or hot cross buns kept for a year – and my old dad allus reckoned a bit of rowan wood or stonecrop would keep fire off. And lightning strikes. There's plenty of things'll stop us catching fire.'

'Charms, you mean?

'Ah wouldn't call 'em charms, not if they work like this 'un does. It's not like carrying a rabbit's foot for luck, is it?'

'George,' I said, 'it doesn't work like that. You can't rely on a firemark to stop fire breaking out, that's not what it was for.'

'Well, say what you like, Matthew, but we've never caught fire yet, and yon moorland sign has been on our smithy wall as long as Ah've been around – my dad allus swore by it.'

I realized I was faced with a task similar to that of telling a bride that blue was really an unlucky colour for her wedding dress, and that the horseshoes presented to her would not make her any happier, or that thirteen wasn't really unlucky and there wasn't going to be a death in the family if a crow sat on the roof of your house.

For that reason, I tried a different approach.

'Suppose that coke fire of yours set a beam ablaze, an old one hidden up the chimney. That could spread to the whole building and the lot could go up in smoke. You know as well as me that beams can smoulder for ages before breaking into flames. You could be fast asleep and never know a thing about it until you got here next morning to find nothing left.'

'It won't happen, Matthew, not with yon sign on t' wall. We're protected, that's what my old dad said. Yon sign gives us protection, all the year round. And it costs nowt. Thoo can't frighten me into takking oot yan o' your insurance things.'

Many old superstitions survived in those moorland villages, but this was the first time I'd come across a notion that a firemark actually protected the building from fire. I tried to explain to both Georges, for young George had now returned, but realized I was wasting their time and mine.

'I'll leave you some literature to read,' was all I could think of saying. 'If you do decide to insure your smithy – or your house – you know where to find me.'

'Aye, lad,' smiled old George. 'We do.'

I must admit that as I rode away I wondered whether he really believed in the power of the firemark or whether it had been a clever ruse to protect himself from having to pay insurance premiums. Yorkshiremen are famous for being rather canny with their money. But neither of the Georges approached me to seek proper insurance cover for the fire risk to either their house or smithy – and, so far as I know, neither their home nor that smithy ever caught fire.

It was a very different story with Baldby Garage. A newcomer called Alan Leckonby, who appeared to have plenty of money, came to live in Baldby a few years after the war. No one was sure where he had come from or why he had selected this rather remote moorland village as the location of his business venture, but he did appear to be a charming man with expansive plans for developing his new business.

Baldby is almost hidden in the depths of the moors, miles from any urban area and well away from any main routes. In spite of its loneliness, there he established a garage, which undertook repairs, bought and sold cars and motor-bikes, sold petrol, diesel and oil, and also provided a taxi service. As it was the only garage in the village, the residents patronized his establishment and welcomed his presence.

In his thirties, tall, dark and handsome, Alan was an enthusiastic sort of person, always busy, always looking for new business outlets, always telling everyone of his wonderful plans, which never seemed to come to fruition, and it was known that he always had a struggle to pay his bills. His small business empire never seemed to generate enough money to meet his expenses, but because he assured every one he would, one day, make a lot of money and provide jobs in the future development of his premises, the local people supported him – and believed in him.

In time, I discovered he was unable to cope with moorland farmers who paid their bills only once a year and people who ran up petrol bills and paid them when they felt like it, not when he wanted, at the end of each month. In spite of this, there is little doubt he lived beyond his means – he ran a very smart Jaguar XK120 sports car for example.

Although he was not married, he enjoyed the attentions of a succession of girlfriends who might have come from the pages of the society magazines. Rarely did he get his hands dirty in the garage; to avoid that he employed a mechanic, and to do his secretarial work and dispense petrol there was a girl in the office. He did not spend all his time at the garage, either; a lot of the time he motored about the countryside trying to persuade people to make use of the facilities he offered – and to share in the expansive plans he was considering.

After a while, I discovered he was planning to build an up-market hotel in the village to cater for tourists, complete with golf course and fishing rights. There was even a hint of a dry-ski slope and an indoor swimming pool. It was this kind of daydream that led me to think Alan was not dishonest or crooked, although most of us realized that his feet were not planted firmly in the Yorkshire ground. Rather, he floated round the moors in a haze of rose-coloured cloud.

By chance I was in the Abbey Inn at Baldby one Thursday lunchtime while Evelyn was still teaching at Graindale Bridge. I was enjoying a pint of bitter after eating my sand-wiches on the moor when Alan walked in. Our paths had crossed on occasions, such as in the post office, and on one occasion when I was visiting a farm he arrived with the farmer's car, which his garage had just serviced. In the pub that day he nodded to me in a friendly manner, for I was the only person in the bar except for the landlady, then he said 'Hello' and brought his pint over, asking if he could join me. I agreed – I had a few minutes to while away before an appointment at a nearby farm.

I wasn't sure whether he had recognized me or was just being sociable, but, knowing a little of his personality, I guessed he would try to impress me if he thought that I was a businessman on some kind of formal visit.

'Alan Leckonby,' he said. 'I've got the garage down the road.'

'Matthew Taylor.' I shook his hand. 'The new man from

the Premier, the insurance company. We've met – in the post office and then at Highfield Farm a few weeks ago.'

'Ah, yes, I thought I recognised you.' He smiled affably. 'Insurance, eh? Maybe, when I get all my plans approved, we can do business. I'm planning an hotel on some land I own near the garage; it backs on to the river so there'll be fishing rights, and I've some rough land I can turn into a golf course . . . I want to establish some kind of oasis on these moors, Mr Taylor, where businessmen can come to relax away from the pressures of city life. Their cars can also be valeted and serviced while they're here. I'll be able to supply cars, too, of the more prestigious kind, of course, and I hope to expand into conference facilities . . .'

I was quite surprised that he would launch into this kind of talk with someone who was almost a complete stranger, but very quickly I realized that he was indeed out to impress me – or anyone else whom he'd just met – and at that point, I decided to treat all his expansive talk with more than a little scepticism. For all that, however, he was an affable and pleasant man and I enjoyed his company. Just as he was launching into his well-rehearsed business chatter, I decided I could not leave him without trying to win a policy from him.

'Before you go,' I managed to say when I saw he was making a move to leave. 'Is your garage covered for all fire risks? It's just that my company is in the middle of a campaign to make business people more aware of the risk of fire. We're offering highly competitive rates for small businesses, and if your hotel idea comes to fruition I know we can produce a very comprehensive and cost-effective cover plan for all elements of your business.'

'My father has seen to all that, Mr Taylor. He has funded my business to enable me to get established, but in due course I shall be independent. I am sure he has insured the garage for fire, flood and that sort of thing, but I'll check. As you will appreciate, the cars I accept for servicing and sale do have their own individual cover anyway . . . Well, I think they do . . .'

'Not always.' I tried to warn him not to accept the word of those who brought their vehicles to him. 'If the place caught fire and the cars inside were destroyed or damaged, you could be liable, you should realize that. You should check the small print on any insurance your father might have arranged; you need to be sure that everything and everyone that comes on to your premises is fully covered for all risks, whatever the purpose of their visit. You could be sued for injury if something went wrong, like a piece of machinery falling on someone's foot, or someone slipping on a patch of oil.'

'Well, the building's not worth much, not as it stands,' he said. 'When I get my plans passed, it will be demolished to make way for a brand new custom-built garage fitted with the very latest equipment.'

'One can't stand still in business!' I said with as much wisdom as I could muster. 'One has to keep abreast of the times.'

'I couldn't agree more. And staff, they're vital. One must recruit the right people. My staff, who will be highly trained, will be able to service every type of motor vehicle from motorbikes to buses by way of articulated lorries and combine harvesters, and I'll have the latest welding equipment, brake-testing facilities, electrical-system testers, paint sprays and repair shop. When all that is in position, up and running as they say, then that's the time for you and I to have a business chat. I must say I don't fancy paying out lots of insurance premiums for an old shed that's on its last legs. You can see the state of it – I bought it for a song, of course, I do have the rare ability to spot the potential of run-down businesses. So keep an eye on things, Mr Taylor, watch my progress and don't be afraid to come and talk to me when you see exciting things happening.'

'Apart from your buildings, you're not with the Premier for your cars or your taxi service, are you? We can do a very competitive rate, inclusive of the vehicles, buildings and grounds, for all risks, fire, flood, damage of every kind . . .'

'My father has seen to all that, too, but he's only given me a short time to get established, then I'm on my own. I think you have found yourself a new customer,' he beamed.

'Let us hope so, for both our sakes,' I smiled.

'Tell you what, Mr Taylor, leave me some literature, give me time to think it over and then we'll talk again. You'll be in the village from time to time?'

'Very regularly,' I assured him, and so he departed with a pile of my insurance leaflets, not only for fire insurance but for endowment policies, life assurance and vehicle cover as well as risks to staff and customers when on his garage premises.

As the weeks passed, I kept an eye on Alan Leckonby's garage, but things never seemed to change. On occasions I filled the tank of my motorcycle with petrol from his pump, but I seldom saw him. The mechanic would usually serve me, breaking from his work on some vehicle inside the dark premises, and sometimes the office girl would operate the pump, then provide me with the necessary receipt. The fact that these two people continued to work at the garage provided me with some kind of confidence; clearly, Alan was paying their wages, which in turn meant he was generating some kind of income – unless his father was bailing him out. Nonetheless, the garage did look run down and in need of a very basic lick of paint. Furthermore, the prestigious cars never appeared for sale on his forecourt, and there was never any sign of activity on the plot of land he'd earmarked for his up-market hotel complex.

As I continued my regular visits to Baldby, I learned that Alan had, over a few weeks, earned a growing reputation for not paying his own bills, and had run up a substantial grocery and newspaper account with the village shop.

Gossip, often a very reliable barometer of local opinion, said he'd had a debt collector chasing him for monies outstanding from a previous car sales business he'd run in Lincolnshire, and his office girl left, saying he owed her three weeks' wages. The mechanic remained, however – local gossip said he'd been paid and had no argument with Alan.

The signs were increasingly clear: Alan Leckonby's grand plan was heading for failure.

For that reason, it made sense to avoid the risk of insuring this man and his business, so I made a conscious decision not to canvass him. I did not want the trauma of dealing with a man who wouldn't or couldn't pay his dues.

It would have been about three months after my first contact with him that I pulled up outside his garage and filled up my petrol tank. This time he noticed me outside – he'd been in the tiny office, trying to catch up with some paperwork.

'Ah, Mr Taylor,' he said. 'Just the fellow. We never did get around to that discussion about insuring my premises. Maybe we can make a definite appointment. My father's part in all this is due to end very soon and I shall need comprehensive cover, even before I begin my hotel development.'

My instinct told me I must continue to exercise a high degree of caution and I knew that even if most of his plans never came to fruition he might decide to implement some kind of modest insurance cover if his father cast him adrift. I was very aware, of course, that some desperate people took out fire insurance and then set fire to their own premises in an attempt to clear their debts through the insurance.

In my view, all the warning signs were present in Alan's circumstances.

'If it's going to be a major development, we need to consider the wider implications.' I was thinking fast, trying to produce some kind of response that did not suggest any kind of mistrust – after all, I could be wrong about him.

'I'd agree with that,' he smiled. 'So what can you offer?'

'We have specialists who deal with large policies of a

commercial nature. They are familiar with all the problems likely to arise, and with the kind of risk you need to be insured against, and, of course, the level of premiums you might be expected to pay. If you can make a firm date in your diary, Mr Leckonby, I'll write to my District Manager and we can set up a meeting between you and one of our highly experienced and specialized commercial managers. I am merely a rural agent, you need a specialist.'

'Oh, well, yes, that seems a good idea, Mr Taylor. With the kind of large development I envisage, I do need the very best advice. So yes, perhaps you can set something in action?'

'Just give me a few suitable dates,' I said. 'Then leave it to me.'

We settled for a fortnight's time, and that evening I wrote to my District Office with an explanation of Alan's intentions and the proposed dates for a meeting with him. I decided to add a note to suggest this proposal be treated with a degree of caution, then awaited the response.

Three days later, a letter arrived saying that a week on Wednesday would be suitable, and Mr Clemminson, the District Commercial Manager, would drive out to call on me prior to our meeting with Alan. He could come to my house at 10.00 a.m., and suggested we meet the client on his garage premises at ll.00 a.m., the drive across the moor occupying half an hour of that time. I was expected to accompany Mr Clemminson – it was part of my learning process – but my presence was also necessary because this proposed large policy was to be actioned within my agency. That preliminary chat would allow me to further express my personal reservations to Mr Clemminson, and I knew that he would lose no time making some discreet enquiries about Alan Leckonby. From the telephone kiosk in Micklesfield, I rang Alan, who agreed to the date and time, sounding very enthusiastic. He even promised to provide me with an estimated value of his current premises, along with an architect's plan of the development. I noted the date in my desk diary and looked forward to seeing how the experienced Mr Clemminson dealt with this man.

But the meeting never took place. On the Sunday before, I was roused soon after 7.30 in the morning by a loud hammering on the back door, and when I peered out of the bedroom window I saw a very distraught-looking Alan Leckonby. When he heard the window being opened, he looked up and saw me; in turn, I realized he was in a dreadful state, with his hair, face, hands and clothing filthy. Quite literally, it looked as if he'd been dragged through a hawthorn hedge, trampled by a bull and beaten with a rolling pin, all at the same time.

'Mr Leckonby!' I was hoarse, having been aroused from a deep Sunday morning sleep.

'Sorry, Mr Taylor, sorry to drag you out like this . . .'

'I'll be down in a second,' I called, not waiting for an explanation.

Jumping into a pair of casual trousers and putting on my slippers and a sweater, I hurried down to admit him to the house. When I opened the door he was visibly shaking, so I took him inside and put the kettle on, knowing that a hot drink with sugar was the best restorative for shock – and he seemed heavily in shock. I led him into the sitting room and told him to sit on the settee, then Evelyn arrived, having dressed hurriedly, with her face showing her concern. Happily, Paul had not been roused.

Evelyn had no idea who Alan was, but, rapidly taking in his appearance, asked, 'Do you want a doctor? I can go and fetch him if you want . . .'

'No, I'm all right, really I am, it's been a shock . . . a terrible shock...'

'I'll talk to Mr Leckonby if you could make a cup of tea,' I asked Evelyn. 'Hot and sweet, and one for me. The kettle's on.'

As she went into the kitchen, he said, 'Look, I don't want to be a nuisance but I had to come here, I've come straight over.'

'So what's happened?' I asked.

'My garage,' he said, almost on the point of tears. 'Burned to the ground. There was a blaze, I don't know how it started, a neighbour noticed it and called the brigade, they got there about three this morning. It was well ablaze, burning like fury, all that oil and petrol and stuff . . . Cars ruined, everything gone, burned to the ground.'

I did not know what to say, except that I was dreadfully sorry for him, but I must admit I had no idea why he had come to tell me about it. We had not insured him, we had not even had our preliminary meeting, so I was not involved officially with his dilemma. As I listened to his sorrowful story, Evelyn arrived with two mugs of tea, and I passed one to him. He took it gratefully and sat on the front edge of the seat, both hands clutching the mug, and stared into space.

'You'll be wondering why I have come to you,' he said after a long pause.

'Yes,' I said. 'I can't see there's anything I can do, except to say how sorry I am that this has happened.'

'It was just that we'd had those talks, you and me, about your company insuring my garage, and then there's that meeting we were going to have on Wednesday, with that official from your District Office . . . Well, I was intending to go ahead with the policy, you see, for the garage, a smaller policy until I get the rest of my project built, and I was just wondering if you could back-date the agreement, so that it would cover this morning's fire . . .'

His voice trailed away as he spoke and I knew he realized he was asking the impossible. He was like a drowning man clutching at the proverbial straw, but I had to shake my head.

'Sorry, Mr Leckonby, you know that's impossible.'

'I just hoped, well, hoped against my better judgement, seeing we'd discussed things and had got something moving, something very positive, I was wondering if your company would cover me, as an act of good faith with a view to the future.'

'The Premier doesn't work like that.'

59

'I know, really I do. I shouldn't have come. I was hoping you could do something for me because I have a big future . . . It was going to be a huge success, an investment for your company . . . I mean, Mr Taylor, I really was going to take out a policy with you, really I was . . .'

'There's nothing I can do. There's no way my company will back-date a policy – not that there ever was a policy in your case . . . Anyhow, I thought you were insured, through your father.'

'No,' he said. 'I wasn't, not in recent weeks.'

'You mean the whole place was not insured?'

'Not for one penny, not against fire, not against anything.' He rose to his feet. 'My own fault, all my own stupid fault . . . I couldn't afford to insure it, Mr Taylor. I took that risk, and now it's all gone.'

He made to leave the room, but extended his hand for me to shake.

'I really am most sorry,' was all I could think of saying.

'I must go, I've things to do,' he said. 'They don't know what caused the fire – the fire brigade that is. If I had been insured, they'd have suspected me, wouldn't they, of starting it, to claim money to pay my debts? Well, that's a non-starter, Mr Taylor. It wasn't paid for, the garage, I had borrowed money to buy it, you see, as you do starting out . . .'

He left the house a very sad and beaten man, and I listened as his car drove away. That same morning, I wrote to Mr Clemminson to cancel our appointment, and later, as a matter of personal interest, I tried to find out what had really happened. But no one knew. The cause of the outbreak was never determined. Alan Leckonby was suspected of starting it to clear his debts, but few knew he'd not been insured. I had no idea whether or not he was instrumental in setting fire to his own garage; perhaps he was deeper in debt than any of us realized and took a gamble that the Premier might look favourably on his plight. But whatever his motives – or however bad his luck – he moved on. He left Baldby very soon afterwards and did not tell anyone where he was heading. Eventually, the land on which his garage had stood was sold and two houses were built on it. I never knew who owned it at the time of that sale, but it brought a good price.

Four

*'I'd been driving for forty-five years when I fell
asleep at the wheel and crashed'*

From a claim form

When I took over the Delverdale agency, I was left several helpful notes by Jim Villiers. One of them reminded me that I should expect occasional visits from senior officials based at our District Office. It was no surprise, therefore, to receive a letter from the District General Manager informing me that Mr M. Wilkins, the District Ordinary Branch Sales Manager – Life, would visit me next Tuesday. He would come in his own car to my house in Micklesfield at 10.00 a.m. and would then accompany me on my rounds until five thirty or thereabouts. The letter suggested I prepare an itinerary based on what I would normally be doing that day, with particular emphasis on existing clients who might be prepared to increase their insurance cover by investing in some form of updated life assurance.

Apart from wondering how on earth this man managed life (and whether the company also had a District Manager – Death), the letter put me into something of a flap because, having served in HM Forces, I guessed his visit would be something like a very official and thorough inspection by the commanding officer, or as daunting as a visit from an income tax inspector. Apart from the trauma of having one's boss joining one's daily round, Jim had told me that such visits had a three-fold purpose – mainly they were advisory, so that if I had any worries, difficulties or problems

I could benefit from the wisdom of these very important gentlemen. The second purpose was that they undoubtedly acted as a type of supervisory exercise, during which my work and understanding of the insurance business in general would be checked and my suitability to remain in the job discreetly assessed. The third purpose was for me to be accompanied by this very experienced senior official, who through his own skills would endeavour to show me how the job should really be done. Thus it was also a tutorial exercise, part of my ongoing training, and I realized I should take every advantage to learn as much as I could from this very professional person.

As I wondered whether I would be expected to carry Mr Wilkins on the pillion of my motorbike, Evelyn fussed around making sure the house was scrupulously clean and tidy, especially our modest lounge, where she would offer him coffee or tea with biscuits before embarking on our tour. I hoped he would take due note of my miniature office in the corner, especially as I had tidied it the evening before, placing my various daily books in strategic places so that he might observe them and note I was up to date with everything.

Evelyn, who had completed her first spell of supply teaching work by this stage, had taken Paul to play with his three-year-old cousin Bernard at Maureen's, so she had the house to herself, with plenty of time to prepare for our important visitor. While she made preparations fit to welcome our new young Queen, doing her best to find three cups without cracks and with matching saucers and plates, I made notes of potential clients who lived along today's route and I made sure that all my publicity literature was relevant and that I had actioned all outstanding claims. So far as I could tell, everything that could be done had been done. I was ready to greet my visitor.

By five minutes to ten, I was standing around and waiting; the kettle had boiled, everything was in its place and outside the sun was shining on this lovely morning in late March. Not having met Mr Wilkins, or any of the officials from

District Office (other than those who'd interviewed me and who had later participated in my three-day introductory course) I had no idea what he looked like, nor did I know anything of his personality or his likes and dislikes.

Anxious to appear keen and efficient, I had made sure I was clad in my newly pressed and vigorously brushed suit, that my hair was tidy and my shoes were nicely polished. I felt sure we would be travelling in his car – the notion of me carrying such a VIP on my pillion was faintly ridiculous, especially in the unpredictable month of March. As I waited for the great man, I created a mental image of a tall, dark and handsome man in his late forties or early fifties; impeccably dressed in a smart suit and a trilby hat; he would create an immediate and highly favourable impression upon anyone he encountered, a figure of undoubted authority and stature, a reassuring and dependable person – a bit like the character in our national adverts, in fact.

When Mr Wilkins arrived, he was not a bit like that.

I answered the knock at our front door to find a tiny man clad in a sports jacket, cavalry twill trousers and brightly polished brown shoes with pointed toes, all of which looked slightly too big for him. The little fellow was also wearing a black beret and carrying a large briefcase. My first impression was that this was a door-to-door salesman. It never occurred to me that it might be Mr Wilkins; clearly, it was a stranger to the area, because he'd come to the front door. Local people never did that unless they arrived upon a matter of great importance. If Mr Wilkins had called regularly on Jim Villiers he would know the local domestic customs, I felt. If this wasn't a salesman, perhaps it was someone who was lost or who had been given my address as a potential client, or even someone about to ask for directions to another house in the village.

'Mr Taylor?' In his late forties, he had a high-pitched voice which sounded rather like that of a jockey.

'Yes?'

'Wilkins, District Office,' he identified himself.

'Oh, yes, well, good morning, Mr Wilkins, you'd better come in.'

'Thank you. The car's on the road, will it be all right?'

'Yes, we don't get much traffic down here . . .' I led him into the house via the front door, which momentarily puzzled Evelyn. She'd expected me to lead him through the back door and was waiting to greet him in the kitchen. He followed me as I led him into the lounge, calling, 'Evelyn, Mr Wilkins has arrived.'

She emerged smiling from the kitchen as he extended his hand and said, 'Pleased to meet you, Mrs Taylor. I do hope you've not gone to a lot of trouble on my behalf. I shall not be staying long, your husband and I have a good deal of work to complete in the course of today.'

It was then I noticed he had not removed his beret. I wondered if this indicated a very short stay or whether he had something wrong with his hair or head that required it to be covered, but Evelyn was saying, 'Will you have a cup of coffee, Mr Wilkins? Or tea?'

'I never drink stimulants, Mrs Taylor, but a glass of water would be most acceptable. I can drink it while your husband and I have our pre-excursion discussion. I always regard these visits as something of a journey into uncharted waters, Mr Taylor, an exploration, that is why I term them excursions.'

I wasn't sure whether this was a modest joke on his part but responded by saying, 'I see. Well, Evelyn will see to your drink.'

'Coffee for you, Matthew?' she asked as I tried to make this odd little man comfortable in our lounge.

'Please.' And as I made that request, I wondered what Mr Wilkins would do for lunch. Evelyn would have packed a sandwich box for me and there would be a flask of coffee, too, to help me through the day – although I did sometimes pop into a pub for a pint after eating my sandwiches.

'A nice house.' His strangely pitched voice reached me as he peered through the window and into my small and rather ill-tended garden. 'Yours, is it?'

'It's rented,' I told him. 'From a man in the village.'

'You should buy your own home as soon as you are able, Mr Taylor, that is one of the finest investments anyone can make. The company will offer you every assistance, you realize. And I note you do not have a telephone?'

'No, the rent's too expensive—'

'Every successful businessman needs the swiftest and most efficient means of communication, Mr Taylor. You need to be at the forefront of modern technology and you must never hesitate to take advantage of the rapid progress in personal communications.'

'Well, I have been thinking about it . . .'

'Don't think, Mr Taylor. Act. A telephone is indispensible . . . So how do your clients contact you?'

'They write letters or come to the door, or leave messages for me.'

'Leave messages?'

'With other people.' I was going to explain that I operated in a community of small villages where few had telephones and contact was often made by mentioning things to people who were always around, like the postmistress, shopkeeper, butcher or milkman. The alternative was to leave messages in the shop, post office or pub. Before I could stress that aspect of my village bush-telegraph system, Wilkins said, 'You do appreciate much of our business is confidential and I am sure many of your clients would not want their personal business to be made available to others. Your system does seem somewhat fraught with danger, and at the very least it contains the potential for embarrassment, Mr Taylor.'

'I'm not talking about leaving confidential information lying around.' I felt I had to explain and decided to use, as my example, the name of the potential client I was preparing to visit later today.

'What I mean is that if someone, say Jack Linshaw from Cragtop Farm, wants to contact me, he or his wife or one of his sons will have a word with the shopkeeper and ask him to let me know Jack wants a chat next time I'm in

Thornhowe. All he'll say is that Jack Linshaw wants a word with me; there'll be no confidential information given. Then I'll go and see him. Our system works quite well.'

'It would be far more efficient if your Mr Linshaw could reach you by telephone, Mr Taylor.'

'Not really, he hasn't a telephone either,' I said. 'And he lives a mile and a half away from the nearest road, and two miles from the village, which is where the nearest kiosk is located.'

'Clearly, your agency is functioning in a time warp; let us hope I can persuade your clients to be more modern,' he said with just a hint of a thin smile as Evelyn brought in his glass of water, my cup of coffee and a plate of chocolate biscuits. I thought he might invite Evelyn to join us over relaxed refreshments but he seemed anxious to get on with his business. As she placed the refreshments on our coffee table, I invited him to sit down in one of the easy chairs as I took the other. Then I slid the coffee table towards him. When he'd settled on the settee, still wearing his beret, I said, 'Help yourself to a biscuit, Mr Wilkins.'

'I never eat between meals.' He lifted his briefcase on to the settee and opened the lid. 'I have some new literature here for you, details of endowment policies, new house-and-contents insurance, a re-designed leaflet about holiday insurance – that's going to become a major source of insurance in the future – and new rates for women drivers. More and more women are learning to drive cars, you realize, and so our company has decided to treat them the same as men – we do not have special rates for women drivers . . . That's all due to the war, of course, and the Land Army. And we have produced a new policy for insuring all electrically powered apparatus in the home – lots of people are buying television sets now and there's a big market in renting them. Things are changing, Mr Taylor, and we must be abreast of, or even ahead of, the trend towards modernization.'

He seemed to be ignoring his glass of water as he produced a succession of leaflets from his case, rather like a conjurer drawing things from a top hat, and then he'd finished. I was just draining my coffee cup and fancying a refill, when he said, 'Well, we must be going. I am sure you have drawn up a busy plan of action for us. You lead the way, Mr Taylor. Shall we use your car?'

'I haven't got a car,' I told him.

'You haven't got a car? So how do you get around this huge agency, all those villages in remote places?'

'I've got a motorbike, a Coventry Eagle,' I told him. 'You're welcome to be my pillion passenger.'

'I think not. We'll use my car. So, where are we heading, Mr Taylor – you realize I am new to this part of the country.'

'No, I didn't know.'

He told me that his last post was on the outskirts of Birmingham, a very active and busy place, but a deterioration in his wife's health meant he had to find somewhere with lots of bracing sea air, so they settled in Scarborough, a place they'd often visited on holiday. He said he was fortunate there had been a vacancy in the District Office; his wife had settled in very well indeed, and he liked the Yorkshire coast as a place to live. The bonus was that his wife's health had improved tremendously.

'And,' he added, 'I do enjoy seeing more of the countryside, which makes this aspect of my job most interesting.'

'Well,' I said, bearing in mind his mode of dress, 'I am sure you'll see a little of it today. We're going to Thornhowe because Tuesday is my normal collecting day there, and there are two farms I need to visit, one belongs to the Jack Linshaw I mentioned earlier, and the other is not far away. I thought we could visit them both today; there may be an opportunity for new business.'

'Is that all? Two calls?'

'There are other places where I'll be collecting, Mr Wilkins, if we have time that is. Places are rather a long way apart on these moors; there are lots of farms whose nearest neighbour is two miles away, and very few are on surfaced roads.'

'Even so, you need to accommodate many more calls in

the course of a day, Mr Taylor, many more, I would suggest.'

'I fit in as many as I can, I assure you.'

'You must be energetic and dynamic, Mr Taylor. Now when I was a young and keen agent in Droitwich, I would set myself a target of six calls each morning, a further five in the afternoon and two in the evening, every working day.'

I felt like telling him that we were not working in an urban area, nor indeed was this anything like suburbia, and it was distinctly unlike the parks in cities or the open green spaces of some towns. The patch of England he was about to visit was one of the remotest areas of the North York Moors, and the people he was soon to encounter were not townspeople but hard-working moorland farmers who did not understand things like bank accounts, investments, interest rates and endowments. They dealt in cash, which they earned by careful trading and which they kept in the house because it was always needed; they and their families did not have time to trek to the nearest bank, which could be ten or twelve very tortuous miles away. They wanted their money immediately available to buy necessities like food, clothes, new machinery and healthy livestock – most certainly it was not used for luxuries like holidays or television sets. If they effected any savings, then the cash would be stored somewhere safe, like a milk churn in the larder or a box in the loft.

After this briefest but very informative of introductions to this odd little man, my apprehension had evaporated and I was now very keen to show him just a little part of my extensive agency. I felt he had a lot to learn from me, and a lot to learn about the countryside and its people. I told Evelyn we were about to leave and that we expected to return around five thirty.

She kissed me goodbye and I could see he was slightly embarrassed by her show of affection. She explained she had packed my sandwiches and flask and they were in my rucksack in the back porch, standing beside my wellington boots and overcoat. That was my reminder to take those items – the coat was not the one I wore for motorcycling but a smart dress coat I used for funerals. When he saw me pick up my rucksack and wellingtons, Mr Wilkins said, 'Do we have to walk a long way?'

'Not necessarily,' I told him. 'But I've got my sandwiches in here . . .'

'Sandwiches, Mr Taylor? I'm sure the company could stand a modest outlay of necessary expenditure for subsistence today. I shall be making a claim for refreshments, we shall find a nice little restaurant and have a pleasant working lunch at company expense.'

'There aren't any restaurants where we're going, Mr Wilkins, but you might get a pint of beer in one of the pubs and a pork pie or pickled egg and a packet of crisps if you're lucky.'

'Nowhere to eat?'

'Some of the farmers will give you a good feed if you happen to arrive at dinner time.'

'Oh, dear I've not brought any sandwiches.'

'I'm sure Evelyn can make you a pack in a few seconds.'

'That would be most kind. You must think I am very naïve . . . Perhaps I am! So while I'm being rapidly educated into the ways of your local people, Mr Taylor, what is the significance of the wellington boots?'

'For walking around farmyards.' I smiled. 'And down muddy lanes, or wading across becks or flooded areas.'

'I'm afraid I haven't got any wellingtons in the car, either. I did dress for the country, or I thought I had, as you might have observed, but I had no idea we might be visiting such very remote places.'

'They're all very remote places.' I smiled again. 'But what size are you? Maybe Evelyn's wellies will fit you?'

Her feet were size five and he said he took a six, but when he tried on her well-used boots he could squeeze himself into them, and I assured him I would do my best to avoid the very dirtiest of routes or long walks.

Evelyn produced a round of ham sandwiches within

seconds, plus a tomato, apple and slice of fruit cake, not forgetting a lemonade bottle full of water, and by ten forty-five we were on our way. Although slightly tempted to avoid the hilliest and dirtiest of routes, I did have a commitment to my clients in Thornhowe because today was my normal collecting day and I would be expected. So Thornhowe it was; a spectacular destination in the depths of the moors.

Thornhowe lay in a deep dale and was about twelve miles from my home by the short route. The short route was an unmade, rugged, steep pot-hole ridden track, which crossed the treeless heights of the heather-clad landscape, eventually descending into Thornhowe, which was a branch of Baldby Dale. Every descent into Thornhowe was via a narrow winding hill with gradients ranging from 1-in-5 to 1-in-3, which meant it had no bus service, no trains and precious few visitors.

There was a small collection of rugged stone houses deep in the dale with a handful of lonely farms scattered around the moors above but no shop, no pub and not even a Methodist chapel. Nearby Baldby provided the postal service for Thornhowe, and other neighbouring villages supplied additional needs like the butcher, doctor, nurse, Church of England vicar, Catholic priest, Methodist minister, garage and policeman.

I opted for the rugged drive, now wishing to firmly impress upon Mr Wilkins that my agency was definitely not the sort of place where you made half a dozen calls before knocking off for lunch in a smart café. However, I did consider returning via the alternative, more sedate route, but would make that decision depending upon how we progressed during the day.

Mr Wilkins' car was a very smart Standard 10 in dark grey of which he seemed inordinately proud, because it was immaculately clean and brightly polished. But with such a plethora of hills and narrow lanes to cope with, and surely a good deal of muck, mud and cowpats, I knew our average speed would be much less than the normal thirty miles an hour or so. I reckoned it would take about forty-five minutes to cover those twelve open miles, even if we did not meet any other cars en route – and not allowing for stops on the way. The first five or six miles were easy. We used tarmac roads and Mr Wilkins chugged along in fine style, telling me all about his career and his adventures in insurance, and as he talked I realized he had no other topic of conversation – insurance was his entire life.

His work dominated his existence and, although I began to feel rather sorry for him for not having any other apparent interest, I resigned myself to the fact I was in for a long, boring ride. For that reason if for no other, I was glad I had chosen the scenic route.

After a few miles, I said, 'Can we pull up here, Mr Wilkins?'

There was a small stone cottage beside the road and he asked, 'This house?'

'I have a monthly collection here, Miss Cummings. Two shillings. It will be left out for me – it makes sense to collect it while we're passing. It means I don't have to make a special journey – petrol rationing doesn't allow for such things.'

'Left out for you?' he puzzled.

'On a shelf in the outside toilet,' I told him. 'She works away during the day, she's a teacher at Freyerthorpe primary school. She leaves the money out for me.'

'You mean it doesn't get stolen?'

'Who's going to steal money out here?' I smiled as he drew to a halt.

'I must see this with my own eyes,' he said, switching off the engine. So he followed me up the garden path and along the side of the house into the toilet. It was an earth closet, which smelled like an earth closet, but on the small window-ledge inside were several amounts of money. Mine was the two-shilling piece.

'Don't you take all that money?' asked the puzzled Mr Wilkins.

'No, it's not all for me. There'll be some for the butcher,

some for the shop when he delivers here, and I think Miss Cummings had a catalogue to pay – she gets her pots and pans from a catalogue, so the fellow must be due about now.'

And so his first discovery was how the moorfolk settled their regular payments while learning a little about their trust and honesty. Now, having completed that modest transaction, we continued over the high and windswept moors towards Thornhowe. After leaving Miss Cummings' cottage, we branched off the metalled surface and began to climb a winding road whose surface was riddled with holes and rocks and whose sides were more rocks smothered with heather. A grouse clattered from the heather, stones rattled against the undersides of Mr Wilkins' precious little car, and I was sure I could hear briars scrubbing the panelling as we climbed, even if we were doing less than five miles an hour as the gallant little car groaned and protested at the punishment being inflicted upon it. Soon we were on the level summit of the moor, where an improved road crossed the heights. We joined it, whereupon he sighed and said, 'Look at those views, Mr Taylor . . . I must bring my wife to see this, really I must.'

'Don't come up here in winter.' I laughed. 'The snow can be ten feet deep and there's nowhere to shelter.'

'So where is Thornhowe from here?' he asked, peering through the windscreen.

From our perspective it seemed we were looking across an endless plateau of heather, but I knew the expanse was broken by deep dales, some deserted, others containing a solitary farm or even a village. I explained this aspect of the local geography and he seemed stunned by the scale of the vast open vista before him, mile after mile of treeless heather with distant views of hills.

The views up here stretched for seventy or eighty miles into far reaches of the Yorkshire dales but it wasn't long before we were dropping down a very steep and narrow hill bordered by high dry-stone walls on either side. There was no room for two vehicles to pass and I could sense his nervousness but, to give him credit, Mr Wilkins did not panic on the incline and eventually we reached the bottom, where the road widened among a few cottages and was once again surfaced with tarmac.

'Nearly there,' I said.

'Now I can understand why you do only two calls a day.' He smiled. 'You must think I'm a simpleton.'

'Not at all,' I countered. 'It's just that this part of England is so different from towns and cities, it's a case of understanding it – and the people.'

'One is never too old to learn,' he conceded, and suddenly I found him rather more approachable than he had been an hour ago. There was no doubt he was experiencing something he'd never encountered either in his work or leisure moments, and I hoped he would enjoy the rest of the day. Already, it was nearly half past eleven – we'd been travelling for almost an hour and, apart from collecting Miss Cummings' modest premium, we had done no insurance work.

'I thought we would visit Highthorn first, it's along our route – well, sort of.' I estimated we would have enough time to talk to Mrs Wellingford before she broke off for her dinner, then we could find somewhere to park for our own sandwiches before going on to Cragtop Farm, home of the Linshaws. I put this suggestion to Mr Wilkins and he agreed.

'Tell me about Mrs Wellingford,' he put to me as he headed for her smallholding.

I explained that she was a widow in her mid fifties, whose husband had been a yeoman farmer at another premises in Thornhowe. Yeoman farmers were a distinct and very industrious group of people on the moors: they were working farmers, often very poor, but they owned their farms. They did not rent them from big estates or landowners, but in many cases had inherited them. Many such farms, often comprising a few tough acres upon very inhospitable land, had been in one family for centuries, and while their income was low their wealth lay in their premises; they owned property but had little cash, and what was the value of an isolated moorland farm to anyone but an experienced moorland farmer, who knew how to cope with it?

In the Wellingfords' case, they'd specialized in black-faced moorland sheep, although they had maintained a milking herd of redpolls and bred a few pigs, the large white breed, chiefly for the fatstock market. Andrew Wellingford, hard working and widely respected, had died suddenly about a year ago. He'd had no life insurance and so his wife had had to sell the family farm in order to pay off her husband's business debts, then buy and stock her own modest small-holding. This now provided her livelihood. It was a tough life, but Mrs Wellingford was determined to make a success of her new role.

'She left a message for me at the post office in Baldby,' I told him. 'Since her husband was not insured, she felt she ought to examine the possibility of her own life insurance. From what I've been told, she's concerned for her children; she wants to make sure all her debts are covered when she dies. The smallholding might be self-sufficient, but she also wants to make sure she has some kind of financial support in case she ever becomes too ill to work. If she suffered something as simple as flu or a broken leg, she'd have to find someone to look after the livestock, or if she became really ill, or just too old to cope, she might have to sell the whole enterprise and move off the moors and into the village.'

'She sounds like a very good potential client to me, Mr Taylor,' said Wilkins as I directed him along the rough track which led to her house. 'Just you show me the way.'

As we wound our way very slowly along the narrow lane that climbed not very steeply from the floor of the dale, I could see Highthorn nestling on the side of the hill ahead of us. It was a long house built of dark granite with blue slate tiles, and it occupied a hillside site below the line of the heather. The house was surrounded by several fields containing sheep, while others roamed the open moors above. The field boundaries were identified by dry-stone walls built of that same dark granite, and I could see a rough track winding its way between a pair of those walls. Such long granite houses were a feature of this moorland, and had a portion adjoining them used by cattle and other livestock, who wintered within those walls, their body heat helping to maintain warmth in the domestic areas. The houses were also built to endure the rigorous climate, having thick stone walls, small windows and most domestic rooms facing south, with places like the pantry and dairy being on the cooler north side.

'That's where we're heading.' I indicated the house with my finger.

'You couldn't say it had neighbours nearby, could you?' Wilkins smiled. 'I've never, in my entire life, experienced living in a house without neighbours just over the garden fence.'

'Up here, neighbours can be several miles away,' I said. He kept his speed very low as he manoeuvred his car across the rough track between the high walls, and soon we were entering an open space, a muddy yard containing hens and ducks among what appeared to be hundreds of lambs and ewes. After this his little car would need a thorough cleansing.

'It's lambing time,' I explained. 'People sometimes bring the sheep down from the moors at this time, so they can keep an eye on them, although a lot of lambs do get born on those heights without any assistance from their owners – or vets. If Mrs Wellingford's working alone, she'll have brought all her pregnant ewes down to the house, to make things easier for her. Even so, she'll have been working day and night, tending her flock, seeing to the poorly ones, feeding lambs if the mother's milk doesn't come, or caring for those rejected by their mothers . . .'

He parked just inside the gate, which I opened to allow him entry, and now he knew why I'd brought my wellington boots.

He pressed himself into Evelyn's wellies and then, after

picking up his briefcase, we splodged through a sea of mud, with hens and ducks running away from us and many sheep ignoring us; then a dog came running from the house, tail wagging but not barking. It was a black and white border collie, hereabouts known as a cur, a wonderful breed for all aspects of sheep farming and general farm work.

'Hello, boy.' I had no idea of the dog's name but I patted him and allowed him to lead us to the door of the house. It was standing wide open and led into a stone-floored passage in which I noticed boots, brooms, spades, shovels and all manner of tools. This passage would lead to another door providing entry to the house. The dog wagged its tail and led us to it. Such was the state of that passage that we had no need to discard our dirty welling-tons. It was more like an outdoor pavement than a corridor inside a house.

I led the way and, passing through another open door, found myself in what some might call the living room but others might refer to as the kitchen. It was a huge square room with a black fire range, complete with an oven. A bare wooden table stood in the centre and the stone floor was covered with clip rugs. One of them lay before the grate.

The noise was astonishing. The room was full of bleating sheep and lambs. Some were lying on the floor and others were standing still and looking up at us with some degree of expectancy.

'Is this where they give birth?' whispered Mr Wilkins.

'Quite likely,' I said. 'It's her kitchen.'

'Her kitchen? I thought it was some kind of birthing unit.'

'Well it is, but it's her kitchen as well, part of the house . . .'

'But it's full of sheep.'

'They're sheltered and accessible in here.' I tried to play down the situation, adding, 'I wonder where she is?' I decided to call out. 'Mrs Wellingford?' I raised my voice to make it heard about the din from the sheep, but the dog merely looked at us and wagged its tail.

'Where is she?' I asked the dog. 'Esme . . . Where's Esme?'

It just wagged its tail and then went out of the kitchen and trotted further along the stone-floored corridor to the door of another room; it looked at me, wagged its tail and went in. I followed the dog, and Mr Wilkins followed me. This was the lounge or what some called the sitting room; it had a carpet on the floor and there was a three piece suite and a picture on the wall above the fireplace. This room was also full of sheep and lambs, all bleating.

Then I became aware that the figure of a fully clothed woman was slumped on the settee. At first I thought she was dead, but quickly realized she was fast asleep. The dog went towards her and nudged her dangling hand with its cool nose. For a time she did not respond, and I felt it might be good manners to leave the room, but then the dog barked and the woman opened her eyes, sat up with a look of surprise on her face and tried to focus her sleepy eyes upon her visitors. She emerged from her deep sleep to the sight of two insurance men standing staring down at her.

I felt that the sight of a little man in the black beret was not all that strange in these circumstances.

'Sorry, I must have nodded off, it's been a busy time, lambing you know, up all night with the little darlings . . . Worse than having children of my own . . .' and she struggled to get off the settee, finally standing up. 'Hello, I'm Esme, Esme Wellingford.'

She was a large lady with iron-grey hair that looked unwashed and was tied back with a blue ribbon; she was dressed in men's overalls and black leather boots. Not very feminine, but highly practical in the circumstances.

'Look,' I decided to take the initiative here. 'We can come back later today if it's better for you. I'm Matthew Taylor from the Premier Assurance Association, I live at Micklesfield, and this is my District Manager – Life, Mr Wilkins. We heard you wanted to talk to us.'

'There's no saying what state I'll be in if you came back, and I can't say what my ewes will be doing, some are due any time . . . I'll have to get round them now I'm awake, just for a quick check . . . And I do need to talk to you chaps . . . How about a cup of coffee? I'm parched. It must be breakfast time – is it?'

'I don't drink stimulants,' chipped in Wilkins, doubtless recalling his impression of the kitchen.

'Look,' I said. 'It's long after breakfast time, it's nearly dinner time. Show me where to find the kettle and coffee, then you go and look at your sheep while I'm brewing something for you; you look as thought you need a stimulant.'

As Mrs Wellingford hurried outside for a rapid survey of those ewes she believed to be about due or even in the midst of giving birth, I found a kettle, which I filled and hung on the hook above the glowing fire. I managed to find some milk, sugar, mugs and a bottle of Camp coffee essence.

Wilkins was not quite sure what to make of all this, so he found a kitchen chair and settled upon it as a lamb came to him, expecting to be bottle fed. All he could do was stroke it and talk to it as if he was speaking to a dog; the cur, meanwhile, had gone outside with Esme to round up the necessary ewes. Esme returned about twenty minutes later and was delighted to find someone had actually made a warm drink for her. As we all found a seat, she warmed some milk for the hungry lamb, found some home-made rock buns, which I accepted and Wilkins declined, and sipped her coffee with obvious relish, as did I. As she drank her coffee with the mug in one hand, she fed the demanding lamb with a baby's bottle held in the other, the lamb tugging at the teat as if it was trying to drag it off. I found myself patting the head of a ewe that appeared to need nothing more than a spot of human affection, while the dog seemed fascinated with Mr Wilkins' wellingtons – my wife's in fact. Maybe the dog realized the scent of this man in the beret did not match that which arose from them.

By this stage, there had been no talk of insurance. Wilkins was very quiet, I noticed, and, I felt, somewhat overawed by this very domestic farming scene. I knew we must not stay too long, and unduly interrupt Esme's shepherding, but we had our own mission to fulfil. I decided to put the onus upon Esme.

'We don't want to get in your way,' I told her. 'Shall we discuss your insurance now, or shall we come back?'

'Let's do it now, Mr Taylor,' she insisted. 'I've enjoyed those few minutes' break and the company of human beings for a change! Now, I really do need to be covered. I learned an awful lesson when my husband died and I need some life insurance. I need the house and contents to be covered, too, and perhaps some of the farm machinery and buildings. I welcome your advice, please, and I know you won't force me into something that's unnecessary or too expensive.'

'Thank you for your trust, Mrs Wellingford. Now, let's start with a look at a policy based on your own life,' smiled Mr Wilkins, now on ground that was much more familiar to him.

Five

*'I was stationary and travelling in the
opposite direction when I hit a car
travelling the other way'*
From a claim form

It was after one thirty by the time we concluded our business with Esme Wellingford, our discussions being interrupted several times by the dog – whom we now knew as
Shep – coming in to indicate dramas among the heavily pregnant ewes both indoors and outside. Fortunately for us, all
were false alarms, but it did make me appreciate the value
of a trained sheepdog. Shep was clearly aware of the importance of what was happening and was very keen to be helpful.

Although Esme invited us to stay for dinner with her –
offering mashed potato, warmed up from yesterday, with
cold home-cured ham, carrots and some rice pudding – we
declined, saying we had to press on to complete the rest of
the day's outstanding engagements.

Mr Wilkins, with his beret still in place, drove to a flat
piece of moorland beside the road above the village, and
there we parked to enjoy our pack-up meals, me with my
coffee and he with the bottle of water. He chattered amiably
about his life in insurance, contrasting this morning's efforts
with his experiences with former clients, and he seemed
quite happy to be undertaking his work in such a different
environment. He asked about my previous work, too. I told
him about my butchering skills, relating how I had killed
seven pigs on my first insurance outing, gaining some poten-
tially useful contacts as a consequence, and adding a note

about my military service as a mechanic specializing in motorcycles.

He listened carefully, saying how he felt my past would prove of even greater value in the future, especially in such a rural agency, where one required a broad knowledge of the people and their way of life.

'I was very impressed by your wife, Mr Taylor,' he said at length. 'I could quote you many instances where I have visited agents and have not been admitted to the house, because the wife did not want me to go inside. I think they thought I would be critical of them and the way they lived. Many times I have had to conduct my business in my car. But your wife made me feel most welcome. I do appreciate that.'

'I think you'll find everyone in the moors is just as hospitable,' I told him.

'Perhaps so, but you must be sure to treasure your wife, Mr Taylor. I treasure mine, which is why I moved here from Birmingham. Her health was more important than my career, but we are so happy now and her health has improved. I might add that excursions like today are a wonderful tonic. Like a holiday in fact. I shall bring my wife out here for a ride to show her the scenery, petrol rations permitting. So is your wife a local girl?'

I told him Evelyn was from a large family in Micklesfield, with her parents owning the Unicorn, and that after she had finished studying at the teacher training college we had married and now had a two-year-old son. I told him about her supply work and our hopes that one day we would buy a house, get a telephone and even run a car. He seemed very interested in our domestic life and implied that a happy marriage was essential in creating a good working atmosphere.

'So how did you meet your wife? I'm interested because there do not seem to be many people living in this part of the world! Villages and houses are so far apart. So how does a young man find his future wife? There can't be many to choose from!'

'Well, I knew Evelyn as a child, our families have known each other ever since our parents were children. That's how it is in these villages. Young people have the same interests, and for entertainment or to socialize we went to Saturday night dances – that's where young people meet each other out here. Each village would stage a dance, in one village one week and in another the next. Even if we moved around the dale, those dances weren't full of strangers, Mr Wilkins, all the boys and girls knew one another, and still do. But, in fact, I was so shy I sent Evelyn a Valentine card!'

'Really? Now that is romantic . . .'

'I was just a butcher's lad, and she was a trainee teacher . . . I thought she was a bit too grand for me – her parents had their own business while my dad was just a gardener at a big house. But it didn't take her long to work out who'd sent it.'

'How did she do that?' He was smiling now and I felt he was more relaxed that I'd seen him so far.

'I was in the Army. I posted it from the barracks. There weren't many Micklesfield lads there! She worked it out from the postmark. So when I came back home on leave and went to a dance she found the opportunity to ask if I'd sent it. I must admit I blushed a lot before admitting it, but the rest is history, as someone once said!'

'Well, I think that is a wonderful story, Mr Taylor, and to repeat what I said, always treasure your wife and work for her as well as for yourself.'

'Thank you, yes I will.'

We both sat in silence for a few minutes, each nursing our own thoughts, and then it was time to continue.

'So, Mr Taylor, what can I expect this afternoon?'

'We're going to Cragtop Farm, but I've not met the family yet,' I had to admit. 'Jim Villiers' note suggested I call on them. They're called Linshaw, and it's a large farm just over that brow. It's been the family farm for generations.'

I pointed to the distant horizon, devoid of trees but covered with a blanket of heather, and could see the sun shining on a silver ribbon of road that twisted and turned up the steep hill before vanishing over the summit. Cragtop Farm lay somewhere beyond that summit, and from its name I guessed there must be more elevated land upon which it stood. At this point, it was hidden from view; indeed, there was no building of any kind on that horizon.

'Am I right in thinking this excursion will occupy us for the entire afternoon?' asked Wilkins.

'It depends what we find when we get there,' I laughed. 'We might find a house full of hens, a kitchen full of cows or a bedroom full of bulls. Who knows?'

'I can see why you selected just two calls, but I must say it's more interesting than talking to people who don't want their neighbours to know their business.' He smiled.

'I bet you can tell some tales, though, from your work in the city.'

'Indeed I can. Here's just a flavour. I had a client in Birmingham who insisted I park three streets away because she didn't think my car was impressive enough to stand on her drive, and another who wanted me to insure her jewellery against theft, except she didn't own any! She just wanted to impress the neighbours by taking out a big policy she could talk about. If we'd gone ahead with her idea, it would have been cheaper than actually buying the jewels, but what she didn't realize was that we need an official valuation. That's how we learned of her deception.'

'You couldn't officially value nothing! I don't think you'll find that kind of person hereabouts,' I told him. 'They're decent people, Mr Wilkins, with no airs and graces, or inflated opinions about their own importance. They're honest and they expect honesty in return. I'd never try to sell them a policy if I felt I was being dishonest or cheating them. I know some insurance men will sell anything just to gain a little more commission, but that's not for me. I want to help them, not impose burdens on them – they've enough burdens to cope with by simply earning their living.'

'I'm glad to hear it,' he said, starting the engine. 'You

must win the trust of your clients, that is vital. So, on we go, show me the way to Cragtop Farm.'

It was ten past two when we departed our picnic site, and I did not suggest going to a pub for a pint. I did not indulge in such luxuries every day, although I welcomed a long drink after a particularly tough session of canvassing. Already, though, I had gained the impression Mr Wilkins was not one for supping pints.

It took a further fifteen minutes to gain the summit we had viewed earlier, then a further ten minutes to descend the other side and locate Cragtop Farm. It stood on its own hilltop site at the head of the dale, almost like a mighty fortress in dark grey granite. It was the kind of lofty position in which one would expect to find a castle, and indeed this was a very large farm, evident from the number of buildings that surrounded it like a litter of pups round a proud mother dog.

As we approached, I could see that one face of the farmhouse – the east front – overlooked a lofty cliff, a sheer drop of several hundred feet to a stream trickling below. I was reminded of those fortified farms one sees in Northumberland, except that this house bore no indication of battlements or other fortifications. As the road ahead left the floor of the dale, it corkscrewed up the hill through a small wood of deciduous trees before entering fields surrounding the complex, leading eventually into the farmyard.

Mr Wilkins parked on a patch of concrete near the rear entrance to the massive farmhouse – everyone used this entrance – and this time, owing to the yard being concreted, we did not require our wellingtons. At close range, the house appeared huge – it was a massive copy of the traditional long house, but had an extra storey and lots of additional buildings attached to it. The yard was surrounded by wonderfully constructed stone barns, shippens and implement sheds, all providing shelter from the winds that would always blow across this exposed site, and it looked for all the world like the quadrangle of a medieval castle.

I began to wonder whether this had ever been a castle – it was quite feasible. The stones of a former building on this site could have been used, and, if so, it would have been sensible to make use of any existing foundations. Maybe, if I had time, I could do a little local research into its ancient history.

Although there was no one in the yard, the house door – the rear entrance – was standing wide open, as most of them were prone to do on such premises, and the yard had the customary complement of hens, ducks, cats and sheep-dogs. One of the dogs barked once as we left the car, then, after wagging its tail as a welcome, settled down in a sunny corner to continue its slumbers.

Mr Wilkins was by now standing on a stone walkway surrounding the base of the house, and I headed for the open door; he followed, and, as we approached, a young man emerged. He would have been twenty-five years old or thereabouts, a shade younger than me, a stocky man with broad shoulders, thick fair hair, blue eyes and a solid tread; he reminded me of a sturdy Viking. Probably he was descended from the Viking raiders who had settled here more than a thousand years earlier – I seemed to recollect that the old dialect word lin, the prefix to the name of the owners of this farm, originated in the name for flax. Linshaw might well have connections with the ancient flax industry. So was this one of the family?

'Hello,' I greeted him. 'I'm looking for Jack Linshaw.'

'Then you've found him. That's me. Animal feed, is it? We're about ready to order another load.' Surprisingly, he did not use the local dialect.

'Not animal feed,' I smiled. 'Something just as important – insurance.'

'I bet Jim Villiers told you to call!' grinned the cheerful man.

'He did,' I acknowledged. 'He said you might be interested in life assurance or some other kind of cover for the house and farm. I'm Matthew Taylor, by the way, your new agent for Premier. I live at Micklesfield. This is Mr Wilkins,

86

our Senior Manager – Life. He's from the District Office at Ryethorpe but lives in Scarborough.'

'Scarborough, eh? I once went there for a school trip. On the sands, just before the war. And we saw King Richard III's house. Ours is older than his, by the way. Anyway, you'd better come in, the missus will fix you a cup of tea, I expect, and mebbe a scone or piece of apple pie. Follow me.'

He led us along a passage almost identical to the one at Esme Wellingford's farmhouse, and we turned into a kitchen that was equally similar, if slightly larger. There were no sheep in this one, but there were three cats on the mat in front of the fire and a young woman was sitting at the table surrounded by piles of paper and account books. She was very pretty, with dark hair and smiling brown eyes, and she rose to her feet as we entered with her husband. It was then I realized she was heavily pregnant.

'This is Jill, my wife,' he introduced her. 'She sees to the book work. I'm no good at that, I'd rather work with cows and sheep than letters and figures. Jill, this is our new man from the Premier, Matthew Taylor – he looks too young to be in that sort of job – and this is Mr Wilkins from his District Office. They've come because Jim thought we might need some insurance, he was always telling us that!'

We shook hands, Wilkins still wearing his beret, and she offered us a chair at the table, shifting her pile of work to one side. Then, without asking, she began to open her cupboards to produce teacups, saucers, plates, sugar and milk, along with a plate of scones, an apple pie, a jug of cream, a large piece of fruit cake and some jam tarts. These were arrayed in front of us like treats in front of a child during a birthday party. I was aware of this instant hospitality for callers and I thought Wilkins found it rather overwhelming. I waited for him to say he did not drink stimulants or eat between meals, but this time he said nothing; he merely stared at the feast before him. In the eyes of Jill Linshaw, of course, this was a mere snack, a quick bite between meals. As Jill busied herself preparing the snack, Jack washed his hands and then, once the kettle was boiling, both joined us at the table. Neither of us had taken any food by this stage.

'You've eaten nowt!' he said. 'You should have been tucking in while she's getting things fettled. Help yourselves, don't wait to be asked, it wants eating up, that's what it's there for.'

Remembering I had so recently enjoyed my sandwiches, I wondered if I could cope with any more, but I knew it was considered ill-manners not to avail oneself of such hospitality when visiting these moorland farms, and so, as Jack told us about the extent of his farm and his produce, I helped myself to a slice of apple pie, poured over it a generous helping of fresh cream and selected a spoon from the pile on the table.

I was moderately surprised to see Mr Wilkins do likewise, and realized he had rapidly learned that this was expected; to refuse would be churlish, and besides I think he had reasoned that refusal might cost him the policy he was dearly wishing to sell to this family. So we tucked in, Wilkins even accepting a cup of weak tea instead of a glass of water. He seemed quite happy to learn our country ways!

'Right,' said Jack at length. 'What's all this insurance you want to sell me?'

'Consider it an investment, Mr Linshaw,' smiled Wilkins. 'What insurance do you have already?'

'Nowt,' said Jack. 'We've never had any.'

'Never?'

'Never in all the time our family's been at Cragtop.'

'And how long is that?' Wilkins asked in all innocence.

'Eleven or twelve hundred years, summat like that,' said Jack without batting an eyelid. 'Mind, my ancestors had another house before this one, on this site it was, mebbe built of wood, but this one's fairly new, built about 1300 or thereabouts.'

Wilkins did not know whether to believe this or whether the man was making fun of him, but he ploughed on. 'So what if your hayshed caught fire, say through a simple electrical fault, and was burned to the ground? How would you pay for a new one?'

'It's happened already, Mr Wilkins, that hayshed of ours did burn down and we salvaged the stone but lost all the roofing timbers. We got a party of blokes from the dale who were looking for work to come and rebuild it, roof and all, and they put tiles on instead of thatch. They did a cracking job, it didn't cost us much and it's better now than it was before it got burned down.'

'And when was this?' asked Wilkins.

'1793,' said Jack. 'Before electric came to these dales, that was. My great granddad heard his granddad talk about it.'

'Well, we must think, in modern terms, of the risks from installing electricity in the outbuildings and the use of modern equipment in old structures; then there's the domestic quarters. There'll be electricity in the house, the risk of theft from your farm or even from the house – we do a good combined fire and house contents insurance. Then there's life insurance to consider for you and for Mrs Linshaw, and, if I may be so bold, for your future child. You might consider an endowment policy, which is a wonderful form of saving for the future, or a simple life assurance. We can offer a very wide range – there's something for everyone, Mr Linshaw.'

'There'll be a cost for all this, is there?' asked Jack.

'Well, yes, there is. As one would expect there are premiums to pay, but the cost has to be balanced against the benefits. In very simple terms, you get what you pay for: the more you put in, the more you get out.'

'A bit like gambling, you mean? You put money on a horse expecting it to win so you'll have more than you set off with, but that rarely happens because the horse comes in last or falls and breaks its neck or summat. The more you put on the horse, the more you're likely to win – and the more you're likely to lose, that's how I see it.'

'Our policies are infinitely more secure than betting on horses, Mr Linshaw, and I suspect the terms are far more beneficial. Now, if you take out a with-profits endowment policy now – at the age of, say, twenty-five – you could pay premiums until you reach retirement age of sixty-five, and then the policy could mature and you would receive all your money back, along with any profits your investment had made over the years. A very wise and effective way of saving, Mr Linshaw.'

'And if I die before I'm sixty-five, what happens?'

'That depends on the kind of policy you take out, but a wise man would make sure it was paid to his dependants. There are lots of options and lots of schemes available – my company is noted for the variety of policies on offer, and we can find one to suit your personal requirements or your family needs.'

'It might be better to invest in a good pedigree bull. He'd fetch in a fairish good income, that's guaranteed, and if I die he keeps going, earning money for the farm.'

With that simple statement, I could see that Mr Wilkins was going to have a difficult time persuading this man into insurance of any kind. Jack was clearly thinking he'd be paying out good money with the risk of nothing in return, and I must admit my thoughts began to drift as Wilkins embarked upon his sales patter.

I was brought back to reality when I heard Jack say, 'Well, our family's not in the habit of dying early, Mr Wilkins. My old great-granddad's notched up his hundred, and although folks said we should be proud of him because he's grown old, I reckon he took a mighty long time about it, and he didn't do much else apart from grow old. When you get to that age, though, you can't expect folks to earn their keep mucking the cows out, you've got to look after them. If that had been a sheepdog we'd have had him put down, so I can't see the sense of having life insurance, not when you live to that sort of age. You'd pay out a fortune over the years and get nowt back. Life insurance is for folks who drop dead early, isn't it? For us farmers, we've stopped earning by the time we get old – you're not expected to earn, the young 'uns take over, like me. So what I'm saying is that it doesn't matter to this family if an old chap dies – he's not earning and in fact he costs less to keep when he's dead and buried than he does when he's alive and kicking. So insurance, with money for when you're old, seems a waste of time.'

'But when a senior family member has retired, he won't be your responsibility, Mr Linshaw, surely? Not if he had a nice endowment sum to cushion him into old age.'

'My dad's still living here, we feed him, give him a roof over his head, let him use the car and keep a few pigs and hens if he wants, and his pocket money comes from his savings, for clothes and things. There's no pension for him, you see. It's my job, now I've taken over the farm, to make sure he's looked after – and my mother, they live along that corridor. He did the same for his mum and dad – it's a family tradition.'

'But if your dad had taken out one of these endowment policies, it would have matured by now and he'd have a lump sum to enjoy.'

'But he'd have been paying into it all those years?'

'Well, yes, that's how the system works.'

'My dad's been doing that in a different way: paying to keep this farm going for me to take over, and now it's keeping him. I reckon that's good insurance, Mr Wilkins. He wants for nothing, neither does my mother – he's got his health and he's happy, and so is she.'

'So how old is your father?'

'Fifty.'

'Is that all? And he's retired at fifty?'

'Oh, aye, that's the family custom. You get your wife pregnant so she gives birth when you're twenty five, then when that baby lad reaches twenty five, like I am now, he takes over the farm and his dad takes a back seat. Dad can be retired if he wants, with everything found for him from the business, and he can keep a few hens and things to earn a few bob while the son runs the farm.'

'It seems an ideal way of life, in theory at least . . .'

'It's more than theory, Mr Wilkins, it's worked all these

91

years and the eldest has always been a lad, always born when his dad is twenty-five, and so the system goes on and on. We look after each other, like we have all these years. I can't see we need your sort of insurance.'

I could see that this logic caused Mr Wilkins to reconsider his tactics and, for a moment or two, he was lost for words. Then he said, 'Perhaps I should leave you my explanatory leaflets, Mr Linshaw, and then you can read them at your leisure, and also allow your father to see them.'

'It costs nowt to look at 'em.'

'When you've done that, Mr Taylor can contact you later to see whether you have made a decision.'

'I can ask my dad now,' said Jack. 'He's still a director of the business. I'll fetch him right away and we can settle this right now.'

Jack's father was also called Jack and he looked exactly like his son, except that he was slightly heavier and his hair was rather more grey. He listened as Wilkins tried to explain the merits of life assurance and the wisdom of insuring one's house and business for things like fire risk and other forms of damage, and then he shook his head. 'Nay, Mr Wilkins, I can't see there's any benefit in spending hard earned money on summat like insurance where you might not get owt back. Our system seems to work, we've been doing things this way right from the start, centuries ago we started, and I doubt if my father would want us to change things.'

'Your father?' puzzled Wilkins.

'Aye, he lives in the west wing, he's a director of the business, and he saw to it all his life, finance and the lot. If you like I could ask him what he thinks.'

'So how old is he?' asked Wilkins.

'Twenty-five years older than me, seventy-five, and as fit as a lop. I'll go and fetch him.'

Five minutes later, young Jack's grandfather – also called Jack – entered the room and listened to his family's account of what insurance might do for the business and the family.

But this man, an older replica of his son and grandson,

shook his head and said, 'If it was up to me, I might consider it, if it was cheap and produced a good return on our cash, but the way I see things is that our livestock brings in a good return, and we don't need house insurance or insurance for our buildings, because we can fix 'em ourselves.'

Wilkins sighed and said, 'Well, if you are the person who makes the decisions, perhaps you should study my leaflets and proposals.'

'Nay, lad, it's not really my responsibility, I think you'd better ask my dad.'

'Your father?' cried Wilkins. 'So where is he and how old is he?'

'He's just turned a hundred but he's as wick as weasel and he lives in the east wing. I'll go and fetch him and you can ask him about insurance, but I can't see he'll be much taken with life insurance, not if you pay into it all your life and then get nowt back when you're dead. It would have cost him a fair bit. He's better spending it on his tot of whisky, and most of us Linshaws have lived to be ninety or more . . . He's called Jack as well, we're all Jacks, all the first-born lads that is.'

Very old Jack was a rather stooped version of the others, but his facial characteristics and his attitude were almost identical. I must admit that after listening to them explaining their way of life, I could not see any reason how or why they would benefit through any kind of insurance scheme. They had a unique way of life, and when we quizzed them in depth their funeral arrangements were also covered, each person 'putting a bit by' on a weekly basis in a special funeral savings box kept in the kitchen.

As I sat back to watch Mr Wilkins deal with the eldest of the Jacks, I wondered if Jim Villiers had sent us here merely to meet this remarkable family rather than to sell them any insurance. Or, perhaps, he'd wanted us to learn something from them . . . Perhaps it was to teach us about family responsibilities, or a way of life which was rapidly becoming extinct. Not surprisingly, we did not sell insurance of any kind to the Linshaws, and it was almost four o'clock when we took our leave.

'I do not know what to make of that family,' admitted Mr Wilkins as we drove away. 'I just do not know. I think you should persist, though, Mr Taylor, and pay them a return visit to see if they have studied my literature.'

'Yes, I'll do that,' I promised, one reason being that young Mrs Linshaw made very good apple pies.

As we headed for my home, I told Mr Wilkins that I had just one more call on the return route but assured him it would be nothing like our previous two. It was merely a case of collecting a tiny premium from an elderly lady who lived on the outskirts of Thornhowe. By my reckoning, we had just about sufficient time if we wanted to return to Micklesfield by five thirty.

The lady in question was Miss Maureen Royle, a retired civil servant now in her early eighties. Her entire career had been with the Foreign Office in London, which meant she was something of a mystery to the local people, especially as she had retired to her Thornhowe cottage just before the outbreak of World War II. She had previously been on the books of a West London agent, and Jim Villiers had attended her when she'd been transferred to my agency on her return in 1938. Jim had mentioned her in one of his notes because, as he put it, there was a certain ritual that had to be performed in collecting her monthly premium.

Today's visit was not my first, therefore, but her March payment was now due and it would be easy to make the collection on our return trip. Apart from that, I thought Mr Wilkins might like to meet this interesting lady, who was very reclusive and rarely ventured from her ivy covered house, Woodside. It stood near the road that led to Gaitingsby, and if she did emerge from her home it was usually on an old pedal cycle with a basket on the front. She rode it to the shop in Gaitingsby, a two-mile trip, and sometimes called at a local farm for fresh eggs and butter. Most of her essentials came via deliveries to the door, and

I had discovered a little about her foibles from others callers to her house, such as the postman and milkman.

Woodside was set back from the narrow carriageway on a steep hill that rose from Thornhowe on the road to Gaitingsby, and it was almost invisible behind a high, dense hawthorn hedge, not yet in leaf. It was a brick-built bungalow of very square dimensions and seemed to be surrounded by trees and shrubs, which flourished in the extensive garden. There was no garage, the only access being a small wooden gate marked 'Woodside', but there was a patch of grass outside the gate. We could park there and walk down the pebble-covered path to the rear door where it continued round the house to the front door.

'A nice bungalow,' commented Mr Wilkins. 'Very isolated, though, well out of the village.'

'She likes it like this,' I told him. 'You could drive past without even realizing it was here, especially when that hedge and those trees are in leaf. It looks completely surrounded by trees from this side, but from the front garden there are wonderful views across the dale – you can see for miles. She's got a telescope set up in the front lounge and spends hours gazing down the dale.'

'A bird watcher, is she? Or star gazer?' he asked as we approached the front door, our feet crunching the pebbles. This was one occasion we presented ourselves at a front door, Miss Royle having worked in London, where such peculiar habits were considered normal.

'No,' I smiled. 'She's looking out for spies.'

'Spies?'

'She worked for the Foreign Office,' I reminded him. 'She thinks there are spies everywhere, she's always on the look out for them.'

As we walked round the house, I noticed the curtains were all closed – again quite normal at this house. As we arrived at the front door I became aware of a curtain fluttering and a pair of bespectacled eyes peeping out, but I did not draw Mr Wilkins' attention to them; I preferred to let her believe she had not been observed. Then I pressed the door bell and we heard it ring in the house. Some moments passed, and then the letter box was raised from within and the same pair of bespectacled eyes peered out.

Knowing the routine, I bent down to gaze into the eyes at their own level as she ordered, 'Identify yourself.'

'Agent Taylor,' I replied.

'Unit?'

'Premier,' I responded with all the solemnity I could muster.

'Password?'

'A pocket full of rye.'

'Wait.'

The letter box closed and we were left outside in silence.

'Is she going to open the door and let us in?' I could see the puzzled frown on Mr Wilkins' face, which made his beret look even more incongruous.

'No, she's gone to check my name on the master list she keeps somewhere inside,' I smiled. 'I'm undergoing a security clearance operation at this moment but I'm not sure how she'll respond to you.'

A few minutes passed and then the letter box was reopened and she asked, 'Agent Taylor, who is your comrade?'

Before I could respond, and much to my surprise and delight, Mr Wilkins, clearly entering into the spirit of the occasion, stooped just a little, put a hand to his beret and said to the letter box, 'Agent Montgomery from Headquarters, Agent Taylor's commanding officer.'

'Montgomery!' she whispered, her eyes now screwing up tightly and seeing only the beret outside her door. 'Everything is present and correct, sir.'

'Thank you,' said Wilkins, not even looking in my direction.

'The material is at box six,' she whispered. 'Ready for collection.'

'Thank you,' he said, and the letter box closed. Then he turned to me and asked, 'What's box six?'

'It's a stone on the rockery near the sundial,' I told him. 'The money will be under it.'

As he followed me across the lawn, I knew she was watching from behind another set of curtains, and I could quite see how the diminutive figure of Wilkins in his beret could be mistaken that of Field Marshall Montgomery. That might be especially so for an elderly lady with poor eyesight, but I was rather amazed that this little man, whom I had thought humourless, had so effectively responded to her. He had displayed a wonderful human side – just as he had when chatting to me about family matters.

I found the stone, the one she always used, and lifted it to find a sixpence underneath.

'Is that all?' asked Mr Wilkins.

'She pays six shillings a year,' I told him. 'It's a long running policy, one she took out many many years ago, a life insurance. I collect it once a month.'

'With this ritual every time?'

'It adds to the joy of my work,' I said with honesty. 'But tell me, how did you manage to understand her peculiarities so quickly?'

'I've come across similar people before. You get lots of them in towns, but, in her case, I'd heard about her. A former colleague of mine, now retired, used to work in the West End of London where Miss Royle used to live. She's quite famous, you know, Bunny Royle she was known as. She did some wonderful intelligence work during the war. They reckon she once saved Churchill's life, very bravely too.'

'I thought she retired here before the war – she was living here throughout the whole conflict.'

'Not all the time,' he told me with confidence. 'That was part of her deception. This was her safe house . . . Now, Mr Taylor, if only you could get her talking to you. She is a legend, you know. You are most fortunate to have her as one of your clients. I am so delighted you have introduced her to me.'

'It seems I must delve a little into her background,' I said.

'I'll see if I can trace my old colleague, he was an agent before the war . . .'

'What sort of agent? Insurance or intelligence?' I asked with a smile.

'Both,' was his surprising answer.

As we returned to his car for the final run home, I couldn't resist asking, 'What made you respond so quickly with the name of Montgomery?'

'It's my Christian name,' he told me.

And now I understood why he wore that beret.

Six

'When I caught sight of my mother-in-law
in the driving mirror, I lost control
and finished up in the river'
From a claim form

I received a very nice letter from Montgomery Wilkins, expressing his thanks for such an interesting day on the moors, even if we had done little business, adding that he had been delighted to meet Evelyn and stressing he had been completely enchanted to learn the whereabouts of Bunny Royle, especially as she had continued to be a Premium policy holder.

Our lack of business that day was not unusual, but fluctuations in premium receipts and new business meant that, on some occasions, my income – through the reduced commission – was smaller than it should have been, if only temporarily. Some weeks, therefore, it was barely sufficient for the family needs, but I had been brought up not to borrow money and not to get in debt. The logic was simple: if you could not pay for something you did without it.

I began to ponder additional means of raising money on a fairly regular basis. There was no doubt that Evelyn's potential income from her supply teaching was a consideration, but the problem was that it was by no means regular. In fact, she had undertaken just a single duty of two weeks at Graindale Bridge school and I had told her to put her earnings into a savings account at the post office. I suggested she should keep the extra money for essentials like new clothes for herself – she'd need decent outfits if her work was to become more regular.

In spite of Evelyn's help, therefore, I began to wonder how I could increase my income other than by relying on earning more commission. There was nothing in my contract of employment to forbid me earning money elsewhere, provided the Premium Assurance Association took precedence in my activities. I could, for example, earn a little by repairing the occasional motorcycle at weekends or even by killing pigs, but it would be far better to earn something while on my rounds, without it interfering with what I was supposed to be doing.

The realization that this was possible came one morning when I called on Kathy Newton, the wife of a farm labourer who lived in a tied house on a large farm near Baysthorpe. Kathy had seven children, whose ages ranged from three to thirteen, and she was a hard-working mother who earned a little extra by working a few hours in the dairy on the farm that employed her husband, Eric. In his mid thirties, Eric worked long hours for his employer and was considered most reliable, hard working and honest. Unfortunately, he had fallen from a ladder while doing some repairs to the roof of an outbuilding and broken his left leg just below the knee. For all their modest income, the Newtons had taken out a small policy some time before my appointment, and it covered them for events such as this. If Eric was unable to work due to any injury suffered at work, or even when not at work, then the policy would pay him £3 2s 6d per week for the first twelve weeks, with a review at that stage. If the incapacity continued, he'd been paid £3 a week for the ensuing twelve weeks, and £2 17s 6d a week thereafter. It was a very good policy, but there was one snag: payments did not commence until one month after the injury had been incurred.

An added factor was that a doctor's certificate was also required to authorize the payments. While the latter condition was not really a problem, the former meant that for an entire month the Newtons would have no income, apart from Kathy's few hours of work. I knew Eric's boss, Les

Dixon, would make sure the family had plenty of food and, of course, their house was rent free but, even so, a young family does need access to ready cash, and on the low wages of a farm labourer few could save for such eventualities, especially with such a large family. It was against this background that I called on the Newtons a week after Eric's accident to confirm that the company had agreed to his insurance payout. Sadly, I also had to tell him that it would be another three weeks before the first payment could be made, and equally unfortunately, the weekly premium of a shilling, which was not suspended during this period, was also due. Both Eric and Kathy were present during these discussions, and I told them I would not press them for their premium until Eric was earning once again.

Eric, however, did not believe in owing money to anyone. He knew that if he got into debt it would be extremely difficult to overcome it, and he said he wanted to pay anything he owed, even if it meant raiding one of the family's savings tins. Most families kept a tin on the mantelpiece into which they popped small amounts of surplus cash, always useful in emergencies. Even if this was possible, I was determined not to let this needy family go short of cash when a little leeway could be tolerated both by me and my company.

'I won't come for any premiums until your insurance comes through,' I told them. 'That'll be in three weeks' time. I'll fetch it as soon as it arrives.'

'Look, Matthew, we haven't a bean right now, but I'll do a deal with you.' Eric struggled to his feet, the huge plaster weighing on his leg, and grabbed a crutch which stood against the wall. 'Come with me.'

Kathy smiled and shrugged her shoulders as if to indicate she had an idea of what her husband was going to do, and I followed him out of the back door and down his garden path into a stone-built shed. It had electricity installed and he switched on the light. He led me into a woodworking shed complete with bench, rows of tools on the walls and several high shelves containing wooden toys,

101

all painted in a variety of bright colours. Most of them were boys' toys: lorries, tractors, cars, a crane and even a train set complete with trucks and a guard's van, all made in wood. Furthermore, they were all painted beautifully. There were a few girls' things too – I spotted a doll's cradle, a doll's cot and some play furniture, a miniature table and chairs and a lovely wardrobe about six inches high.

'Wow!' I breathed. 'Are these all yours?'

'Aye,' he said. 'My hobby. Making toys. I started with a tipper lorry for one of my lads, then another, then a doll's house for one of the lasses followed by some bits of dolls' furniture . . . It's gone on from there. Friends and relations have asked for 'em an' all, so it keeps me busy when I'm not on the farm. And it gets me out from under Kathy's feet. I enjoy the peace and quiet down here sometimes, when the house is full of noisy bairns.'

'Do you sell any of these? I mean, Eric, judging by the number of toys on your shelves, you're making far more than you need for your family.'

'I am. Sometimes, if I'm asked to do a tractor and trailer for somebody, I'll make two and put one on the shelf, in case somebody comes in a rush wanting a birthday present, so, yes, I do sell a few.'

'So who buys them?'

'Relations mainly, some friends. Word gets around. If any of our relations want one, they'll give me summat, usually enough to cover the cost of the wood and paint.'

'You should ask a toy shop to display them for sale,' I put to him. 'In Whitby, Guisborough or Stokesley, one of the local towns, I bet they'd stock your stuff and give you a good price, more than just the cost of paint and wood. And I'd bet they would come back for more.'

'I did think about it, Matthew, but I've no car to get about in, and working on the farm means I don't have any spare time when the shops are open, so I only sell to folk who know me and call here. There's no way I can deliver to a shop. One cousin said I should go full time – he reckons I'd make more from this than from labouring – but it would mean finding another house to rent or buy, setting up a shed with more tools, getting a car or a van to carry stuff to the shops. That's a lot of expense just to get started, so I'm happy as I am, just for now. It's a good hobby. I mightn't like it so much if it was my living. If I had to depend on it for everything, there'd be a lot of extra pressures.'

Eric was right and I sensed he had not brought me to his shed merely to look at his impressive creations. He said, 'Have you any family, Matthew?'

'A boy,' I told him. 'Paul, he's two.'

'Here.' With an effort, owing to his temporary incapacity, he reached up to one of the shelves and lifted down a smart green tipper lorry. It was about a foot long with a rear section on hinges so that it operated like a genuine vehicle, and it even had a steering wheel, front wheels that steered and two seats in the cab. It was one of three similar lorries on the shelf. He passed it to me. I took it, not realizing he intended to give it to me.

'How much do you want for this?' I asked.

'Nowt,' he said. 'I thought we might do a deal. I owe you a shilling for this week's premium, and if you leave it a month it could be four or five bob by the time you come back. So take this lorry instead of that money.'

'I can't do that!' I said. 'This is worth far more than four shillings – it would be at least fifteen bob or even a quid in any toy shop.'

'Then you'll have gained summat and I'll have cleared my debt,' he said dourly. 'We'd both be happy.'

I looked at the toy. It was beautifully made and was very strong, certainly strong enough for a boisterous child to play with in safety, and I thought Paul was quite capable of handling it. He loved things like tractors and lorries.

'Tell you what,' I said. 'I'll buy it off you.'

'No, that's not the idea. Just take the truck and write my payments off for a month in your book, Matthew, then we're quits, you and me. That would be a big load off my mind.'

'Eric, with a stock of toys like this you've no need to go without money. You could sell one or two a week and it would keep you in ready cash . . . Look, I'll give you 12s 6d for this lorry, right now. If it will keep your conscience happy, give me four shillings back and I'll mark your account as paid up for a month. That means I've paid a fair price for the truck, you've cleared your account and I've got a toy for Paul. That would make me happier, I don't want to take advantage of you.'

'And I don't want you to think I'm pressing you to part with your own money or that I need charity. I can pay my way, by bartering if I have to.'

'I reckon we understand each other, Eric. Consider it done. If you're happy then so am I.'

We settled for that. It meant his debt to the Premier was paid and he had 8s 6d in his pocket. It wasn't much, but it was more than the cost of the wood and paint he'd used and he was happy with the deal. I was happy because I went off with a very handsome addition to Paul's growing collection of toys.

When I got home with it, Paul's little face showed his delight, and Evelyn was equally pleased. 'Where did you get this?' she asked.

I explained, whereupon she said, 'Matthew, you mustn't take advantage of Eric. He must be paid a fair wage for what he does. This is a real craftsman's work.'

'I know, and I told him so. At the moment he just wants to cover his costs and have a bit in his pocket, but if he's off work for very long he'll soon learn to charge a fair price for his toys.'

'When Paul's friends see this, I'm sure they'll all want one!' She smiled. 'Can I pass the word around the mums I meet?'

'You do that, then I can get Eric to produce the toys. He has a big stock of things but I'm sure he would make something special on request, like a tractor or a crane. And now's the time to ask him, while he's off work.'

The following Wednesday evening a client called at my house to renew his car insurance. As I completed the paperwork at my desk, he noticed the tipper truck on the floor of the kitchen, where Paul had been playing with it.

'That lorry,' he said when we had concluded our business. 'Where did you find it? I'd love one for my little lad, he's mad about tippers.'

'I know a man who makes them,' I said. 'You'll not find them in the shops, they're hand-made locally.'

'Could you get me one?' was his next question.

'I think so,' I said. 'He had two left when I got that one. A green one and a blue one.'

'Right, I'd like one, green if possible,' he said. 'If I give you the money now, can you get it for me? It's Richard's birthday a week next Friday and I could call any evening.'

'Fair enough,' I said, doing a rapid mental calculation to determine when I would next be near Baysthorpe. 'How about next Wednesday night?'

'Right, done. How much are they?' was his next question.

'Thirty bob,' I said, thinking that if I was to buy and deliver the lorry, I needed a little more than Eric would charge. With no more ado, my client produced a pound note and a ten shilling note, and the following Wednesday afternoon I rode out to Throstle Nest Farm Cottage to find Eric working in his shed.

I explained what had transpired and he said fifteen shillings would be a good price. I still thought he was undercharging and offered him twenty-five shillings, saying it was for the time involved in creating such a toy. It was a wonderful profit as far as he was concerned. He was amazed at the prices people would pay for a good quality toy, but, with some pressure from me, he agreed – and I earned myself five bob into the bargain.

In the following days and weeks, Evelyn's friends also placed orders for trucks, trains, tractors and combine harvesters, and so began a very fruitful relationship, with me selling Eric's toys around my agency to earn both of us a modest extra income. I bought a few of them for stock so they were readily available if anyone asked. Evelyn grumbled that they were taking up too much space under our bed, but I was delighted when word of his skills began to reach a wider audience and people began to approach him directly. His skills earned him a very welcome few pounds and eventually he bought a large second-hand car, both to transport his family and to deliver toys when he had the time.

I continued to sell a few of his toys during my rounds, for a small commission, which helped me meet my domestic expenses, but Eric never gave up his day job.

He was still a farm labourer when he retired many years later but he did not retire from his toy making. In fact, Eric's toys can still be seen in houses and farms around the moors, a tribute to their quality and masterful construction.

Another example of mutual aid occurred when I was collecting in Graindale. Inevitably, about half of my clients were away from their homes, either at work or shopping, when I called, and they would leave their premiums in pre-arranged places. That day, I was collecting shillings, florins, half crowns and even ten shilling notes from their usual places in outside toilets, garden sheds, on rear window-ledges and under flowerpots or doormats. One advantage of this system was that I did not have to spend time talking to lots of people, but the disadvantage was that I rarely spoke to them at all, which in turn meant I could not generate much new personal business. New business inevitably arose through person-to-person chats.

It was while walking down a narrow alley between two stone cottages in Graindale, having collected two shillings from Mrs Harrison's washhouse window-ledge, that I encountered Roger Crossley. He was walking towards me carrying a small box of what looked like groceries, so I stepped into a recess to let him past.

'Morning, Matthew.' He was a cheery man with a shining bald head bearing a monk-like tonsure of thin white hair about his ears. Roger, in his late forties, was the keeper of the village shop in Micklesfield, and he habitually wore a white smock, even when delivering from his small van to customers in other villages. 'Is Mrs Harrison in?'

'It's her day for seeing her sister in Crossrigg,' I reminded him. 'She'll have gone down on the ten train, and she'll be back on the four.'

'Fair enough. I'll put this in her washhouse,' he said. 'She's expecting it.'

'The money's there for you,' I told him, having noticed the coins alongside my dues. 'On the window-ledge inside. I've just got mine.'

'If I'd known you were coming here, you could have brought these groceries for her,' he laughed, halting beside me while still carrying the box. I noticed it contained very few items, stacked round a bottle of HP sauce, and thought I could have accommodated all of them in my rucksack or even in my panniers on the bike.

'And if I'd known you were coming here, you could have collected my premium for me!'

He paused, pursed his lips and then said, 'You know what, Matthew, maybe we've got the makings of a good idea here. Look, let me put this in the washhouse, then I'll have a chat with you before you leave.'

I returned to my bike, made an entry against Mrs Harrison's name in my collecting book and then waited for Roger. He came back, whistling and beaming as he hurried to his van, which was parked next to my bike.

'Matthew,' he said, 'that was my only delivery in Graindale today, a tiny order to say the least, but it meant a special journey, and that's expensive in terms of time and money, not to say how much it's drinking into my petrol ration. It's true, isn't it, that with a bit of advance planning you could have brought it for me and left it at Mrs Harrison's?'

'Well, yes,' I had to agree. 'If I'd known you were coming, I could have saved you a journey.'

'I'd have given you something towards your petrol,' he offered.

107

'That wouldn't be necessary, not if I was coming anyway,' I countered.

'Ah, yes, but one good turn deserves another, so in return, I could collect your premiums for you from places that mean a special journey or a long trip for you.'

'Well, there are one or two places where I call regularly that involve a long trek over the moors, very time consuming . . .' Already I was seeing the sense in his suggestion. 'If I delivered your groceries and you collected my premiums in these cases, especially the long-haul calls, we'd both gain in saved time, expense and petrol, wouldn't we?'

'Why don't we give it a try?' He waved his hands in a gesture that suggested there was nothing to lose. 'Look, one day when you've a few minutes to spare, pop into the shop with a list of a few of your clients like Mrs Harrison, and I'll see if any of them are on my delivery round for that day or the next. If they are, we can join forces.'

'If this becomes a big job,' I laughed, 'I'll have to get a car!'

'I reckon it won't be long before you get one anyway,' he said in all seriousness. 'A chap in your position needs a car, Matthew. After all, you are a businessman, you need to be smart and you also need to show some confidence in yourself. A nice car will go a long way towards that. Anyway, mustn't hold you up, think over my proposal and call in for that chat when it's convenient.'

His idea set me thinking and over the next few days I pondered his suggestion, visualizing those of my clients who habitually left money out both for me and for other tradesmen. In many ways, it made sense for only one of us to make such a journey. It would require very careful book-keeping so that mistakes and confusion were avoided, and we would have to inform those clients of our new system so that they were not puzzled or alienated by the new situation.

As Roger had suggested, I called at the shop and he led me into his domestic quarters where, over a cup of tea and a cream bun, we compared our itineraries for the next few days. The following Monday, I was going collecting in Crossrigg, which was always a challenge, and I did not think our system could function satisfactorily there, but, perhaps fortunately, his rounds did not include that village, which had a shop of its own, a Co-Op store in fact.

I knew the Co-Op manager always had difficulty getting some of his customers to pay their bills and was also very aware of the kind of problem that might arise if any of the people involved in our proposed scheme were like Miss Gibbons and her meat order on that very first day of my insurance career. In spite of a few minor difficulties, however, I felt the suggestion was definitely worth a try.

Tuesday was my day for collecting in Gaitingsby, with both weekly and monthly premiums being due, and it was also Roger's day for delivering there, so I provided him with my list of client names. Checking it against his planned deliveries, we saw that four of his customers were also on my list of calls and three lived in remote places on the moors, well over a mile out of Gaitingsby village. These were Mrs Tyreman, Mrs Harland and Mr Freeman. The other customer, Mrs Cole, lived near the joiner's shop, so he could accommodate her and collect her insurance premium for me at the same time, thus saving me one call. I said I could cope with the others, provided there was no large order to carry around, and discovered that Mrs Tyreman had telephoned to ask him to bring her a penn'orth of boiled sweets, Mrs Harland had earlier told him she wanted a 3lb bag of plain flour, 1lb of sugar, half a pound of butter and a 1lb jar of strawberry jam, while Mr Freeman had ordered a 4oz tin of his favourite Golden Flake ready rubbed tobacco and half a dozen wire pipe cleaners. I could easily carry those items, so the deal was done. They had all been employees of Gaitingsby estate, and lived in estate cottages on the moors some distance from each other. None owned or drove a car and each house was at the end of an unmade track on estate land. It was a rough trek in each case, but I thought my bike would cope with the terrain more easily than his van.

On that Tuesday morning, therefore, I collected all three orders from the shop and made sure each was clearly identified and that I knew how much was owed for each. There was ample space in my panniers and haversack and so, having told Roger how much premium was due from Mrs Cole, I sallied forth.

My morning routine was as usual, and eventually it was time to venture on to the moors with my grocery orders. I had no qualms about this – I'd been to all the houses on previous occasions and knew the people quite well. I thought it would be a simple task.

I began with Mr Freeman because his house was furthest away, a rugged single-storey stone cottage hidden in a cleft of the moors. From the approach road, the tiny house, appropriately called Rock End, looked a natural part of this ancient landscape; indeed, in some conditions you could barely see the house among the rocks and rough terrain in which it was situated, so well was it camouflaged.

Ted Freeman was a retired gamekeeper who had been employed all his life on the estate, and in retirement he continued to live rent free in his home. A bachelor in his seventies, and a Scot, he was a fit man who walked the moors every day, just as he had when working. He was an authority on the red grouse and an acknowledged expert on the management of the heather moors. Whenever I called, he insisted I have a tot of whisky, which seemed a means of persuading me to stay long enough to listen to one of his tales of keepering for the estate, especially the one about the time he was almost accidentally shot by George V during a grouse shoot, and the one when a visiting foreign president put in foot in a pothole and broke his leg.

I parked my bike in the usual place near his peat shelter, saw that the house door was open, unpacked his order, then went to the door and called out to him. There was no reply. I ventured deeper into the house, calling with each step forward until I found myself in the tidy front lounge, without any sign of Ted's presence.

I thought he must be around the place, because the door had been standing open, so I shouted again, becoming slightly concerned and wondering if he had been injured or taken ill. Then, with a good deal of relief, I heard his response.

'Comin' de noo.'

I called back in a louder voice, giving my name, and soon a door opened and Ted appeared.

'Sorry aboot tha',' he rolled his 'r's in his strong brogue. 'Ah was watching an osprey an' could nea tear myself awa'. Ah've a telescope set up in the spare-bedroom window. Ospreys are very rare roond here, Matthew, very rare indeed, and Ah'm sure that's what it was, passing through and flying south. Fish eagles some call them – he'll be heading for an inland water somewhere, on his way doon fre' Sco'land as he heads awa' ti Africa.'

Without waiting to ask, he went to the sideboard and poured two generous tots of whisky, handing one to me. Then he led the way to the armchairs where we would sit while he reminisced. This time, I interrupted his sequence slightly by saying, 'I've got your tobacco and pipe cleaners from the shop, Ted, me and Roger are sharing our jobs just a little,' and passing them to him. He placed them on the mantelpiece.

'Oh, dear, does that mean he's nea coming?'

'Not today, he'll collect your money next time he comes, or I can take it with me.'

'Och, man, that's no problem, the money.'

'Did you want to see him for something else? I can get a message to him,' I offered.

'Nay, Ah should nae bother you, Matthew.'

'Look, if it's something you want doing, just ask. You're very isolated up here . . .'

'Aye, Ah've everything a chap can want – except a bookmaker!' His eyes twinkled. 'Ah've overcome my strict Scots Presbyterian upbringing aboot betting, Matthew, and fra' time to time Ah have a wee flutter. Roger puts it on for me, you see, and there's a good yan running this Saturday, at Ayr . . . King's Shot . . . Noo, Ah thought that was an omen, you see, bearing in mind that stuff wi' King George. Ah was going to ask Roger to put a wee bet on for me, two shillings each way . . .'

'I can ask him to do it,' I offered. 'In fact, I might put some on as well!'

And so we chatted as we sipped his wee dram, then he gave me his insurance premium, his money for the tobacco and pipe cleaners and an extra four bob for his each-way bet. I assured him it would reach Roger in good time to place the bet. He also added that he wanted the same order next week, and then I left, determined to remember to put a little on the horse for myself.

Miss Tyreman – Gertrude – was also a former employee of the estate and, like Ted, lived rent free in this remote moorland cottage. She had been a nanny and now kept goats, hens and a few sheep on her plot of land.

A tall and majestic woman with a mop of grey hair tied into plaits across the crown of her head and a penchant for wearing long black dresses that swept the ground as she walked, she had a look of old Queen Mary. Certainly, there was an aristocratic air about her, which some felt she'd cultivated during her long life as a nanny to Lord Gaitingsby's family; but, although she continued to make regular social calls at the big house, she had adapted quickly to life in this tiny and rather lonely place on the moors.

When I arrived she was making a clip rug with the oblong wooden frame on the kitchen table and piles of coloured cloth cut into strips, which she was expertly threading into a pattern on to the sacking backcloth. She was using a clothes peg that she'd adapted by cutting a hook on to one of its prongs and was working with impressive speed. As I knocked and entered upon her loud 'Come in, the door's open' she completed a small section, then said, 'One minute, Matthew, then I'll make some tea.'

I sat in silence as she finished her piece of the rug, then

112

made small talk while she boiled the kettle on the hob, found some slices of fruit cake and made the tea. I collected her small premium – an insurance to cover her should she become too ill to care for herself – and then handed over the penn'orth of boiled sweets, explaining how I had joined forces with Roger Crossley.

'So he's not coming today?' She frowned. 'That's a shame, a real shame. Oh dear.'

I saw the sorrow on her face. Clearly she'd been expecting him.

'Is there something I can do? I get easily get a message to him.'

'Well, I do want to repeat my order for next week, but the other's not all that important, Matthew. It's just that Lord Gaitingsby's son has a horse running on Saturday and I thought I might have a little flutter – Mr Crossley would have put it on for me. I can't get to the betting shop, you see – not that I am a regular gambler, Matthew, but I feel this is one way of showing confidence in my former employer, if you understand.'

'It wouldn't be King's Shot, would it?' I smiled.

'Well, yes, it is, as a matter of fact.' Her face showed pleasure at this tiny piece of knowledge I'd so recently gained.

'I'm going to have a flutter myself,' I told her. 'I'll get Mr Crossley to put it on for me, and Mr Freeman over at Rock End is also risking a couple of shillings each way, so I can ask Mr Crossley to place your bet, too, if you wish.'

'Would you be so kind? That would be nice. Yes, I think I can risk a shilling each way, Matthew. You've heard of King's Shot, have you, and the reason for our interest in the horse?'

I told her that Ted Freeman had related the tale of nearly being shot by King George V during a grouse shoot on these moors some years ago, and agreed the horse was worth a gamble. Half an hour later, I left Miss Tyreman's with the money for the sweets, the money for my insurance premium, and a couple of shillings to invest on King's Shot.

When I delivered the flour, sugar, jam and butter to Mrs Jessie Harland at the remote Ling Hollow Cottage, the same thing happened. Her husband, Dick, had been a forester on the estate and they lived in retirement in this idyllic place near a moorland stream where they had developed a wonderful garden, regularly selling flowers to local shops and markets. I declined her offer of tea and biscuits because I was still feeling well fed after my visit to Miss Tyreman, but after settling the matter of paying for her groceries, her insurance premium and her repeat order, she said, 'Matthew, Dick and me would like to put a bet on King's Shot at Ayr on Saturday, Mr Crossley always sees to that for us.'

'No problem,' I assured her, already comfortable with the system. 'I'm going to see him about putting some more bets on, so I'll add yours to it.'

The Harlands, not short of money from their flower-selling business, wanted to invest half a crown each way on the horse, so I left those three remote houses with three distinct payments, each one resting in a separate pocket of my commodious overcoat. It was rapidly approaching finishing time as I left the Harlands, and I was anxious to catch Roger Crossley before he closed. Half an hour later, standing at the back of his shop, I unloaded the pockets I'd reserved for him, reminding him of the repeat orders and settling the cash for the deliveries. In return, he gave me the premium he'd collected from Mrs Cole.

'Now,' I said. 'Betting! There's a horse running at Ayr on Saturday, King's Shot, and it seems very popular with those retired estate workers, Roger. I've got some bets here they want you to place for them.'

'I can do that.' He nodded. 'Every time Lord Gaitingsby's son has a horse running, you can guarantee most of the estate workers, retired and still working, will place a bob or two on it. Not many of them win, I have to say, but it creates a bit of interest among the staff and keeps the bookies happy. Mind, one of the estate's horses did win the Grand National near the end of the last century, so anything can happen.'

And so I gave him the bets, along with a slip of paper detailing the amount from each punter, and then, almost as an afterthought, I said, 'I might as well have a bet myself. Can you add a couple of shillings each way for me? On King's Shot?'

'Are you sure? I ought to tell you it's a rank outsider, Matthew, hardly in with a chance.'

As I had already made up my mind, I passed him four shillings for the bet, and, after an interesting day's work, went home and told Evelyn all about my adventures. She listened intently as always as I expressed my belief that Roger and I could work together in a limited way, even if it required a bit of effort from both of us. I felt sure our mutual system would save both time and expense as we went about our respective businesses in this remote and widespread part of England.

'So how much do you think you'll save each week, if you share visits?' Evelyn asked.

'I'll know on Saturday,' I told her, and then explained about the horse race.

'You haven't wasted good money on a horse, Matthew!' she cried. 'We can't afford that sort of thing, we've no spare money for gambling. You know how tight things are just now, and we're supposed to be saving up for a house or a car or even a telephone! And Paul needs some new shoes!'

'It's just the once,' I tried to appease her. 'The estate workers think it's in with a chance . . .'

Unfortunately, King's Shot was unplaced. It meant I was four shillings worse off through that part of the joint enterprise, but I still felt our new system was worthy of persistence – provided I didn't follow the example of others by betting on horses.

There was a happier outcome, however. In thinking about the tale of George V's near miss with the shotgun and the foreign prime minister's foot down the pothole, I did wonder whether the estate was insured for accidental injuries to its guests while they were on its land and premises. Within

115

the week, I made a point of calling at the estate office, where I spoke to Alastair Dowling, the agent. He told me the estate was well covered for such liabilities but said it was fortuitous that I had called, because they were unhappy with the current insurer of their fleet of motor vehicles. They had refused payment when the windscreen of a jeep had been smashed by a stray shot.

I listened to the problems, said the Premier would cover such accidents if the vehicles were comprehensively insured and then completed a proposal form for the entire fleet. Out of that little adventure, therefore, I won some valuable new business. That four shillings turned out to be a very good investment – and King's Shot won at odds of 8-1 at Doncaster a month later. The estate workers were delighted – as always, they'd backed him.

On that occasion, of course, I didn't have a bet on him.

Seven

*'The horse just flew over the wall and landed
right on my bonnet'*
From a claim form

A large proportion of my business involved the insurance of private motor cars, and one of my continuing battles was to persuade policyholders, for their own long-term security, to invest in fully comprehensive cover rather than the basic third party, fire and theft policies. Certainly, the latter fulfilled the statutory requirements imposed by the Road Traffic Acts of 1930 and 1934, but it did not cater for a wealth of possible claims, some bizarre and some straightforward, that might arise from a combination of the car's presence on a road, other drivers' behaviour and various unpredictable factors. A simple example might be the cost of replacing a smashed windscreen and a more extreme one might involve the car running over a rare and valuable prize-winning cat, and the driver then being sued for some huge sum in damages.

The snag was that the majority of car owners within my agency were not at all wealthy and many were young men who ran their cars on a shoestring, doing running repairs and urgent maintenance themselves, or getting experienced pals to do it for them. Many were very practical and could efficiently cope with welding equipment; they could effect repairs to the bodywork, deal with rust and with the mechanical side of things, adjust the brakes or fit new brake pads, strip an engine, change the oil, rebore it and repair the clutch

117

or gearbox, fit new gaskets and adjust the timing or air/fuel mixtures.

Motor vehicles were not very complicated pieces of machinery and most owners could learn what to do when simple things went wrong. There is no truth, however, in the rumour that most country garages were equipped only with a big hammer and a bit of string. Some had a little hammer as well, and even two bits of string!

Car owners of a practical nature could not see the merit in paying extra money for fully comprehensive insurance, which covered matters like damage to the bodywork of their own car or even to roadside furniture, or injury to animals like valuable dogs, cattle or horses; indeed, few thought their driving bad enough to warrant such insurance or to generate such claims. The prevailing attitude was that if the law wanted third party, fire and theft insurance, then that's all they themselves considered necessary, firmly believing, too, that the county council would insure things like bollards, signposts and roundabouts, while caring animal owners would ensure that their precious pets or valuable livestock were covered for such risks. It was far more complicated than that simplistic view would have it, of course, especially when the liability of persons involved in accidents was brought into question – but try telling that to a keen young man who wants a car merely to impress his girlfriends or to take himself out of the village on some excursion or other.

I had such a discussion with David Baker, the twenty-one-year-old son of a local builder whose fleet of vehicles I insured. The Bakers lived in a fine house built into the hillside above Micklesfield, above and behind which was open moorland.

Several well-used paths passed close to their house and extended right up to the distant heights. These routes, always popular with ramblers, were also used by hundreds of free-roaming blackfaced sheep when they trekked down from the moor to invade the gardens of the village; this regular invasion of sheep was said to be a sign of impending

118

bad weather, but most of the storms were created by irate gardeners whose prize crops were destroyed by these black-faced invaders.

The Bakers' house, one of the finest in the village, had wonderful south-facing views across the dale and it was high enough to overlook the trees that marked the course of the river below them. Their builders' yard was some distance from the house, well beyond that fabulous view, and there is no doubt they enjoyed the prestige of living in such a splendid place. Evelyn had often said it was the sort of house she would love to own – not that particular one, perhaps, but something as spacious and splendid on a lofty site with fine views. I could never envisage myself in such superior surroundings! My dreams were much more modest.

Although David Baker had driven dumper trucks on his father's building sites long before leaving school, he had learned to officially drive cars in his father's comprehensively insured Rover and, for this, he had been taught on public roads. There is little doubt he was a most capable driver. The time had come, however, once he reached twenty-one, for him to acquire a car of his own. His father, Dennis, a sensible man, had told David he must save up to buy his own vehicle, and then pay his own running costs.

Wisely, he told David, who was employed by the family business, to attend to his own insurance, too, the logic being that if the lad's name appeared on the policy – which would cost rather more than a similar one in his father's name – he would eventually accrue a useful no-claims bonus of his own. The earlier a person started to build up a no-claim reputation, the better it was financially in the long term, even if the starting period was rather more expensive. Apart from that consideration, it placed the onus for all aspects of his motoring and all the responsibility for his actions firmly on his shoulders. And so it was that David came to see me at my home.

It was a Sunday afternoon and I was in the garden trying to make one of the borders look as if it was not given over entirely to dandelions, buttercups and other weeds of an amazing prolific tendency. His arrival offered a welcome break from hoeing and digging, and, as Evelyn found us a glass of beer apiece, I took him into the lounge, which doubled as my office. He told me had bought a used Austin Healey Sprite, an open-top tourer in bright red, and it had cost him £45; sports cars, even second-hand ones, were much more impressive than saloons, and David would use it to impress and attract the girls. He wanted me to arrange the necessary insurance. I explained that as it was a sports car with an open top, and this was the first policy in his name, it would be rather more expensive than if the car had been added to his father's policy, and certainly more expensive to insure than an ordinary saloon, but I convinced him that by negotiating his own insurance he was doing the right thing in the long term.

In five years' time, provided he had no claims, he could considerably reduce the cost of today's premium. The no-claims bonus was a valuable saving. David listened carefully as I prepared the proposal form. When I began to explain the merits – and costs – of taking out fully comprehensive cover, he shook his head.

'Third party, fire and theft will do me,' he affirmed. 'That means I'll be legally covered, and I'm a good driver, Matthew, I'm not daft enough to take unnecessary risks.'

At this point, bearing in mind he had bought a sports car and that other drivers were liable to do stupid things, sometimes in uninsured vehicles, I endeavoured to explain the wisdom of taking out fully comprehensive insurance even if it was rather more expensive than third party cover. I soon realized David's mind was closed to my suggestions. I'm not sure whether he thought I was trying to impose more expensive cover upon him merely so I would benefit from the commission, but I tried to convince him that was not my motivation. Quite genuinely, I believed in the best possible cover for any motorist, because one never knew what might happen on the open road or even when off the road, often through no fault of one's own.

In one final attempt to win his trust in my recommendation, I said, 'All right, David. Let me put a set of circumstances to you – it's pure fiction, but it illustrates the point I'm trying to make.'

As he had not yet finished his glass of beer, he smiled and issued the challenge, 'Fair enough, Matthew, try and persuade me!'

'Imagine an old car coming into this village,' I began. 'It is driven by an elderly gentleman who has not been as careful with his maintenance as he should have been, and, on top of that, he's going rather too fast down the High Street because his brakes aren't very good. His car is long overdue for a service, it rattles and groans and there are lots of loose bits that need attention. Unfortunately, when he gets to the corner near the pub, his front wheel comes off. The wheel nuts weren't properly tightened and over time have come off, one by one. The car slews across the road, knocks down the wall of Mrs Featham's garden, damages her drains and knocks down her outside toilet. The car is also very badly damage as a result – it might even be a write-off – but that's not all. The detached front wheel now has a life of its own; it careers across the road, through an open garden gate belonging to Mrs Browning, and hurtles down her garden path where it smashes through her goldfish pond and kills all the fish, knocks the sundial over then bounds ever onward and demolishes her heated greenhouse, ruins all her prize orchids, which she sells all over the country, and kills the cat. My question to you, David, is: who's going to pay for all that? I can tell you it's not the old man's insurance company, because he had only the cheapest minimum third party, fire and theft cover.'

'A nice story, Matthew, but it's all fiction. That sort of thing's never likely to happen. Besides, I'd never let my car get into such a state that the brakes failed or a wheel came off. I do look after my vehicles! You know that.'

'The point I'm making, David, is that if that story was true, the old man – whose insurance wouldn't cover such things – could find himself sued for the damage he had caused, and if he had no other insurance to cover him he'd have to find the money out of his savings, perhaps all he had in the world. And if it was something very serious – like that wheel making an invalid out of someone who happened to get in the way – he might finish up selling his house and becoming destitute to pay the compensation.

'What I am trying to impress upon you is that with the right type of policy the insurance company would foot the bill. That's the difference it makes for only a few pounds in premiums. A vital difference, in my opinion.'

'Fair enough, Matthew, you've made your point, but the sort of person you're talking about isn't the sort who'll make sure his car is always in the peak of condition, who's proud of his driving skills, who'll not take unnecessary risks. I believe what you say, Matthew, but it doesn't apply to me. So third party, fire and theft is what I want, just as the law demands. It's all I can afford anyway, Dad's not helping me with this, you know, it's all down to me.'

'It's your decision.' I conceded defeat and wrote him a cover note bearing the date and time of issue, then sent him on his way with a reminder that the necessary insurance certificate would be sent to me in due course, along with details of the full cost. It would arrive in about a week's time, I told him, and I would make sure he received it immediately. I could understand his decision, for it was one made by most of the young car owners of the area, except that I thought David, being involved in a successful business, would have exercised a little foresight.

I thought his father would have advised him about the merits of being comprehensively insured, but I could see that in this case Dad had left his son to learn his own lessons.

Fate, however, has an odd way of dealing with some people. Some three or four months after David bought his car, a local farmer called Archie Bolton, aboard his tractor, towing its trailer, was chugging along the elevated moorland track. It was early afternoon one Friday and he was using the unsurfaced track that ran above the village, behind the Bakers' house.

The track emerged into the village at the top of the hill close to the post office, but it looped around the upper part of Micklesfield as it ran behind one of the pubs, the Angel, to connect two farms and a few isolated cottages, before emerging near the church.

Archie Bolton lived at one of those farms – Hagg End – and his younger brother, Ben, lived at the adjoining premises, Haggside. Both properties had been in the family for generations and were owned by the brothers, whose sheep ran freely across the surrounding moorland. They also kept a few Highland cattle and bred turkeys and geese for the Christmas market.

It so happened that Ben's tractor had suffered a puncture when one of its rear wheels ran over a sharp piece of flint, and the damage to the tyre was so severe (it was, in any case, a very old and well-worn tyre) that Ben decided to replace it. He had words with the garage owner, Danny Randall, who assured him he could obtain and fit the correct tyre if Ben brought the wheel to the garage. When the huge new tyre, some four feet six inches in diameter with a width of more than a foot, was delivered to the garage, Ben asked Archie if he could help by taking the entire wheel into the village on his trailer, which Archie duly did. And it followed that when the new tyre had been fitted, Archie was asked if he would transport it back to Ben's premises – between them, he and Archie would re-fit the wheel to the waiting and disabled tractor.

It so happened that Archie was chugging homeward with his brother's newly tyred wheel aboard his trailer that Friday afternoon. The massive wheel was lying flat on the trailer and its immense weight meant it was not secured – it was so heavy it would take several men to shift it.

Precisely what happened next was never determined with accuracy but it seems that as Archie was sedately propelling his tractor along that elevated route, quite at home with nature and the brisk breeze that blew from the heather, it so happened that Crocky Morris was nearby with his basket of pots on his head and several pints of bitter inside his belly.

By all accounts, he had been in the Angel and had found his way up the footpath to the moorland track, probably intent on visiting the neighbouring farms in the hope of selling a few cups and saucers. According to Archie's account, which circulated the village and grew better with every telling, he'd been chugging along minding his own business when Crocky had suddenly leaped up from the gutter where he'd been lying, or doing something else; but the amazing thing was that the basket of crockery was on his head.

As he had appeared directly in front of Archie's tractor, Archie had taken the only possible action by swerving rapidly, and this swift movement took his tractor off the road and into the very ditch from which Crocky had emerged. And everywhere the tractor went, its trailer was sure to follow.

The jolting of the trailer and its accompanying tilting to one side caused the huge wheel to slide off and, as if managed by some unseen hand, it landed upright on its big tyre. Before Archie could dismount from the driving seat and reach the wheel, the impetus of the accident caused it to roll away. As there was a gentle downward slope, the wheel quickly gathered speed until it was bounding along faster than a horse could gallop. That made any pursuit pointless – the thing would be far too heavy to halt anyway – and as Archie stood and watched with his mouth gaping in soundless shouts, Crocky continued to sway at his side with the basket of pots still balanced on his head. The wheel continued to gather speed and was soon bouncing over the rocks and forging through the heather as it headed down the slope – directly towards Micklesfield.

'I wonder where it'll come to a shhtop,' muttered Crocky, ceaselessly swaying backwards and forwards beneath his basket, adding, 'But Ah've neea tahme ti stand and watch, Ah've business ti attend to at yon farm houses. Where there'sh a wheel, there'sh a way, so they say, so it'll finish up shomewhere. Thoo won't lose it, thoo knaws.'

And as Crocky departed in his attempt to sell a few cups and saucers at those lonely farmsteads, Archie found himself in a dilemma. At this stage, the wheel had disappeared from view, its path marked only by occasional cries from startled grouse, baas from bewildered ewes and the sound of crashing through tangled undergrowth – but one thing was certain: it was still bounding down the hillside like a giant child's hoop propelled by some colossal but unseen hand. The snag was there was nothing to stop it until it arrived in Micklesfield, and then, depending upon how it steered itself, it might terminate its run at the rear of the Angel among the crates of empties. Alternatively it might end up among nearby gardens and cold frames or even come to rest against the wall of some other house or, worse still, in someone's lounge or conservatory.

There was a distinct possibility it would demolish a few hen houses and greenhouses en route; it could cross the road safely or it might strike or merely startle a passing cyclist, car, lorry, bus or tractor. With a bit of luck, though, it would reach the railway station to end its trek in a coal bunker, waiting room or signal cabin – or it could even reach the river to float away to the North Sea like a dinghy. The fate of a runaway tractor wheel can never be certain.

In fact, it did none of those things. In hurtling down the side of the moor it managed to avoid everything along its way, missing cottages by inches, somehow passing through an open gate in a dry stone wall, narrowly avoiding a passing car by bouncing over its roof and then it ended its trip by colliding with the wall of Dennis Baker's house. It struck the wall some fifteen feet from ground level. Fortunately, the house was very solidly constructed and the wheel bounced off like a rubber ball, when, with its energy spent, it dropped like a stone – and landed fair and square upon David's nice little sports car, which was parked near the house. The weight of this huge wheel dropping from above smashed the bonnet, the windscreen, the seats and the doors, pushing the bases of the seats through the floor and crushing the boot until it looked like a well-used Christmas cracker.

Archie, meanwhile, had decided he should alert his brother, so the pair of them rushed into the village as only tractors can rush, and began their efforts to find the wheel.

From what I learned later, several people had witnessed this amazing run from the moors – something akin to the cheese-rolling custom of Brockworth in Gloucestershire, albeit on a substantially larger scale. All had marvelled that the wheel had remained upright as it bounced with gigantic leaps to clear obstructions without demolishing them, until its final resting place on (or rather in) David's car. As a consequence, Archie had little difficulty in tracing the wheel to its final destination

I knew nothing of this drama, however, until I responded to a knock on the door later that day and found David standing there, looking as if the whole world had collapsed about him.

'David!' I was shocked by his appearance. 'Come in.'

He followed me inside and just stood in the middle of the room, as if in a daze.

'What is it?'

'You know that unlikely story you told me about the car wheel running amok . . .'

David's third party, fire and theft insurance most definitely did not insure him against tractor wheels dropping from the heavens, but when he bought a new car he decided to take out fully comprehensive insurance cover – just in case it happened again.

One would hardly imagine that this set of circumstances would repeat itself, but although I did not encounter the same situation I did experience one with remarkable similarities.

Algernon Glover was an upper-crust bachelor gentleman who lived alone in modest circumstances, having managed to spend most of his inheritance on oceans of malt whisky. In his late seventies, he was an affable old cove with an

Oxford accent, a mop of silvery hair, a trim white moustache and horn-rimmed spectacles, which complemented the huge briar pipe that was always present in his mouth. Always dressed in plus fours and brogue shoes with a heavy tweed jacket, Algernon employed a housekeeper to deal with matters like cleaning, washing his clothes and preparing his evening dinner, and he drove a wonderful old two-tone Rolls Royce coloured like coffee and cream.

His family had been in the distillery business in Scotland, a profession in which he had trained before inheriting the business and then selling it to a large conglomeration. The very profitable sale had provided an income for the rest of his life – that he enjoyed to the utmost and during which he never lost his devotion to Scotch whisky, which, he claimed, he found more interesting and warming than a wife might ever have been. Algernon was one of my clients, inherited from Jim Villiers, and he had always insured his house and his car with the Premier. There was no canvassing to worry me in this case – all I had to do was renew his policies every year, an automatic process, although the premiums did rise slightly from time to time.

However, there was a problem with Algernon. It was one that Jim Villiers had known about and that he passed on to me, but it was something I knew about already, because I had lived in the village all my life. In fact, everyone in Micklesfield knew about Algernon's little problem – two little problems to be exact, three even – and everyone coped with it.

The first was his famous love of malt whisky. Local gossip, initiated by a succession of housekeepers and others who knew Algernon, claimed he had a tot for breakfast, a tot with his morning coffee, several tots at lunchtime, another tot with his afternoon tea, and a tot or two as an aperitif before dinner. Then he had another after dinner to make him sleep. And Algernon's tots were quite substantial. When driving his splendid old Rolls about the district, therefore, it was inevitable that he would be under the influence of alcohol – or the affluence of incohol as he might have put it.

The snag was that when he was under the influence he drove perfectly well, but if he missed a noggin or two for any reason then his driving became very erratic. Withdrawal symptoms certainly made their impact upon Algernon. There were several stories of people having to leap to safety as Algernon's Rolls sped towards the pub on one of his urgent whisky buying missions, and on one occasion he even sent Crocky Morris spinning into a cottage garden – but Crocky's basket survived, as always.

The police had, with impressive regularity, stopped Algernon and had taken him to the police station to be tested with a view to establishing whether or not he was under the influence of alchohol to such an extent that he was unfit to be in charge of a motor vehicle. The highly scientific test, which comprised walking along a white line without overbalancing, calculating something like the seven-times table, spelling chrysanthemum or quoting 'the Leith police dismisseth us', were easy challenges for a man of Algernon's capabilities, and for someone as practised as he. The outcome was that he was never prosecuted for being drunk in charge of a motor vehicle – even if he was well plied with whisky, his ability to drive was never impaired. In fact, the more he drank, the better he drove. In some ways, he mirrored Crocky Morris, for the more beer Crocky consumed, the less likely he was to unbalance the basket on his head.

Another weakness in Algernon was his eyesight, which most of the villagers suspected was not as sharp as it should be. Confirmation of that came one evening at the annual cricket club dinner when Algernon, as president, leaned across the table towards a vase of russet-coloured chrysanthemums and said, 'How wonderful you look this evening, Mrs Carstairs.' Mrs Carstairs was the well-known red-headed wife of the captain.

Because the majority of villagers were aware that Algernon could not see very well, they took the simple precaution of keeping out of his way whenever his splendid Rolls appeared in view, whether from in front or behind, although from time to time unwitting tourists came to grief in ditches, hedgebacks, fields and ponds when the presence of the coffee and cream Rolls had necessitated their leaving the road in something of a hurry if they were to avoid a collision. But no one thought of checking his eyesight, and the odd thing was that he never hit anyone or anything, and his ability to drive was never challenged, either in court or anywhere else.

His third little problem was his age; as his insurance agent, my records said he was seventy-eight at the time of the incident that follows, although some said he'd knocked a few years off when originally discussing his insurance with Jim Villiers. Some claimed he was over eighty, probably around eighty-four or eighty-five, and this was supported by another source, who said Algernon had been too old to become an officer at the outbreak of the First World War. In spite of his age, however, he had never suffered from any illness, and his only recent visit to the doctor had been for an aching back as a result of trying to unearth a boulder in his garden. All these factors considered, I must admit that each time I renewed his car insurance I was increasingly worried that his recorded data was inaccurate or, at the very least, misleading.

Strictly by the letter of the law, it was true, however, that he'd never been convicted of a drink-driving offence, that he did not wear spectacles, and that he had never received medical treatment or hospitalization for any matter that might adversely affect his ability to drive. On paper, therefore, he was a good risk – and he was comprehensively covered.

That was a wonderful comfort when a cart horse leaped on to his car.

The cart horse in question was a massive Shire, a handsome black stallion called Nero, who lived in a field at Cam Farm along Cam Lane on the eastern outskirts of Micklesfield. His owner was called Jacob Etherington. It was difficult to establish exactly what happened, because the only witnesses were Nero and Algernon, neither of

129

whom could give a truly coherent version of events, but it did seem that, for reasons unknown, Nero had leaped over the wall to land fair and square on the bonnet of the passing Rolls.

Remarkably, neither Nero nor Algernon was injured, although the Rolls suffered from badly dented bodywork, especially upon the bonnet and roof, and several hoof marks were also found on the doors, imposed when the frightened horse had lashed out with its huge feathered feet. Subsequent enquiries showed that as Algernon had motored through the village he had been very close behind a horse box, and it was theorized that the horse box had contained a mare, to whom Nero had found himself instantly and dramatically attracted.

One expert thought Nero had scented the mare as she was wafted past his field and he had rushed out to greet her, taking the wall in his stride. His actions were in good imitation of Pegasus, as he headed for what might have been a romantic encounter, but unfortunately Algernon's Rolls had got in the way to thwart his lovestruck inclinations. There is no reason to believe that the Rolls was the true object of Nero's affections. In fact, Nero could probably have leaped completely over the car if he'd had enough time and space. Shire horses, in spite of their size and weight, are very capable leapers and can jump over very high fences when the mood takes them.

As Nero was not injured, and neither was Algernon, there was no requirement, under section 22 of the Road Traffic Act, 1930, to report the accident to the police. Having personally survived this incident, Algernon eventually arrived at my house to make a claim for repairs to his car. As I quizzed him, he assured me he had never seen the horse, never seen a horse box and was quite stationary when the thing had landed on his bonnet, but I felt that if I wrote down everything he said my bosses might conclude either that he'd been drunk, or that he was blind, or that he had fallen asleep at the wheel. After quizzing him soundly, it did seem he'd had absolutely no chance of avoiding the flying steed and so, in the fullness of time and after due consideration by our assessor, it was decided no liability rested upon Algernon. The Premier would attend to his claim for repairs of the Rolls and would consider any liability by the horse's owner – and so I was provided with another story that illustrated the merits of fully comprehensive insurance for motor cars. Later, I succeeded in securing insurance of Nero, just in case he fell in love all over again and performed something even more dramatic and expensive.

Even that incident did not persuade Algernon to have his eyes tested, although I did hear he disliked black animals from that time onwards, thinking they brought bad luck instead of good luck when they crossed the road. I also heard that his dislike of black horses was such that he changed his bank and started to drink White Horse whisky in addition to his range of malts.

In spite of these accidents to motor cars, I began seriously to consider the merits of buying one to replace my Coventry Eagle motorbike. One evening, when Paul was in bed, I put the idea to Evelyn. I knew she would support me because she'd often said she wanted a car, but it would be a question of cost. Could we afford one?

'It wouldn't have to be anything expensive or very big,' I began, hoping my words would convince her it was a sound idea. 'An Austin 10 would do, it would be large enough for you and me, and we could put a carry cot in the back if Paul wanted to go to sleep. There are some very good second-hand ones for sale. I could make sure the tyres and brakes were in good condition, and I know enough about cars to make sure I don't buy a heap of rusty junk.'

'And could you maintain it? To save on garage bills? Doing the brakes, changing the oil, putting new plugs in or whatever needs doing for regular maintenance?'

'Well yes, of course. There's not a lot I can't do in the way of vehicle maintenance. I can even weld bodywork if

I have to. And for my work, of course, it would make things much easier.'

Having a car would mean I didn't have to get togged up like a man from outer space every time I rode out to meet a client. I could arrive at people's houses quite neat and clean, very professional and smartly dressed, and I could carry all my papers and files in the car – which would mean less paper and leaflets cluttering up our lounge.

But Evelyn was not to be easily persuaded. 'It would mean you'd bring home more of those bits of rubbish you seem to collect on your rounds. You can get more into a car . . . bigger things. And what about those riding boots. What on earth do we want with second-hand riding boots?'

'I took them from a chap who couldn't afford his premium – the idea is to sell them, then I will make a profit.'

'But they've not been sold, have they? They're cluttering up the scullery because you don't want them to get damp in the washhouse. You've brought such a lot of rubbish home lately, Matthew. I think some people see you as a soft touch, palming you off with unwanted junk on the pretext they can't pay their premiums.'

'It's not rubbish, there's some valuable things there, like those toys Eric makes . . .'

'And,' she smiled with all her feminine guile, 'there's another thing if you buy a car. You could teach me to drive and then I could take myself to work if I've got to do any more supply teaching, or go into Whitby or Guisborough to do some shopping. It would be much easier than relying on the train or buses, especially with Paul and shopping bags.'

'That might be difficult if I was using the car for work,' I commented.

'You could always keep the motorbike.' She grinned. 'You could use that when I wanted the car.'

At this, I did not know quite what to say. I felt sure she was teasing me, but there was no sign of a smile on her face or mischief in her eyes.

'I didn't intend keeping the bike,' I said. 'I don't think

I could afford to keep two vehicles, what with their insurance, tax and running costs, and if you were classed as a driver it would add to the cost of the premiums . . .'

'But you'd have two petrol rationing books, one for the bike and one for the car – that would help if we wanted a day out at the seaside or something. But there is one other thing, Matthew.'

I wondered what she was going to say next. 'Yes?'

'Where would you keep it? We haven't got a garage.'

'Well, if we get a bigger house we'll have to make sure we buy one with a garage.'

'Ah, so is that the promise? I agree to you having a car if you promise me we'll get a bigger house?'

I knew she had manoeuvred me into a corner and so I nodded. 'I've always said I would like a bigger house, one of my own instead of a rented place.'

'All right, if we get a nice house, you can have your car, but it would have to park on the road outside if you got it now. It would get rusty and I can see some of our neighbours would grumble if it got in the way of their washing lines.'

'I can cope with all that. I'd keep it clean and stop it getting rusty and I'm sure I can cope with washing hanging out to dry. Most Mondays I would be away early, in Crossrigg. But don't forget I might have to sell the bike to pay for it. I really doubt we could run two vehicles.' I felt I must state my own case. 'I honestly believe I need a car before we think about a house of our own.'

'But whatever you decide, you will teach me to drive?'

'Yes, darling,' I said, and kissed her.

Eight

*'I warned the cow by blowing my horn but it
just stood there and said "moo"'*
From a claim form

Like most working people, I found Monday the most
difficult day of the week, but in my case it was not due
to a dislike of my job; it was because I had to go collecting
in Crossrigg. Collecting in Crossrigg was something of a
misnomer because I was never able to abstract money from
everyone on my client list. I did achieve a few successes,
but these were very few, for it was something of an achieve-
ment to persuade any of my Crossrigg clients to settle their
debts or even to pay anything off the arrears they owed.
The people of this defiant village with its thriving brickyard were renowned for not paying anyone if they could
possibly avoid it and so I considered my Monday mornings far worse than any of those suffered by other people.

A day in Crossrigg was not the happiest of starts to any
week, and there were times I wondered why these people
bothered to take out insurance at all, when they seemed to
have every intention of avoiding payment of their
premiums.

Saving anything, putting cash by for the future and paying
their dues were all alien customs to these industrial
labourers. For that reason, I must admit I did not try to
canvas the people of Crossrigg, preferring to let them decide
to approach me if they felt they needed an insurance policy
of any kind. The fact was that all those on my books had
been the result of Jim Villiers' work, and most were small

134

industrial policies to cater for being off work through sickness or injury. And there was one Crossrigg resident whom I was sure would not have any insurance: Crocky Morris. I felt sure that neither he nor his tiny terrace house, nor indeed the basket of crockery forever upon his head, would be insured. One day, perhaps, I would find time for a chat with him, but I did not regard Crocky and his problems as high priority.

The main problem within the village was not one of poverty; it was the habit of the hard-working menfolk to spend their wages on what they felt worthwhile – and for their wives to do likewise – all as quickly as possible after receiving their pay packets; for them all, money was wisely spent if it was done so in the pub or at the betting shop. That was the culture in this village, and both man and women seemed to accept it.

It was true, however, that some unfortunate women had to do their best on a very inadequate amount of housekeeping money, and had to make ends meet by buying second-hand clothes, taking in washing for others, doing odd jobs for cash, relying on the kindness of relatives, especially grandparents, or simply doing without. There is no doubt a lot of the men did not adequately provide for their wives and families even if they could afford to spend each evening in the pub or visiting betting shops.

Although most insurance policies were held in the names of the husbands, it was the wives with whom I dealt in most cases. I called regularly at their homes in the hope of balancing my books while not impoverishing them, and did my best not to allow them to get a long way in arrears. Although I hated having to collect money from the poorer of these women, it did not seem right that I should try to catch the menfolk when they were at work in the brickyard, or coming home after just being paid, even if most of the insurance money I collected was really for their ultimate benefit. I was very aware that in the unlikely chance I managed to catch any of them at their place of work, I would be told that they did not pay insurance premiums

135

out of their pocket money; that sort of thing was 'house-keeping' and therefore the responsibility of the wife, which meant it had to be paid out of her share of the man's wages. If she could not manage on what he gave her, then she was considered inefficient and wasteful.

Most of these men would spend their leisure time – and their pocket money – on drinking, playing darts and dominoes, or cricket and football, shooting rabbits and pheasants, going to the races or playing three card brag for high stakes. They would also bet on the horses, using a local landlord as the bookies' runner. That was their way of life, the normal masculine behaviour, and none could see any reason for changing, even if their wives struggled to save a pittance each week for some kind of very modest family insurance.

Although I had a great deal of sympathy for those who found it genuinely hard to maintain their payments, I was equally aware they had voluntarily taken out their insurances in full knowledge of the cost of the premiums, plus the fact that if they persistently failed to maintain the payments, the insurance could become void at the very time it was needed. For that reason, I endeavoured to ensure they paid their dues, however painful it was for them – and me, on occasions.

Each time I visited Crossrigg, I knew my presence was expected – Monday was insurance day. This gave the bad payers time to formulate their plans to avoid me, the simplest dodge being to arrange to be out of the house when I called. Either they went out or pretended to be out – and few left their monies for me in outhouses and on window-ledges as people did in the other more rural villages. Inevitably, there were the regular excuses for non-payment: husband not at work due to sickness, a sudden demand for money elsewhere, children needing something extra at school such as money for an outing, a purse lost on the way to the shop, thieves pilfering while the householder was making the beds upstairs, unexpected rent increases, new clothes needed for a wedding or funeral – there were always plausible excuses for the lady to be short of cash, and when I first began these visits I must admit I believed most of them.

As payments fell further and further behind, to the extent that some clients were seriously in arrears, I realized I must harden my heart. In time, I became aware of those that were the genuine cases and those who were skilful dodgers.

I knew when to say, 'I'm not leaving until I get the sixpence you owe for this week,' or, 'All right, let's stay here until Jack gets home and see what he says about paying your shilling.'

For many women, however, there was a battle of conscience on Mondays, because Monday was also wash day. Wash day meant staying at home to do the family washing, followed by the ironing if the weather had been kind enough to allow the clothes to dry. Convention dictated that women must do the family washing on Mondays – those who did not were considered sluts. No one wanted that kind of dubious distinction and so they all worked in the house on Monday mornings. Even when it meant dodging lines of washing hanging across the back streets, Monday was by far the best day – indeed, it was really the only day – to collect in Crossrigg, for it was vital that the washing was done. There is an old verse which sums up this attitude.

Them that wash on Monday, have a whole week to dry;
Them that wash on Tuesday, are not so much awry;
Them that wash on Wednesday, may get their clothes clean;
Them that wash on Thursday, are not so much too mean;
Them that wash on Friday, wash for their need;
Them that wash on Saturday, are clarty-paps indeed.

Although this odd verse, which was commonly quoted in the rural North Riding of Yorkshire, makes very little sense, it does show that those who washed on Sundays were too depraved to be even mentioned.

The cult of the Monday wash day, therefore, was extremely

advantageous because the sight of washing hanging from the line was a strong indication that the lady of the house was at home. All I had to do was walk along the paved lanes between the back-to-back terrace houses and head for any house with washing on the line. My strategy was aided because soot from the brickyard chimneys and the railway station was ruinous when it settled on the clean clothes, and that threat meant the women did not leave the washing unattended on the line. They didn't dare – they had to keep a sharp eye on the brickyard chimneys and railway station, particularly if the wind was blowing from the west. The moment they saw signs of rising and drifting smoke, it was the signal to rush out and bring in the washing before it became blackened – and a heavy blackening meant washing it all over again, not the easiest of jobs before washing machines and spin driers. Clothes were washed by possing them with a poss stick in a large tub filled with boiling water taken from the copper in the washhouse, and letting them dry in the wind after squeezing them as dry as possible through the wooden rollers of a mangle. It was a mammoth operation, so very rarely did a woman leave her house on Mondays when there was washing on the line – and I knew that, and took full advantage of it. In addition, few wives had the opportunity by Monday morning to spend all the wages received by their husbands, because the shops were shut on Sundays.

Saturdays were often spent on local shopping for the weekend, with cash being retained for other necessities later in the week. And part of that cash was for me! It was my job to acquire it.

Most of the time my strategy was successful, but there was one young woman from whom I collected absolutely nothing, even though I called every Monday morning and even though the premium was a mere threepence per week, and, for simplicity, a shilling per four weeks. Jim Villiers had secured the policy, and he had managed to square his books with her before retiring, but since my appointment she had paid nothing. I collected from her only once a month, on the first Monday, sometimes a shilling and sometimes one and threepence if it was a five-Monday month. A problem soon developed, however, because her debt was increasing month by month. When it reached six shillings and sixpence I was determined to abstract some money from her, not necessarily the entire amount but enough to persuade District Office not to cancel the policy. It was an industrial policy on behalf of her husband, a plumber employed by the brickworks, and in the event of his being off work for more than a month due to an injury not sustained at work, or any certified illness, he would receive £2 5s 6d per week until he was fit to return – a modest amount, but enough for food on a temporary basis.

I decided I must confront this lady, who had three children at primary school, and I selected wash day for my unpleasant task. Most of the menfolk worked shifts but I was not sure of the hours worked by the handful of plumbers, so I decided to call on her just after nine, when the children would be at school.

Her husband would surely be at work – and she would be coping with her pile of weekly washing.

Her name was Sandra Baines, and she was around thirty with a pale, rather putty-coloured face that never seemed capable of producing a smile, framed with long dark hair that always looked ready for a wash. She had lovely dark eyes but her thin and rather gaunt figure, and her cheap blue cotton frock – apparently her only one – made her look permanently ill or underfed. On previous occasions she'd either been out when I called or she'd produced some acceptable excuse, so on this occasion I made doubly sure I would find her.

If she was out, I would ask people at my other routine calls whether Sanda had been seen and, if so, where. Then I would go and find her, or wait near the house. The Baineses' home was in one of the terraces near the railway station, Station Rise, and it was a modest rented two-bedroom brick-built house with a living room and kitchen downstairs, and an outside toilet in the back yard. There was no bathroom – a tin bath hung on the outside wall, for use in the living room when required. Although it was sparsely and cheaply furnished, Sandra kept it clean and tidy, and her children always looked well fed and adequately clothed. It seemed she spent most of her limited income on them rather than herself, even to the exclusion of her regular bills.

I knew from local gossip that she owed money to the Co-Op for groceries, and to the butcher for her weekly meat order, but I did not know whether her husband, Derek, was aware of those debts.

I had never met Derek, and consequently had no idea what sort of man he was – whether he was fair with her, or whether she was habitually left short of housekeeping money. I guessed that if she was kept very short of money she would be afraid to tell him she had got herself into debt, but my job was not to interfere with their domestic problems. I had no wish, however, for her insurance policy to lapse: that might aggravate her situation should Derek be unable to work. And so, at nine fifteen that Monday morning, I went to the back door and knocked. Seconds later Sandra answered, still looking pale and harassed and wearing her flimsy blue dress.

'Oh, Mr Taylor.' Her face revealed her surprise and there was the merest hint of a nervous smile. 'You're early, I wasn't expecting you.'

'I got an early start,' I said. 'And I wanted to catch you.'

'You'd better come in.' She stepped back to allow me to enter. I followed her into the kitchen, where she'd clearly been washing the breakfast pots. Before I could say anything about her overdue payments, she said, 'I know why you're here, Mr Taylor. I'm sorry you've had to wait so long, but I've got the money.'

'You have?' I must have sounded surprised, because she chuckled and looked infinitely more relaxed than I'd ever seen her. She opened a kitchen cupboard and lifted a tin from a shelf, then emptied the contents into her hand.

'Six and sixpence brings us up to date.' She smiled again,

a sort of Mona Lisa smile, before adding, 'And another shilling makes seven and six, and that puts me a month in hand.'

'Well, I must admit I'm surprised and delighted, this solves a problem, so thanks.'

'I've got a little job,' she said. 'Two mornings a week in the Co-Op.'

'Good for you.' I marked her as 'paid' in my collecting book and wondered if she was really doing the job to pay off her debts, but said, 'I'm so pleased for you, I hope it makes things easier.'

'Derek's not on a big wage, Mr Taylor, and with three children things do get a bit tight, money wise, even though there's always the divi at the Co-Op and I do try to be careful. I do think insurance is so important, if anything happens to him.'

'That's what concerned me, Mrs Baines. My bosses don't like policies to become too far in arrears and they hate having to lapse them – but I'm sure you know all that. Anyway, don't let me hold you up, I've got calls to make and I'm sure you're busy as well. So I'll give you a miss next month.'

I left feeling very relieved that her account with me had now been settled, then set about visiting my other clients. My next call was the washing line with the tea towels hanging between brassieres and knickers, 4 Station Rise, then the one with the double white sheets and pillow cases at Number 2. As always, I ended that day's collecting with several accounts remaining incomplete, but the majority had paid their due, and I felt particularly pleased that Sandra Baines had done something so positive about her situation. I felt it had been a good day – certainly, a very good one by normal Crossrigg standards.

Although I went to Crossrigg every Monday, I gave Sanda Baines a miss the next time, and after a largely fruitless morning making unproductive calls in the village I found a quiet corner with a bench to enjoy my sandwiches. Then I popped into the pub, the White Hart, for a pint – a pint

141

was always welcome after a morning in Crossrigg. Being midday, the bar was quiet and I was the only customer. The landlord, Dave Brown, knew me well – in fact he was one of my clients through his car insurance, although the inn itself was insured by the brewery that owned it – and we chatted about inconsequential things; then he stunned me by saying, 'Sad about Sandra Baines, wasn't it?'

'Sandra Baines?' I must have sounded very puzzled. 'Why, what's happened to her?'

'She got arrested, for pinching from the Co-Op. Money was disappearing and so the police set a trap. They thought it might be a sneak thief nipping in when the staff's backs were turned, so they marked some money, but it was Sandra. Pity really, she's a very nice girl and had got the job to work off her debt . . . but she couldn't keep her fingers out of the till.'

I did not tell anyone that I thought Sandra had paid her premiums with stolen money – perhaps she hadn't – but I was very concerned for her, and when I called the following month to collect her premiums she did not smile as she said, 'You've heard?'

'Yes, I have, and I'm so sorry, Sandra.' I used her Christian name, which I felt was appropriate on this occasion. 'You must have been very desperate.'

'They were very kind – the police, I mean – but I feel awful, letting the Co-Op down like that . . . But I was so desperate . . . They took me to court last week, I got put on probation and they've had a word with Derek about giving me more housekeeping.'

I think she needed someone to talk to, someone who was not the police or the probation officer or even a friend, and so, over a cup of tea, she told me the whole story. What it boiled down to was that Derek had given her housekeeping money when they had married, but when the children had arrived he hadn't increased it . . . and she'd never asked. She'd been brought up not to question her husband's decisions on money matters, and, because he had no idea of the cost of running a house or the demands created by the arrival

142

of children, the idea of giving her extra housekeeping had never occurred to him. It should have – but it hadn't.

In view of the trauma she'd endured, however, Derek had been given a lecture by Sandra's probation officer, after which he had started to give her extra housekeeping. I believe Derek had been quite shocked at this outcome in his own household, and the result was that he had told Sandra to be sure to approach him whenever she felt she could not cope, financially or otherwise. When the Co-Op manager discovered the reason behind her uncharacteristic behaviour, he said he needed someone to work in his private house, for a few hours each week, and he offered the job to Sandra – wisely making sure she did not have access to cash. I understand she did a very good job with the washing, ironing and cleaning – and she always paid her premiums on time.

Another collection problem arose with Geoff and Greta Simpson, a busy couple who lived in a spacious detached house halfway up the long and very steep hill at Crossrigg. It was called Hillside and was originally built from the local bricks, but a previous owner had pebble-dashed it, and it was now an off-white colour, always looking as if it needed a coat of fresh paint. Geoff owned and ran a popular seaside café in Whitby, and drove in every day in his gleaming navy-blue Austin 16, while Greta was a secretary in the rural district council offices. Although she worked in the same town, she travelled to and from work by train and invariably arrived home ahead of her husband – his busy enterprise often necessitated staying late to balance the books or prepare for the following day, and so she avoided the long waits that might develop.

With both of them leading such busy lives, and with Geoff having to work most weekends while Greta caught up with her shopping and socializing, they were rarely at home. For me, as their insurance agent, it would have made life somewhat difficult if they had forgotten to leave out their monthly premiums. But they never did. They always remembered, so I did not have to make special trips during the evenings or weekends.

Their house and its contents were comprehensively insured; it was an all-risks policy covering housebreaking, burglary, fire, damage from various causes, and it even covered them if, say, Greta lost one of her valuable earrings while away from home.

Both were insured for sickness and injury, too, and they each had a substantial endowment policy to save for the future. In addition, Geoff had his car insured with me, although his business premises were insured through another company as part of the deal through which he obtained his business mortgage. It was clear that Geoff and Greta believed in insurance and were not afraid of paying the market rate for full cover and serious investments.

I called at their house only once a month, on the first Monday, and their money was always placed in the summer house at the end of their spacious garden. The house was very private, being on the outskirts up that long and steep hill, and well away from exploring children, who might have found the money a temptation.

When I questioned their habit of leaving cash in the summer house when a cheque through the post would have been acceptable, they assured me there had never been any attempt to steal their money. Geoff could even have left a cheque in the summer house, but he told me he'd started this cash system years ago, long before I arrived, and saw no reason to change it. At one of our rare meetings he explained that because he dealt in cash at work it was a simple matter to use it at home for paying small and regular bills. Each evening he brought home cash bags full of loose change, from the day's takings from his café, and it was convenient to make use of it, chiefly to avoid the need to carry it all back to work for paying into the bank the following day.

Jokingly, he would say that if he left a cheque in his summer house, the front of which was open to the elements on a very windy site, it might blow away or get eaten by

144

mice or rained on so that the ink figures were obliterated. He'd thought it through, he told me, and for all sorts of reasons he much preferred to leave cash. So cash it was: several piles of half-crowns, florins and shillings totalling the amount due, with not many ten shilling notes or pound notes – in case they got blown away.

Unlike the working-class people of Crossrigg, the Simpsons' premiums were susbstantial – not surprising bearing in mind the number and type of policies they held. So instead of collecting something like four or five shillings a month, their amount was £3 12s 6d every month – more than a weekly wage for some. As Geoff told me, 'While I'm earning, I want to prepare for when I'm not earning. There's no pension with my job.'

And so it was that I fell in with his wishes, calling at the summer house every first Monday, checking the amount put out for me and making the necessary entry in my collecting book.

Then, in December, there was no cash waiting for me. I let myself into the unlocked summer house, a spacious wooden construction with a window-type opening with no glass and a single door. Inside, Geoff had stacked his deck chairs, lawnmower, a cane settee, three cane chairs and a small table, all employed during their summertime leisure periods in the garden. The cash was not in its usual place, a small shelf just inside the window, and so I checked else-where, thinking it might have fallen off or been knocked down, but there was no sign of it. I assumed Geoff or Greta had forgotten to leave it out for me but did not regard it as a problem.

I saw no need to remind them, or to call in one evening to collect it. I was confident it would be there the following month, along with the overdue amount. But it wasn't. There was no money that February, either. Although I felt a slight touch of concern, I had no reason to believe they were avoiding me or that they were suffering from some kind of financial problem. They'd forgotten, I felt, or perhaps there'd been some family drama like a death, something

145

drastic that had obliterated any thought of leaving money out for the insurance man. Or they might have taken an overseas holiday, something a seasonal businessman in Whitby might do. An additional factor was that, in cases of monthly premiums, three months' grace was not at all unusual and so, once again, I did not pursue the matter. I would allow them the full three months without chasing up the payments, substantial though they were.

During this time, I did not have any contact with either Geoff or Greta for any other reason – which was not unusual – and so it was with some trepidation, on the first Monday in March, that I chugged up the hill, parked my bike against their boundary wall and prepared to enter the garden. It was just after two thirty in the afternoon. As I made sure the bike was safely resting against the wall, who should come swaying past, with his basket of pots on his head, but Crocky Morris. He stopped when he saw me, swaying on his feet like a reed blowing in the wind, then he hiccupped, burped and sighed, all the time with his basket of pots remaining aloft in defiance of gravity and balance.

'They're out,' he shouted, with more than a hint of a slur in his voice. 'They're allus out.'

'I know, Crocky, but I have to call anyway.'

'Nice people,' he slurped. 'Very nice people. Out of the top drawer.'

'Yes, they are. Very nice, very hard working, very busy, too.'

'Like me, Mr Taylor, very busy, very hard working, very businesslike.'

I was rather wary of letting Crocky see where I went and why, but he did not appear to want to stay, because he said, 'Mishush Sshtringer along the road wantsh a new shet of tea cupsh sho I musht be off . . . niesh to talk . . .'

And off he wandered. I watched his basket weaving along the hillside lane behind the wall, an odd sight – it looked like a basket-weave boat, the sort that Moses was probably put aboard for his trip down the Nile, for I could not see

Crocky's head, just a basket floating and bobbing along the hillside.

When I reached the summer house my heart sank because there was no money; this meant the Simpsons were now three months in arrears and I must take the unwelcome action of confronting them about it. That meant returning in the evening when they had finished work, and, as I had no telephone, I could not ring in advance to notify them of my intention. I returned to my motorbike with a heavy heart, wondering what had gone wrong with this couple – and then, perhaps with Crocky in mind, a thought struck me. Was someone stealing the money? I did not think Crocky would do such a thing, and, besides, he had no reason to enter the garden or visit the summer house. Children perhaps? I dismissed this, chiefly because the money would be put out on Sunday night, and the children would be in school on Monday, thus denying them the opportunity to even find the waiting cash. A passing thief? It was a possibility, so I decided to ask Crocky if he'd seen anyone hanging about; he was around this village more than anyone else simply because he lived here and spent most of his time on Mondays in the pub. If there had been unwelcome strangers around, he might know about it.

I caught him before he reached Mrs Stringer's bungalow.

'Crocky . . .' I switched off the engine to talk to him but remained astride the bike, still marvelling at his balancing skills as he swayed alarmingly without moving his feet. 'Has there been anyone around lately? Wandering into people's gardens? Checking houses, that sort of thing?'

'Awd Willie'sh been about,' he said. 'It'ssh hissh time of year.'

'Awd Willie?' I puzzled.

'Comeshh every year about now, sleeps in haysheds . . . does a bit of ditching and drain clearing on farmssh . . .'

'A tramp, you mean?' I asked.

'A gentleman of the road,' retorted Crocky. 'A real gentleman. One of the few, like me.'

147

'Would he be likely to come to the Simpsons'?' I asked, not wishing to suggest Awd Willie might be a thief.

'He'sh been there, he'ssh left his mark near t' gate,' said Crocky.

'Left his mark?'

'On a sshtone near t' wall bottom, you've got to look hard for it but it's hish mark all right . . . It meansh they're good folksh here and will give you money.'

'You mean he's been getting money from here?'

'Tha's what hish sign sayssh, Mr Taylor, very generoush folksh . . .'

When I returned to the entrance gate and parked the bike once more, I searched the stonework of the surrounding walls and then, very close to the ground, I saw a white chalk circle with a cross in the centre, followed by three empty circles. I was later to discover this was the tramps' sign that indicated the people here were nice and charitable (the circle with the cross indicating Christian charity) and would give you money (the three rings representing coins). A series of crossed lines like cell bars meant they were liable to call the police, and a simple letter T meant 'nothing doing here'.

I discovered there were many other signs used by tramps, some indicating food or a dangerous dog, and even one to suggest the householder would first refuse any charity but would relent with persistence! It now meant I had something positive to tell Geoff. When I returned that evening, he invited me to have a glass of beer with him, but I thought I had better clarify things first. I told him there had been no money since the December collecting day and he shook his head, saying, 'But, Matthew, I put it out as always. Same place, exact amount due, in coins.'

I knew this was a difficult topic – I did want to believe him, and I also wanted him to believe I was not being dishonest either, and I think we both, at that stage, realized that a cheque in the post would be a far safer system. As I outlined my problem, though, he listened, and then I said, 'I think it's been taken from the summer house, Geoff,' and gave my reasons.

148

After my explanation, I added, 'I can show you the tramps' sign near your gate.'

'That's it!' he snapped his fingers. 'I knew somebody had been in there, the sofa had been slept on! But look, I'll square up with you, Matthew; I had no idea you weren't getting the money. You should have told me earlier.'

I explained the reason for my reticence, then told him the tramp's name was Awd Willie and that he worked on farms in the vicinity at this time of year. Geoff smiled. 'I hope he takes it as a gift of charity from me. He's welcome to it and I don't regard it as a theft – I won't claim off my insurance.' He smiled.

'You could, you know,' I told him. 'You are covered for theft from the house and grounds.'

'That old tramp wouldn't think he was stealing it, especially if he's left a mark saying we're generous,' he said. 'He'd think it was left out for him, especially when it appeared again and again. No, let's forget it, Matthew. I'll put your books straight but I won't leave cash again. If he wants something from me, he'll have to knock on the door. But I suspect he'll be on his travels by now . . .'

To cut short a long story, Awd Willie had left the village to continue his annual rounds, and Geoff began to pay his premiums with a cheque, posted to my address. And he also arranged a covered window for his summer house, and a lock for the door, then he insured it against fire.

'I don't want gentlemen of the road using my summer house as a camp site,' he laughed.

Nine

*'In the thick fog, I turned into the wrong
driveway and collided with a tree I don't have'*
From a claim form

When collecting money from clients, I was constantly
reminded that many were extremely short of cash, but
there were others who were unbelievably mean. Many were
true misers, who would do their best to save a halfpenny
or even a farthing while having thousands of pounds in the
bank. I knew one family, for example, who made a pot full
of tea and who then reused the tea leaves repeatedly until
the resultant outpouring was almost pure water. There was
another man who never put stamps on his letters, believing
the Post Office would take great care of them in order to
retrieve the money from the addressees – so it was the
addressees who then had to pay if they wanted their mail.
That miser thought he had found a means of securing free
postage. Some of his recipients, however, became wise to
his scheme and refused to accept any letters from him –
they were therefore returned to him, whereupon he had to
pay the excess. In respect of those cases, his plan backfired
and he ceased his activities.

When electricity came to the moors, there was a farmer
who placed a solitary light bulb on his upstairs landing
because it would remove the need to have a light in every
bedroom. In another case, a villager bought a house
adjoining the newly installed street lamp so that its light
shone into the bedrooms and he could avoid switching on
the lights.

Many moorfolk had grown up accustomed to oil lamps and candles, and it made sense not to light these until it was competely dark – and, of course, a single lamp or a candle could be carried from room to room as required, unlike the newfangled electric bulbs, one of which hung expensively from every ceiling, and was very likely to run up rather worrying bills. Examples of rustic frugality could be seen in every shed and outbuilding in my agency; they were full of things that could be reused, such as old bikes, cars, tractors and agricultural machines kept for spares, old mangles and fireside ovens, chairs and tables, beds and picture frames, chests of drawers and wardrobes, knives and forks, bits of string and wire . . . Nothing was thrown away, because there was a belief that everything came in useful once every seven years. The truth was, though, that such items were seldom reused, most lingering there until a sharp-eyed antiques dealer spotted them and made an unbelievably silly offer or they got thrown on the bonfire.

In addition to this kind of frugality, there were tales of moorland ladies going into town to shop, saying, 'We might as well look at summat expensive because we're not going to buy it,' as well as the sheep farmer who sold some lambs to a friend at a very low price, but who then discovered the friend would not pay him. After some weeks of fruitlessly requesting payment, the seller said, 'If Ah'd known thoo was nivver gahin ti pay, Ah'd have charged thoo twice as mich.'

Money, or perhaps the lack of it, was undoubtedy a dominant factor in the life of all moorfolk whether they were genuinely poor, temporarily hard up or misers of renown. I recall one lady who, every summer, hoarded every ten shilling note and pound note that came her way. During the hot weather she made savings through not having to buy coal for the lounge fire, and over the years these unspent few pounds had accumulated to become a substantial hoard. In time, she became worried that this secret cache of paper money might be stolen, so she hid it. One year she chose the last place she reckoned any thief would search: the lounge fireplace, which was likely to be out of use throughout the summer. She heaped wood, coal and some newspaper upon and around the pile of notes – a perfect disguise. We can guess what happened next. When the first chill of autumn made its presence felt, she decided to air the lounge and put a match to the paper, completely forgetting the true nature of her ready-laid fire. It was a while before she realized she'd burned all her precious savings. It doesn't need me to relate her deep distress, made worse by the fact that she was not insured. Even if she had been, a claim for accidentally setting fire to lots of money in a fireplace might have had some difficulty in being accepted by Head Office.

In many instances, this kind of meticulous care of money was not miserly. It was necessary. There were times where it was evidence of a deep respect for money earned with considerable difficulty and hard work, so that the need to conserve it for future use was vitally important. Waste of any kind was almost a mortal sin.

During my rounds, I regularly experienced a prevailing sense of caution where money was concerned. Because it was so difficult to earn and accumulate, nothing was to be spent on frivolous things, not a penny must be wasted. Every penny or part of a penny had to earn its keep and even tiny-value coins like farthings were hoarded in case they were useful in the future. Farthings, valued at one quarter of an old penny, remained in circulation until 1956, but at the height of their usefulness they could purchase considerable domestic necessities, vegetables in particular, and children found them very convenient for buying a few sweets.

As I toured my agency, experiencing genuine poverty in some households, I was reminded of my own circumstances. Evelyn and I were by no means well off or affluent, yet, compared to so many other rural people, we were comfortable and we had security. My work was unusual in that I continued to receive my salary even when I was off work through illness or while on holiday, something not many rural people could enjoy. For them it was no work, no pay.

I knew my regular income and positive prospects for earning more meant that my job was considered by many to be a very good one: I wore a suit and my bosses operated from offices in London. In the eyes of some, therefore, I was a member of the professional class, even though Evelyn and I were sometimes desperately short of ready money.

I was always aware of my own father's struggle as a low-wage earner, and my mother's difficulty in providing the necessities for me and my elder sister, now married and living in London.

I was determined not to let my family suffer financial hardship as I had done, and there is no doubt that my background coloured the way I dealt with my clients. I could sympathize with those who found it hard to make ends meet – but I would work hard and I would earn enough to give us a comfortable life. That was my aim in life – and I certainly had no intention of being miserly!

It is quite understandable, therefore, that I found misers were very intriguing. Perhaps the most curious of those I encountered was a man called Louis Noble, who lived at Ingledale, high up the valley. He was a retired railway linesman whose wife had died shortly before his retirement, and he continued to live on a very modest railway pension in a brick-built cottage by the lineside. Of sturdy build, with iron-grey hair cut short and no sign of baldness, his black suit and highly polished black shoes, although showing signs of age, were well kept if a little on the ancient side. He'd worn that suit and those shoes for as long as anyone could remember, and on almost every occasion when Louis appeared in public he wore them. There is no doubt he had little or no money to spare for new clothes, and most of us appreciated that. The only sign that he ever spent money on luxuries was his curved tobacco pipe, which sometimes remained unlit in his mouth.

Louis was not one of my clients, however, so it was some time before I learned who he was, and I became aware of him through attending a succession of funerals in villages up and down the dale. I made a point of attending the funerals of my deceased clients on the advice of one of my supervisors.

He'd once said, 'Matthew, it makes good business sense to attend the funeral of any of your clients. It shows genuine concern for the family in their grief and it also provides an opportunity for the mourners to come to you discreetly if they wish, to ask advice on any outstanding matter concerning the welfare of the deceased, and, of course, the financial comfort of the surviving relatives. So get yourself to those funerals, Matthew. Show yourself, express your concern and sympathy, and you'll find it will pay dividends.'

Being keen to do my best for everyone, I had followed his advice, even to the extent of attending the funerals of those who were not my clients, and there is little doubt that my presence was noted and, in most cases, respected and appreciated. A moorland funeral was always something of a showpiece, with the ham tea afterwards being the supreme mark of respect. To be 'buried wi' ham' was a sign of true worth for any deceased person in the moorland communities, and it was customary for all mourners, family, friends and mere acquaintances to attend the funeral tea after the interment. A funeral tea comprising anything less than the best ham was considered almost insulting.

There was a wonderful variety of funerals in the length of Delverdale because the three main faiths were all represented in roughly equal proportions: Catholics, Church of England and Methodists, with the Methodists proving the best at singing and arranging funeral teas, the Anglicans being the best at simplifying things and burying anyone who had no particular religion, and the Catholics being the best at ritual and solemnity.

A Catholic funeral was always memorable because the Requiem Mass contained an air of mystery, spoken as it was in Latin and accompanied by incense and rich black vestments – although some of the moorfolk thought it smacked of foreign practices.

In most cases, however, it was the same undertaker who

arranged all the funerals, the same florist who provided all the wreaths and the same taxi firm who provided all the transport. The undertaker, skilled at dealing with all faiths, was J. W. Stoker and Son of Micklesfield, established 1839, with extensive premises at Paradise House, where they also conducted a joinery business.

The current incumbent was Jedd Stoker, a descendant of the founder. He considered his name somewhat appropriate should he ever have to officiate at a cremation, although he did maintain it bore no relation to the fiery destination of some of his customers. Stoker's provided a very sound and efficient funeral service, even providing a glass and ebony hearse drawn by six black horses – or a more modest (and less expensive) mode of coffin transport, a wheeled hearse hauled by six men. It resembled a flat-topped barrow, on four spoked wheels, rather like those of a bicycle. The hearse house (t' eearse oose in local parlance), in which both vehicles were kept, lay a discreet distance outside the village on the edge of the moorland, and as I began my insurance career in the village there was talk of Stoker's buying a motorized hearse.

Many potential customers, however, felt that being carried to one's final resting place in a motor vehicle was somewhat undignified, and lost no time expressing their views to Jedd. 'It's hosses for me, Jedd,' they would say.

In the meantime, therefore, the choice for all was the horse-powered hearse or the man-powered hearse and, to date, none had expressed a wish to be cremated – necessitating a journey by hearse to Middlesbrough or Scarborough. Cremation was not at all popular among the moorfolk, probably because it had echoes of burning in hell; lying still and cold in the earth among one's ancestors was infinitely more acceptable than being roasted in some distant oven. One old woman said to me, 'You know, Mr Taylor, I don't want cremation. I hate being too close to open fires, they make my legs go a funny colour,' while another said, 'I hope they don't put me in that tiny chapel of rest before my funeral, I'm claustrophobic, you know.'

Cremation would have been a long drawn out affair if either of those transport methods had been used to cover the thirty miles or so to destinations in Middlesbrough or Scarborough, and the thirty miles back again. With cremation becoming more acceptable, however, particularly since the end of the war, one could understand why Jedd was thinking of modernizing his undertaking empire. If people did not relish the idea of a motor hearse, there was always the possibility of using the train – with the funeral coach suitably attired in black of course. It could carry a coffin to the station closest to the crematorium, with a horse-drawn hearse at the other end to complete the journey. I was never sure whether that option would be acceptable to the majority of moorfolk either; even if they were relatively poor, they insisted on preserving their dignity. 'Thoo can't beat a black horse or two drawing a black hearse with white roses and glass all aroond t' coffin,' was the widely held view.

It was through attending such funerals that I became well acquainted with Jedd Stoker. He appreciated my company's swift response to the death of a policy holder, having done his best to facilitate proof of death and formal identification of the deceased so that the Premier would release funds into the deceased's estate in the shortest possible time, and thus aid the turnover of Jedd's thriving business. Jedd was a rounded sort of character in his late forties, a capable and cheerful joiner but a solemn undertaker when the occasion demanded; with a happy moonlike face, a mop of light brown hair and a slightly overweight figure, he was not the stereotype of the typical cadaverous undertaker, but he was both liked and respected by all.

It was also through attending a series of moors funerals that I became aware, too, of Louis Noble, although I did not know his name initially. I had attended funerals at Arnoldtoft, Avensfield, Graindale, Annistone, Gaitingsby, Baysthorpe, Ingledale, Micklesfield, Crossrigg, Walton, Lexingthorpe, Hillbraithe and Freyerthorpe, some Catholic, some Anglican, some Methodist and others of very doubtful faith, some with the Stokers officiating and others with different undertakers, but in every case I had noticed Louis Noble among the mourners.

I knew that many moors families boasted a huge array of relatives and friends because so few of them left the area for work, but it was unusual to see them all at every funeral. More often than not, a representative selection attended. But Louis attended every one and was a familiar figure in church and at the graveside with his black suit, polished shoes and, when decorum permitted, his distinctive hooked pipe.

When I first set eyes on him, I wondered if he was an insurance man like myself, or some other businessman, like a bank manager or solicitor, who was showing sympathy to the bereaved families, but upon closer examination I thought he was rather too old to be a member of those professions.

An opportunity to find out more about him came at the funeral of an old man called Harry Reynolds. A resident of Lexingthorpe and a staunch Methodist, Harry had passed away at the age of ninety-two and was being buried following a service that I found memorable due to the splendour of the rendering of 'The Old Rugged Cross' by a choir of chapel singers, an experience both moving and unforgettable.

After the service and interment we all adjourned to the village hall for the funeral tea, a colossal feast laid out on trestle tables. It comprised the inevitable ham sandwiches, along with lots of pork pies, cheese sandwiches, egg sandwiches, jellies, apple pies and ice cream, and a glass of sherry for those who insisted upon an alcoholic drink. Not many Methodist funerals catered for drinkers of alcohol but some of the more modern families respected the customs of mourners of other faiths. Urns of tea sat at the end of each table for those who were teetotallers, and jugs of orange squash were sometimes available.

It was during this tea that I spotted Louis at the distant end of the room. He was helping himself to a huge plateful of ham sandwiches, pork pies, hard-boiled eggs and pickled

157

onions. He seemed to be alone, wandering among the mourners without chatting to anyone, while appearing more interested in the food than the company. As it happened, Jedd was standing near me, it being customary to invite the undertaker to the funeral tea. Having helped himself to a plate of food, he joined me.

'Client of yours, was he, Matthew? Harry, I mean.'

'He was. I thought I'd come and pay my respects.'

'He had plenty of money, I don't need to wait for the insurance payout, Matthew.'

'He had a substantial life policy,' I said. 'More than enough to pay for his funeral. You'll let me have the necessary documentation in due course?'

'No problem,' he nodded, for such people did not bother with solicitors for these matters. 'It'll all go into his estate and his nephews will benefit eventually.'

We paused as we munched the ham – home-cured if the salty taste was anything to go by, and then I asked, 'Jedd, the chap over there, under that picture of King George VI in his coronation robes, who is he? I see him at every funeral.'

'It's Louis Noble,' he told me. 'From Ingledale.'

'A smart-looking man,' I complimented him. 'Bank manager, is he?'

'No, he's a retired linesman, he used to work on the railway.' I realized Jedd knew I was being inquisitive, fishing for information, because he added, 'You'll be wondering what he's doing here, all by himself?'

'He doesn't seem to know anyone,' I agreed.

'Probably not,' he smiled. 'You've seen him at other funerals, you said?'

'I attend quite a few, as you know, and I think he's been to most of them, if not all.'

'Louis goes to all the funerals he can manage. He's been known to attend three in one day.' Jedd laughed. 'That's providing the train times fit in with the time of the service, or, more likely, the funeral tea.'

'So why does he go to them all?' I persisted.

'For the free food,' stressed Jedd. 'He's as tight as a Yorkshireman's wallet. He comes for the day out but more especially for the free food and drink, although he does like a bit of a chat. Once he's been fed and watered, he goes home.'

'That's a bit of a cheek!' I laughed. 'Freeloading like that!'

'Oh, I don't know. Anyone's welcome at a funeral, the more the merrier, and some folks reckon a large turnout is a measure of the respect held for the deceased. Louis checks the *Gazette* or *Northern Echo* for deaths, decides which funeral or funerals to attend, dependent upon train times, then off he goes in his best suit and polished shoes to mingle with the mourners and have his free feast.'

'Don't the families object?'

'Not really – as I said, everyone's welcome and most local people expect Louis to turn up nowadays. One more mouth to feed isn't going to make any difference to this kind of event, the food's got to be eaten up anyway. And I believe Louis takes some home with him as well, he's a bit of a scavenger on the quiet.'

'The old skinflint!' I laughed.

'He's had that suit for years,' chuckled Jedd. 'It was passed down to him by his father, and his grandfather before him. It's seen a few funerals in its time!'

'But if Louis is as mean as you say, surely he'll have worked out that it costs him quite a lot in rail fares to get to the funerals? That must make him out of pocket at the end of the day.'

'Not Louis,' smiled Jedd. 'He's a retired railwayman, remember, he gets a free pass for some if not all of his trips, so it costs him nothing to get here.'

'So he's having all those days out without spending a penny?' I frowned.

'That's Louis!' smiled Jedd, helping himself to a slice of pork pie.

'I wonder who'll turn up at his funeral tea.' I laughed.

'I bet he doesn't have one,' said Jedd. 'I'll bet he's got

159

hundreds of pounds stuffed away in his mattress but he'll be too mean to spend a penny on food for his mourners – that's if he has any.'

'So his relatives will benefit from his meanness?'

'He hasn't any,' Jedd told me. 'He's got no one to leave his money to, so what happens to it when he dies, when his funeral expenses have been paid?'

'I'm not sure,' I admitted. 'Doesn't the state get it, unless he's willed it to someone, or to a cats' home?'

'Something like that,' he said. 'Well, now you know who the man in the black suit is. You'll go to his funeral, will you?'

'I think we should pass the word around when he goes – everyone in the moors should turn up to see him off, and spend all his money for him!'

'Then you'd better go and get him insured,' he laughed.

As I settled into my job on the moors, and continued to support the families of my clients, Louis continued to attend every funeral he could possibly accommodate during his daily rounds. I managed to visit him one day when he was free from his funeral duties, and I put the possibility to him that he might like to invest in an endowment policy, but he shook his head.

'Nay, Mr Taylor,' he emphasized. 'I want for nowt, and I've enough tucked away for my funeral, when it comes. I'll invite everyone. I've been to a lot of funerals in my time, for company really, living on my own, so when I go they can all come to mine; I've eaten all that grub, so they can come and eat mine.'

'I'm sure you'll get a good send-off!'

'I would hope so. They can eat as much as they like when I'm gone, I shan't be there to worry about what it costs and I'd rather they eat the lot and spend the lot than have my hard-earned savings go to t' government. My funeral will be a right big 'un, you'll see, the biggest hereabouts for years . . . There's a lot'll want to get their own back on me for eating their grub. I've had words with a local pub landlord I know well, and he'll see to things – he knows what I want and where to find my money. I reckon I'll have a right good send-off, even if I haven't got a family. It'll be ham, the best, I'll make sure of that. You'll be there, will you?'

'I wouldn't miss it for the world.' I smiled, thinking he was not so mean after all. I could understand him going to funerals for little more than the company he found there, and I though it was an odd but very clever way of ensuring a big funeral for a man with no family.

I encountered further incidences of miserliness within the domestic sphere and I am sure there were many that never became known outside the family home. One case I did come across involved a couple called Carter who lived in Hillbraithe. The husband was Charlie and his wife was Irene; they were in their mid forties with a nice home in the centre of this remote village. Charlie, a tall, thin and unsmiling man with lanky black hair and sunken cheeks, worked as a bus driver for the United bus company and Irene, rather more plump and definitely more cheerful than her husband, had a part-time job as a waitress in Guisborough.

On the days she worked Charlie would drive her across the moors to the hotel that employed her, sometimes fitting her times in with his own shift and sometimes making a special journey. With no children, the couple were very quiet and spent all their free time at home where Charlie's hobby was woodwork and Irene spent a lot of her time knitting. It follows that Charlie was always well kitted out with cardigans, socks and Fair Isle pullovers. The couple did not venture into the local pub, nor did they seem to socialize, rarely being seen at village events such as whist drives and socials, although Charlie would sometimes display an article of woodcraft at the annual village show.

My only contact with them was once a month when I called to collect their life insurance premiums – seven shillings and sixpence per month – and Irene was usually at home. If she was at work then she would leave the money on the kitchen window-ledge.

One Tuesday morning, when their monthly premium was due, I called as usual; it was shortly before 11.00 a.m. and Irene was at home. As she responded to my knock on the door, I could see that my arrival had flustered her and for a time I wondered if I had mistaken my dates, but she soon gathered herself together and offered me a cup of tea and a bun.

I settled down in the living-room chair, a perfectly normal practice for me, and then, as she waited for the kettle to boil, she stood before me and said, 'Oh, dear, Mr Taylor, I feel awful about this and Charlie will be furious, but I haven't got the money.'

'Not to worry.' The couple had never allowed themselves to get behind with their payments and I did not regard them as a problem family. I knew Irene was not the sort to get into debt and I could wait until next month, or, if necessary, call the following week. I explained this to her.

'I should have budgeted for it.' She came and sat on the edge of a chair opposite me, nervously rubbing her hands together as we waited for the kettle to boil.

'It can wait, I know you won't run away!' I tried to make light of this but Irene seemed to be extremely anxious and I began to wonder why she was becoming so upset about such a trivial matter. She seemed to be getting herself into a real fluster about it.

'Charlie will be so cross with me,' she whispered. 'I should have accounted for it when he asked what I wanted this week . . . I just forgot it was your week, Mr Taylor, I do hope it hasn't inconvenienced you too much . . . Charlie always asks what I need for the week, you see, when he gets his pay packet, and I have to work out what I want, then he'll give it to me, the exact amount. I just forgot about the premiums. Now I'll have to budget for it next week and Charlie will ask why I need the extra seven and six, and he'll be so cross when I tell him. He hates owing money, Mr Taylor, he really does and he's so careful.'

I think Irene suddenly felt she had to tell someone about the way she spent her housekeeping allowance from Charlie, and she must have brooded over things as she made the tea. When she returned from the kitchen a few minutes later, she poured out her story to me, almost tearfully at times, and I began to realize Charlie was something of a monster, or at least very miserly. Irene had to work to buy things for herself like clothes and cosmetics, and her wages had also to cater for any luxuries they might enjoy, such as a day trip to Scarborough or an outing to the Yorkshire Dales.

Charlie's wage paid for the day-to-day household expenses such as the rent, rates, food, electricity and other routine outgoings, such as insurance, and he also bought his own clothes out of his wage. The cost of their car also came from Charlie's income.

As she explained all this to me, the overdue premium being the catalyst for this saga, it became clear that when Charlie came home with his weekly pay packet he expected Irene to present him with a list of all the things she required during the coming week, itemized with the precise cost, and it was then that I began to understand her misery at omitting to account for my seven and sixpence. What amazed me was that he totted up the amount even down to the last halfpenny or even farthing, and that is precisely what he gave her for the week's housekeeping. She would list things like a bag of flour, bag of sugar, stone of potatoes, jar of marmalade, and so on, and if her anticipated grocery list, plus her other household expenses, came to £2 13s 6d for that week, then that is precisely what he gave her. It could be more the following week, or perhaps less. While most other wives received a set amount each week to use as they felt best and to effect some savings whenever they could, Irene had to present a budget to Charlie, and this week she'd forgotten to include the insurance money. Charlie's system meant she could never effect any savings because he checked everything she bought, especially the cost, and even though her lapse did not bother or inconvenience me unduly, I could see that she would receive a thorough telling-off from Charlie. I thought what a miserable life she must lead, and, as we sipped our tea, I wondered if Charlie knew she spent money (the cost of tea and milk with a bun too) on the insurance man, but I must admit I was trying to think of some way to prevent her suffering from Charlie's wrath when he came home.

During one of those long moments of silence that inevitably characterize an embarrassing chat of this kind, I spotted a pile of knitting on the sideboard and recalled that she spent a lot of her spare time at her hobby. On the top were a pair of woollen gloves, several pairs of socks and a scarf. As I'd bartered with other people on lots of previous occasions, this gave me an idea.

'Mrs Carter,' I said. 'Suppose I bought some of your knitting for seven and sixpence? Like those gloves over there, and that scarf.'

'Well, yes, you could have those,' she said. 'I did them for old Mr Wragby down the road, for his birthday from his daughter, but he died before I finished them and I didn't want to force her to take them, so they are spare.'

'And does Charlie keep a check on those?' I smiled.

'No,' and her eyes laughed now. 'I have to buy the wool out of my own waitressing money and he will let me keep what I earn if I knit something for a friend, so I can sell some things without him wanting me to account for them. He's not too worried about me spending my own money, so long as I don't waste it or grow reckless; it's me spending his wages that bothers him.'

'Right,' I said. 'I'll buy those gloves, socks and that scarf. I need some new ones anyway, and then I can mark you as paid in my collecting book. How's that?'

'You don't have to do that, Mr Taylor, it was my fault and I should be the one who pays.'

'You've paid with your own skill in handicraft,' I said, lifting the book and marking her down as paid up to date.

She looked relieved and left her chair to get my purchases, all exquisitely done and well worth the money, in my opinion. Although no money had changed hands, I felt it was a good commercial deal. I drained my cup and said, 'Well, there we are. We're up to date once more.'

'So what shall I tell Charlie if he asks?' She frowned. 'He does carry out very careful checks on what I spend and I'm sure he'll find out I didn't ask for that money this week. You don't know him like I do, Mr Taylor. He'll be furious if he thinks I kept something back from him – he doesn't like secrets in a marriage.'

'When does he do his audit?' I asked.

'On pay day,' she said. 'When he comes home with his pay packet, on a Friday. He's bound to remember about the insurance.'

'Well, it's Tuesday now, you'll be at work before Friday?'

'Yes, tomorrow morning as a matter of fact.'

'Well, you could tell him you received a good tip at work, from a party of bus trippers who came into your café, or you could tell him you found a ten shilling note in the street three months ago and told the police, who said you should keep it at work in case it was claimed, but as three months have passed without anyone claiming it, it's now yours. You used it to pay the premium and made half a crown for yourself as well as saving him some money . . . he might like that.'

'Isn't that being deceitful?' she asked, clearly unhappy about any sort of dishonesty so far as Charlie was concerned.

'Yes,' I said. 'It's a white lie but one told in a good cause. And do you know what Charlie does with all his money?'

'Oh, no, and I daren't ask.'

'Well, it's up to you,' I told her. 'Or you could tell him the truth – say the insurance man got his eyes on some socks and gloves, and gave you seven and six for them, which meant you didn't have to ask him for the premium money. I'd have thought that would please him.'

'Yes, I think I will do that.' She smiled. 'It's nearly true, isn't it?'

The next time I called she had the premium money ready, and when I asked whether Charlie had discovered her lapse last month, she smiled.

'He did – I knew he would, Mr Taylor, he knows everything I spend. But when I said you'd paid me for my knitting, he was cross with me, saying I was spending my own money on household expenditure, and I shouldn't do that. I don't think he really knew what had happened exactly, but he said he was quite able to pay his way, that I shouldn't have relied on you for the insurance payment and that the family insurance was his responsibility. So he gave me the seven and six. I've got it in a money box now.'

'So after all that you've made a nice little profit! If I was you, I'd keep it somewhere handy,' I said. 'Just in case you need it again.'

'An insurance against the future?' she said, and she laughed.

If Charlie Carter suffered from his own particular streak of domestic meanness, then Raymond Pollard was just as bad, if not worse. A small man with a dark moustache and black, darting eyes, he worked in a chemists' shop and travelled daily by train to Whitby from his home in Micklesfield. In his early sixties, he had worked in the same shop all his life, rising from boy cleaner and message runner to become part owner. It was a successful shop in which he had a thirty per cent share, and this form of security, plus his own careful attention to the value of money along with a legacy from an aged aunt – and with some considerable and shrewd investing on the stock market – meant he'd been able to buy a nice detached house overlooking the river. It had a large south-facing garden with a conservatory and a pond full of goldfish, but the garden itself was not given over to flowers and shrubs; instead, it was full of vegetables of every kind, and I later discovered that Raymond supplied the local shop with fresh produce. That was yet another form of business income for Raymond.

There is no doubt that Raymond Pollard was a successful businessman who had done very well for himself. His wife, Jacqueline, a rather plump lady with greying hair, was in her late fifties and very pleasant. She did not have any outside job, because she looked after the accounts for the shop and dealt with most of the correspondence, sometimes travelling into town with Raymond but more usually working from home. She was designated the company secretary for business purposes and drew a modest salary, which, together with Raymond's remuneration and other money-making schemes, meant they lived very comfortably.

With no children, they enjoyed a fairly active social life, with Raymond being on various village committees and Jacqueline acting as secretary for the parish council of Micklesfield, in addition to being president of the Women's Institute. Being very financially aware, Raymond had always been a keen supporter of insurances, and was wise enough to have taken out several policies in his youth, including some large endowment schemes. He had started these long before I inherited the agency and would gain the maximum return on his investments when he decided to retire. I had to call on the Pollards every month to collect their premiums, which included sickness cover, comprehensive insurance for the house, including fire, theft and damage, and the annual car insurance for the small vehicle they used at weekends. I had tried to persuade them both to consider increasing their portfolio of policies, but Raymond considered himself well covered for all risks, and reckoned his endowment policies would provide a useful amount of capital when they matured upon his retirement.

'You can be over insured, Mr Taylor, please remember that during your canvassing activities! Don't ask people to pay too much.'

Whenever I called, Jacqueline would be at home and Raymond would be at work, which meant that, for most of my simple collecting duties, I dealt with her. Then one summer morning, a Friday, I called but there was no reply. I rang the bell several times and went around to the back of the house just in case she was outside, and I realized she was down the garden.

She had a large basket beside her on the ground into which she was placing freshly pulled lettuces and spring onions. Not wanting to surprise her, I shouted to warn her of my presence, and she stopped her chores and turned to see who it was. Then, with the basket on her arm, she climbed the path to my side, invited me into the kitchen for a coffee and placed the basket of greens on the table. I saw it also contained some early new potatoes.

'We're having friends over for a meal tonight,' she explained when she saw me looking into the basket. 'They love fresh vegetables, and there's nothing nicer than ones taken straight out of the garden. It'll be salads for everyone tonight, you can be sure of that. I might even find some ripe tomatoes in the greenhouse.'

'I'm no gardener,' I admitted. 'My wife is better by far, not that we have much of a garden, it's more like a pocket handkerchief, but we are hoping to find a bigger house one of these days.'

'Raymond would advise that – he believes in buying the most spacious house one can afford, he considers that to be a very sound investment. Usually it means you have a large garden, too, like we have. Raymond loves his garden – it's his responsibility and these vegetables are all his work,' she said with some pride. 'It's his passion once he leaves work, he says it makes him relax.'

She made the coffee and we sat at the table chatting about inconsequential things, and then she asked how much she owed for their premiums that month. The total was £2 12s 6d, for which she gave me three £1 notes.

I found the necessary 7s 6d change and passed it to her, then she surprised me by saying, 'Thanks for the change. I was short of loose change and this means I can put three shillings in the tin for the garden.'

And on the kitchen mantelshelf there was a tin with the

word 'Garden' written on a label stuck to the front, and she went to it with the money in her hand, lifted the lid and dropped in three shillings.

'That's a neat way of saving up for new seeds and tools,' I commented.

'Oh, it's not for that, Mr Taylor. It's payment for the things I have picked today.'

At first I did not fully comprehend what she was telling me, thinking it was some kind of personal joke, so I said, 'Wages for the gardener, eh?' and laughed.

'Oh, no, we don't have a gardener, except Raymond of course, but I pay him for everything I take from the garden for our use in the house.'

'You've paid him for these vegetables?' I cried. 'For your own use at dinner tonight?'

'I'm afraid so. He runs things very tightly, Mr Taylor, like separate compartments of his business, with each compartment having to make a profit. He buys things for the garden, seeds, tools, fertilizer and so on, and then the garden has to make a profit by the end of the year. His logic is that if the village shop buys things from him, then he's prepared to sell produce to anyone else who asks – including me! I'm part of his business plan for the garden, you see. No free gifts!'

'I've never known anyone charge his own wife for produce taken from their own back garden!' I heard myself say, perhaps a little rudely, then added, as if to make light of it, 'I must try it myself.'

'Raymond pays scrupulous attention to detail when it comes to financial transactions.' She smiled. 'He knows where every penny, halfpenny and farthing goes, and that applies to the shop as well as the house. I used to call him skinflint and Scrooge when I was younger, but it made no difference. He hasn't changed at all. Raymond is Raymond!'

'It seems to have worked,' I said, rising to leave. 'You've got a lovely home, a nice garden, a thriving business – everything you want, in fact.'

'I have,' she sighed. 'Except children. I don't think

169

Raymond could fit those into his profit and loss projections!'

'They can be very expensive,' I commiserated with her.

'They can, but they're an investment, aren't they? Sometimes I think they're the only investment Raymond has not been able to understand.'

I left, feeling that she was rather sad about that. But it did seem odd to me, a woman of obvious financial security having to pay for food taken from her husband's domestic garden. I must admit I wondered what else she had to pay for.

Ten

*'When I saw smoke coming out of the engine, I
knew the car was on fire so I took the dog out
and smothered it with a wet blanket'*
From a claim form

Shortly after my appointment to the Delverdale agency, there was a worrying outbreak of thefts of lead from the roofs of parish churches. Fortunately, none of the churches within my agency was attacked, but nationwide newspaper coverage managed to highlight the problem, prompting Head Office to issue circulars exhorting agents to visit all vulnerable premises with a view to their owners taking out specific types of buildings insurance in addition to increasing their security.

A new policy had been rapidly drawn up by the Premier specifically to cover such cases, but it also included an updated version of the more usual forms of house and property insurance, particularly as large country houses and some public buildings like town halls or entertainment centres were also vulnerable.

It was a puzzle how the thieves managed to strip the church roofs of lead without anyone seeing them in action, especially as a vehicle and either scaffolding or ladders would surely be required. Although no one ever saw the raiders, it was evident the crimes were committed during the night. Because most parish churches were situated away from the centres of population, and often some distance from the vicarage or presbytery, it was not too difficult for a determined gang to assemble their vehicles and ladders, strip the lead and be away from the scene with their precious load before anyone realized what they'd done. After all, few people ventured into churchyards during the hours of darkness – although the presence of the dead did not appear to deter these thieves, nor did they have any conception of the historic value of the goods they were removing for their own selfish purposes.

The large sheets of lead that protected the roofs at their joints with the stonework and also formed impressive medieval gutterings and fallpipes invariably added up to several tons of valuable metal, all with a ready resale value on the illegal market. No one was quite sure how or where the stolen lead was disposed of, although unscrupulous builders were thought to be one source – I heard they would buy the stolen material at a knock-down price and then incorporate it on the roof of some building they were repairing or building, only for it to be stolen once again. Dishonest scrap dealers were also considered to be a means by which the stolen lead was distributed. Whatever its journey from legitimate roofs, it was an unwelcome form of recycling – but it was popular among thieves because of the money involved and the difficulty of identifying sheets of lead. How could anyone say that a certain piece had come from a particular roof, especially if all identifying marks had been removed? The thieves were very difficult to identify and prosecute.

Some thought pieces of stolen lead were used to make weights for fishing lines while others even reckoned some was sold to model makers for the manufacture of lead soldiers and model armies. But whatever its destination, lead was undoubtedly disappearing from church roofs, and indeed from the roofs of stately homes and country houses, at a quite remarkable rate.

Unfortunately, in some cases its absence was not noticed until the arrival of a heavy rainfall, and then urgent repairs had to be effected to protect the contents of the building and the exposed roof timbers. In many cases, there was an additional problem because some insurance companies did not cover that kind of theft. They insured their policy holders against theft from within the house or grounds, but not for theft of what might be termed part of the building. This was perhaps an oversight by those who drafted the terms and conditions of policies, but some parochial church councils and householders found themselves without insurance when their roofs were stripped and their guttering stolen. Some did try to suggest the act was one of malicious damage to the building, and although I believe some insurance companies honoured such claims there were many who did not.

The Premier, therefore, decided to launch a policy specifically drafted to cover all types of damage to buildings, and all thefts from buildings, whether inside or outside, and whether forming part of the structure itself or not. Thus, if someone stole a chimney pot the owners would be insured, just as they would if thieves stole roofing tiles, ridge stones, thatch, lead flashings, guttering, fallpipes, gargoyles, flagpoles, weather vanes, lightning conductors, clocks and other external attachments or adornments. Damage to all such items was also covered, whether or not it had occurred during a theft or attempted theft, and, of course, malicious damage was included.

The cost of such policies would clearly depend upon the type and method of construction of each building insured and the extent of the required cover, particularly if goods within the building were included.

Armed with this information and fired with the enthusiasm of a missionary, I set off to visit all the churches and chapels within my agency, making sure I was up to date with the latest case of theft from a church roof even if it had happened several hundred miles away. I fully appreciated the value of a newspaper photograph of a stripped roof together with a graphic report of the reaction of the priest in charge and members of his congregation.

The first difficulty was deciding which church to visit first, and on the basis that I thought all those of the Anglican communion would have some form of joint cover through the parish network or Church Commissioners (a mistake, as I was later to discover), I decided to start with St Eulalia's Roman Catholic church at Graindale Bridge. A small village nestling in the dale below Graindale, Graindale Bridge was known as the village missed by the Reformation, and although it was a tiny place tucked away in the moors it had been a centre of Catholicism for centuries. Its role was marked by a colossal parish church, the size of a cathedral, with a statue of St Eulalia outside. Almost adjoining it was St Eulalia's infant school, where Evelyn had been educated and where more recently she had undertaken her first two weeks of supply teaching. It was here that Evelyn and I were married, and Paul was baptized; Evelyn continued to attend Mass here each Sunday, being brought by her parents in their car, for I was not a Catholic, and I stayed at home to look after Paul until we felt he could usefully accompany her to Mass, but I also cooked the Sunday lunch – always roast beef, Yorkshire pudding, potatoes, vegetables and gravy with rice pudding to follow. That was my modest contribution to domestic bliss!

The parish priest was Father Seamus O'Hagan, a dark-haired Irishman in his fifties with a fiery temper and a loud voice whose flock obeyed most of his edicts and whose church was therefore full every Sunday and most other days too. He seemed to think all sinners and tax gatherers were infected by the devil himself, and I wondered what he would make of me now that I was an insurance agent. I'd been a butcher when he married us; he'd considered that quite an acceptable profession and talked about things like fatted calves and prodigal sons.

Not having a telephone, I could not ring to make an appointment and so I went unannounced one day when I was canvassing in the village. I parked my motorbike outside the church and leaned it against the railings near the main door, removed my huge overcoat and then gingerly opened the door of the church. I thought it wise to acquaint myself with the church, both inside and out, before seeking Father O'Hagan in his presbytery. I knew the church quite well but had never examined it from an insurer's viewpoint.

I found myself inside a massive nave within a light and airy church. The walls were adorned with magnificent carved figures of the Stations of the Cross while the roof was ribbed and painted blue with golden stars; the altar, I was to learn, was of Belgian terracotta.

When the church was built in 1866, to replace an earlier one, which was now the school, its debt was paid immediately and so this church was not struggling to pay off any parish debt or bank loan. It was an enviable position to be in.

As I moved slowly towards the interior, the thing that struck me more than anything was its immense size: it could accommodate the entire population of the village with ample room for hundreds of others. I must admit I walked around in awe, gazing at the statues, the altar and the sheer scale of the place in its height, length and width. Then a disembodied voice boomed, 'Good morning to you, 'tis a lovely day and you've come to see a lovely church. Ah, I recognize you, do I not? Matthew Taylor, to be sure. Your wife comes to Mass, and sometimes your lovely child, but not you, not since your wedding, or was it the baptism?'

'Both, but I'm not a Catholic, Father.' I spoke to a vaccuum. Where was he?

'That's no excuse, everyone is welcome in the house of God. So what can I do for you now? You must have come for some reason, even if it's only to offer a prayer or two.'

For a few moments I was baffled because I could not sense from which direction the voice came, then I realized the priest was standing behind and high above me, in the choir loft, which spanned the rear wall. I turned to face him on his lofty perch some twelve feet above.

'Oh, you're up there, Father,' I said, staring up at his impressive figure. I felt like a little man on the ground gazing up at God himself in heaven. 'I wondered where the voice was coming from.'

'I'll be down with you in just one jiffy,' he said, then he

175

vanished from my view and moments later I heard his footsteps clattering down the wooden stairs. Then he reappeared below the choir loft and emerged from the shadows to greet me.

'So is it something you want with me, Matthew? You want to join my flock, is it? Or another baptism? Have you had another child, please God.'

'No, Father, we've not had another, there's just Paul at the moment. I'm not here about baptisms or weddings or anything like that . . .'

'So if it's not a wedding or a baptism, Matthew, what can I do for you? Or is it just looking round that you are?'

'I was hoping to find you here, Father, although I must admit I wanted to look closely at the church before I came to the presbytery.'

'Sure it is a wonderful place, so follow me, young man,' he said, and promptly gave me a guided tour of the entire church along with a potted history, in his rich Irish brogue, then he took me outside to a shrine bearing a statue of the Virgin Mary holding the dead Christ on her lap following his crucifixion, and from there he led me past the coloured carvings of the Mysteries of the Rosary that lined the south wall and finally to the presbytery, which adjoined the church.

'Come in and join me in a coffee, then tell me why you are here. I must admit I am intrigued and I do enjoy company. You do drink coffee?'

'Thanks, Father, yes I do.'

He led me into a simply furnished lounge with holy pictures about the walls, a case full of books and a whopping crucifix above the fireplace, then he picked up a brass bell from a central table and rang it. An aged lady with the humble presence and bearing of an arthritic nun then appeared through an internal doorway and smiled. 'Yes, Father?'

'Ah, Miss Sullivan, coffee for two, if you please.'

'Yes, Father.'

'You remember Matthew Taylor? He got married here, to Evelyn. You'll remember Evelyn, Evelyn Mead that was. From that big family of Meads in Micklesfield. A lovely girl – she came here recently to teach, supply she was. Did a good job for us, Matthew, a very good job and the children loved her. You've got a fine young woman there, you know, you must look after her.'

'Thank you, Father, I will. She enjoyed her time here.'

'Then I hope she will come back to us. I am sure we shall be asking for her.'

While Miss Sullivan, the priest's housekeeper, creaked away to organize our coffee, he chattered amiably about the parish, the people in it and how I was coping with married life and a young family, albeit a small one at this stage. I realized he still thought I was the local butcher. I knew I must quickly correct that assumption.

'I've left the butchering profession, Father. I wanted to do something different with my life. The reason for my visit today is that I am now the local agent for Premier Assurance.'

'Ah, a career change! No bad thing, Matthew. Changes can be good for the soul.'

'Yes, I think you're right. I'm fairly new to the job, but our company is very concerned about the increase in the number of thefts of lead from church roofs, not just in this area but throughout the country. I am visiting all churches within my agency to warn them and to suggest they make them as secure as possible and also take out insurance cover. I started with you because I knew you from our wedding and Paul's baptism.'

At this point, like a magician producing a rabbit from a hat just to catch the attention of his audience, I flourished a newspaper cutting complete with photograph about a church in Lincolnshire that had had all its roofing lead removed by thieves.

'We are conducting a vigorous campaign, both in the press and through agents like myself, to persuade those responsible to increase the security of their churches, the

177

roofs in particular, and we hope we can attract some of them to take out insurance cover with us. Acceptance of a proposal by us would, of course, require some proof of the security measures that are in place, or that will be put in place should a proposal be approved. I might also add that our insurance would cover other things on the outside of the building, such as the clock face, roofing tiles, gargoyles and so forth. Now, I do not know whether your church is insured . . .'

'Oh it is, Mr Taylor, to be sure it is. I have the best insurance possible.'

'Oh.' I felt slightly deflated at this news. I thought the Premier had been first off the mark as far as specific roofing insurance was concerned, and now I wondered which company had reacted more speedily than mine. 'Might I ask who with? I may be able to offer a more comprehensive cover on very competitive terms.'

Had I looked him straight in the face, I would have surely noticed a twinkle in his eye because he said, 'Well, Matthew, my insurance costs me nothing apart from my prayers and daily Mass, because God himself is looking after this church for us and I know He will give it every possible protection against every possible risk. And He is assisted by an army of guardian angels – we all have a guardian angel you know – and on top of all that, there is my congregation, Matthew. Lovely people who love their church, and if I lose a tile or two, or get a piece of guttering blocked, or need the woodwork painting or repairing, or want someone to keep watch at night in case the thieves pay us a visit, then all I have to do is ask. The congregation care for their church, Matthew – after all, they built it – and so they will come along and care for it or repair it for nothing. Now, if I was to take out an insurance with you, it would cost me quite a lot of money, am I right or am I not?'

'Yes, of course, I don't know how much, that will depend on the extent of the cover you require and . . .'

'But I get all the cover and protection I want, and it costs nothing.' He smiled, and then the coffee arrived on a tray, complete with milk, sugar and chocolate biscuits.

'Ah, Miss Sullivan. Now, are you insured?' he asked with a chuckle.

'Insured, Father?' I could see the puzzlement on her face.

'Against death or sickness or whatever.'

'No, I must admit I am not, but the Lord will care for me, Father, you know that and I know that. I would not think you could be insured against death, we all have to die, it is the will of God.'

'Thank you, Miss Sullivan, well said, and thanks for the coffee. Now, Matthew, milk and sugar?'

He poured me a coffee and I helped myself to milk and sugar, took a chocolate biscuit and said, 'Thanks for the coffee, Father.'

'It's nice to have a visitor, Matthew, and I do appreciate your interest but I do have complete faith in God, you see – there is no need for any other kind of insurance. Besides, if I did take out one of your policies, it would cost a considerable amount of money each year and who would pay? My congregation, of course, and they help to care for the church already, in various ways. It is not a good thing to keep asking them to pay more and more and more.'

'But if the church caught fire, say . . .' I was struggling to think of some dreadful example that might illustrate the value of insurance. 'Suppose one of the altar candles fell and set fire to the altar cloths and destroyed the altar then set fire to most of the church . . .'

'That's a hypothetical scenario, Matthew, one which will never happen. God would never allow it to happen to one of his finest churches.'

'All right, but can I ask you to imagine that it did happen . . .'

'In that highly unlikely event, we would rebuild it, Matthew, me and my congregation. We would not depend on insurance or outside help, we would do it ourselves, just as this congregation built this church with their own hands nearly a hundred years ago. We have every necessary

179

craftsman in this village and we would do it far cheaper, and far better, than any contractor imported by an insurance company.'

'It would take time . . .'

'Of course it would. Rome was not built in a day, Matthew, and remember it took hundreds of years to build those abbeys of ours like Rievaulx, Whitby and Byland, just in time for the English Protestants to knock them all down again, so the rebuilding of a village parish church is not beyond us. We can do it without insurance, Matthew, with all due respect to you and your company.'

'But if those abbeys had been covered by insurance . . .' I laughed.

'The claims would have made the insurance companies go bust!' He smiled. 'So they were left in ruins, for the locals to take the stones and build their own houses . . . But seriously, Matthew, I do not believe this church needs your kind of insurance. I have total faith in God – and so have my congregation.'

'Fair enough,' I said. 'I accept your reasoning and I respect your faith in God, but should you ever decide to risk a few pounds of your collection upon a worthy cause, don't forget the Premier.'

'I won't, Matthew, please God I won't, but if I do ever decide I need insurance, then I know where to come.'

'I'll be pleased to hear from you.'

We talked about my family as I finished my coffee, and when I left he walked with me to the gate, which led me back to the front door of the church and my waiting motorcycle.

'You know,' he mused when he noticed my bike, 'I am thinking of getting myself a small car, paid for out of my own funds, I should add. Some of my parishioners live in very outlying places and the days of walking for hours to visit them are over, I feel.'

'You'll need insurance for it,' I laughed.

'So God will not watch over me when I'm in a car?' he smiled.

180

'St Christopher might, or your guardian angel, but you'll still need insurance,' I told him. 'It's the law – the law of the land, I mean, not of God.'

'Then we must obey the law of the land, Matthew, so when I get my motor I'll get in touch. Your visit was not wasted, then, was it?'

'No,' I said, climbing aboard my old bike. 'It was not.'

It was a different story when I called at the first of the Anglican churches. For a time I pondered the best one with which to open my bidding for roof insurance, and decided to make the Church of All Saints at Lexingthorpe my first call.

I chose it because Lexingthorpe was one of the larger villages within my agency, a stone-built collection of pleasing houses on a hillside, along with shops, inns, garages, chapels and an impressive church on its elevated site overlooking the dale. On the distant side of the dale, tucked into a fold on the moors, was Lexingthorpe Reservoir – known as Lexmere and covering about fifty acres – which served an area around Middlesbrough. Some boating and fishing was permitted, and there was a picnic site on the eastern shore. It brought people into the village, to the inns and shop, while the church served several smaller hamlets too. It had been built on the site of a former castle, all signs of which had been obliterated, and although the church appeared to be Norman or have Norman origins, it was in fact Victorian, built in the image of an older edifice. The vicar was the Reverend Thomas Redhead, a jolly Friar Tuck character in his mid forties with a happy round face and a portly figure; the sort one imagined had been nurtured on a diet of good food and wine.

His wife was Julia, likewise cheerful and plump, and, like the wife of any good vicar, she took an active part in countless village activities, occasionally smoothing ruffled feathers among the lady members of committees, or else being firmly in charge of the catering arrangements for the annual fête or jumble sale.

When I rattled the huge knocker of the vicarage front door – I went to the front because I was on formal business – it was answered by Mrs Redhead, who asked my business, and then said, 'Tom's in his study, I'll take you in. Can I offer you a coffee, Mr Taylor?'

'If it's not too much trouble,' I replied.

She opened the door and I saw the rounded figure of Thomas Redhead seated at a large round table overflowing with books and papers; with a pair of rimless glasses perched on the end of his nose, he seemed to be lost among it all – there were books on the floor, the window-ledges, the mantelpiece and even in the easy chairs – but he rose and smiled a welcome, holding out his hand for me to shake as he left the security of the table to greet me. I noticed he was wearing carpet slippers, even though he sported a clerical collar and a grey waistcoat.

'Tom, this is Matthew Taylor from Premier Assurance, he'd like a moment of your time. I'll organize some coffee.'

'Ah, yes, well, come in, Mr Taylor, help yourself to a chair, one of those armchairs beside the fireplace, that's if you can find a space not covered with books.'

I made for one of the chairs, shifted a couple of tomes to a coffee table beside it, and sat down.

'Forgive the mess,' he said. 'I need all these books for reference, sermons you know, and the occasional article for church journals, and I find if I stack them all neatly on shelves I can never find the one I want. Here, on this table, the floor and in those chairs, I know exactly where they are. Those you've just moved are Cruden's *Concordance* and Kitto's *Encylcopaedia of Biblical Literature*, indispensible in my work, Mr Taylor. I knew that, you see, I knew exactly where they were. But I must not waffle on, must I? You are here for a purpose?'

I launched into my sales patter about the thefts of lead and the need for better security for church property, adding that the Premier was offering first class cover for churches, including their roofs and other external fittings.

He listened intently, with his glasses threatening to fall

into his lap and his lips pursed whenever the question of money or funds arose.

'So there you are, Mr Redhead, that's why I am here.'

At that stage his wife appeared with a tray of coffee, milk and sugar, along with some home-made rock buns, and so we paused for a few moments as she played hostess. When she had finished, he said to her, 'Julia, Mr Taylor is here to suggest we – the parish that is – take out insurance in case some thieves come along and steal the lead from our church roof. A sensible precaution, I think.'

'There's been a lot about it in the papers,' she agreed. 'Thieves have spirited away tons of lead, leaving roofs open to the weather and parishes with big repair bills. It is something you need to consider, Thomas. If you recall, I showed you that newspaper report last week. A church in the Midlands, completely stripped.'

And, thus informed of my purpose, she left the room.

'Damage of that kind is something we can ill afford, Mr Taylor,' continued the vicar. 'So, let me see. In essence, I am in favour of your proposal, it does make sound commercial and practical sense to let insurers deal with something as costly as this. But I fear it is not my decision.'

'As I thought. I guessed there would be some kind of national insurance policy for all Anglican churches.'

'No, no, not at all, not at all,' he said. 'It is much more complicated than that, Mr Taylor. It is the responsibility of each parish, but there is always the vexed question of cost; such insurance will not come cheap, I would imagine. Now, where's Dale?'

And, with that, he moved across to a huge pile of books untidily thrown in the corner of the room, rummaged among them for a few seconds, and then abstracted a modest volume about the size of a small hardback novel.

'Dale,' he pronounced with pride, holding it aloft. 'Dale's *Law of the Parish Church*. A sort of Anglican legal encyclopedia. Now, let me see. Insurance,' and he began to flick through the index at the rear. He found the right reference, turned to the page and began to read, his eyes darting over the print and his forefinger occasionally appearing from somewhere to return his ever-slipping spectacles to a reasonable site upon his nose.

After a while, he said, 'Just as I thought, Mr Taylor, just as I thought. The responsibility for the care, maintenance, preservation and *insurance* of the fabric of the church used to be the duty of the churchwardens, but in 1921 it was transferred to the Parochial Church Council. However, in 1923 the Ecclesiastical Dilapidations Measure provided there should be no obligation upon any incumbent – me that is – to repair or insure the chancel, and that it should in all respects be repairable and insurable in the same manner as the remainder of the fabric. I talk of incumbents, not lay rectors, Mr Taylor. I might add that the Parochial Church Council is also responsible for the care, maintenance, preservation and *insurance* of the goods and ornaments of the church, and, of course, it follows that it is the duty of that council to raise the necessary funds for such things.'

Every time he came to the word 'insurance' he paused and looked at me over the top of his spectacles, as if to emphasize that it was of some relevance. Then he continued.

'I do suggest, Mr Taylor, that the roof and the lead upon it and around it can be regarded as part of the fabric of the church, and so you should approach the secretary of the PCC. But I will do that for you. There is a meeting two weeks on Wednesday, at which I shall raise the matter of insurance. And, I might add, this might make a good subject for my Sunday sermon: the value of insurance, or is God's care sufficient?'

And he then looked at me over the tops of his spectacles once again as if to say it was the conclusion of our meeting. I was not quite sure whether it was my cue to leave so I said, 'So shall I come back here after your meeting, to see what decision the council has made?'

'I fear they will need a little more information before

they can reach a decision, Mr Taylor. Facts and figures: we shall need to know what it will cost per month or per annum; we shall need to know exactly the extent of the cover available; we must be made aware of any conditions that might be imposed, such as greater security measures . . . so you need to provide us with some kind of proposal, Mr Taylor, detailed as far as possible, so that our PCC is able to conduct a very thorough debate.'

'Thank you, I understand. I will contact my District Office and get their legal department to compile a proposal without delay,' I told him. 'Then I will come back to you in time for the meeting.'

'Thank you, and thank you for your time. Now I must get back to work, Mr Taylor, a short article about the adaptability of melons as revealed in the Old Testament. Now, where's Kitto?'

For a moment, I thought he was talking about his cat, then realized it was one of the volumes I had moved. I picked it up and handed it to him, and he was already studying it, his spectacles threatening to drop off his nose end, as I bade him farewell. As I left, I realized it would be sensible to wait for the response from my District Office before visiting any other Anglican churches; if each had to go through this kind of formal ritual to gain insurance, I had to be prepared to present the councils with the necessary information – and on this occasion I had not been in full possession of that information.

I had learned from the experience, and as I rode home I began to mentally compile the necessary letter to my District Office.

Within a week I had their response. It was a well-presented folder outlining the costs, the cover and the conditions of a policy that could insure the roof of Lexingthorpe parish church against lightning strikes, fires, gales, thieves and other risks, and before I took it to the Reverend Redhead I made notes on the contents so that I could provide other church councils with the basic facts. In many ways, this was a blueprint that could be adapted for other churches, and indeed country houses or any other premises with vulnerable roofs and exteriors.

I made a special trip to Lexingthorpe with the document, found the vicar at home and presented him with it.

'Well done, Mr Taylor.' He peered at me over his spectacles. 'The PCC meeting is on the 17th as I mentioned. Will you call back to see me about the outcome or shall I ring you?'

'I don't have a telephone,' I told him. 'I am in Lexingthorpe quite regularly, so I'll call in after your meeting.'

'Good, I look foward to seeing you then.'

At this stage I had no idea who the members of Lexingthorpe PCC were, so I was content to leave the matter with the Reverend Redhead and, on the morning after the scheduled meeting, I returned to the vicarage. Once again his wife greeted me and took me into the book-littered study; once again the reverend greeted me over his spectacles, but then shook his head.

'So sorry, Mr Taylor,' he apologized. 'I've no news for you. The PCC did not debate the question of insurance. They ran out of time because the chairman's Labrador started to have pups, and he had to leave in a hurry. It will be on the agenda for the next meeting.'

'And when is that?' I asked, wishing to note it in my diary.

'Three months' time,' he said.

I left without having a coffee and without any positive news about this proposal, but made a note in my diary to check for any progress in three months' time.

When I returned three months later, the Reverend Redhead apologized once more. 'The PCC could not proceed with the question of roof insurance, Mr Taylor, because the budget had already been agreed and the matter of insurance premiums was not taken into account when estimating our expenditure for the coming year. The matter will be carried forward to the next meeting, in three months' time.'

My heart began to sink. I knew enough about committees and councils to know they seldom reached a speedy decision, and I was very aware that a camel is really a horse designed by a committee.

'I'll wait to hear from you,' I said, leaving the vicarage.

The moment I said that, I realized it was a mistake. If I left the matter in the hands of this council there would never be a decision, and I would spend far too much time pressing the vicar for one when none was likely to be forthcoming. However, I felt I had done what I could to ensure Lexingthorpe parish church did not risk massive loss through theft or damage to its roof. I suppose I could have repeated my calls on the vicar each time I was in the village, but decided I would wait for him, or his PCC chairman, to contact me.

In the meantime, however, I could approach other vicars, but I decided not to wait for the outcome of parochial church council meetings. Instead, I would leave brochures at each vicarage or manse, along with my business card, and would then follow up that action with a visit during one of my routine canvassing days.

It is fair to say that most of the vicars contacted me to express interest in insuring their church roofs and exteriors, not only against theft but against other forms of damage and, with some PCCs being more efficient than others, I won a few policies. But over the months I heard nothing from the Reverend Redhead of Lexingthorpe. Then, one Saturday morning, there was a knock on my back door. When I opened it, a large florid man was standing there, dressed in a thick tweed jacket and jodhpurs and carrying a whip. He'd clearly ridden on horseback to see me, although there was no sign of his horse.

'Taylor?' He almost snapped my name.

'Yes, Matthew Taylor,' I acknowledged.

'Gardner, High Hall, Lexingthorpe,' he announced himself. 'Chairman of the PCC, you've talked to our vicar about lead insurance for the church roof.'

'Ah, yes,' I said. 'Come in, Mr Gardner.'

I took him into the lounge and settled him on a chair beside the desk; he refused a drink of any kind, saying, 'Can't stay, got to be off, but as I was in the village, thought I'd call in.'

'So how can I help you?'

'Your idea of insuring the lead on our church roof is good, Mr Taylor, so I thought I could take out a policy for my house – the roof is heavy with lead, dammed vulnerable it is, too, out where I live. You'll be able to do something for me?'

'Yes, of course, I can fill in a proposal form right away,' I said, reaching for one that was lying on my desk – I could not miss an opportunity like this.

After we had completed it, he said, 'Now, this church business, the confounded roof insurance. My council is getting itself into quite a tizzy about it, they want it to include lightning strikes as well, subsidence, too, dammit, and I know that'll add to the blasted cost. Some councillors don't want to spend money on that sort of unlikely happening, they've a tight budget to consider for the next financial year. As for me, well, I'd settle for the theft business, deliberate damage and nothing else, but they ignore me, you know. Time was when chairman's word was law, but thought I'd pop in to explain the delay. We do wish to go ahead with some insurance, Mr Taylor, rest assured about that, but it's the detail we can't agree upon. Confounded committees!'

'We don't ordinarily cover things like lightning strikes, subsidence or earthquakes,' I told him. 'The policy I was offering to your church was really against theft and subsequent damage to your church roof or fabric, nothing more. That's all you need for basic cover.'

'Well, dammit, I'm glad I called. So insurance of things like earthquakes would cost a small fortune, eh? Not really relevant in this neck of the woods – I've never known an earthquake in these parts, and lightning strikes are mighty rare, too, although we do have a conductor on the church tower.'

'I'll have to check but we might not cover that sort of thing at all,' I said.

'And why not?'

'We don't insure against Acts of God,' I told him.

Eleven

'I was thrown out into the ditch when my
car went out of control, and I was found
there by a herd of cows'
From a claim form

During my first year in the Delverdale agency I had been
reasonably successful, and my accounts books
confirmed that. My income had increased steadily and was
far more than it would have been had I remained in the
butchering business or found work as a garage mechanic.
My list of new clients had grown, too, and I found the inter-
action with them much more interesting than in my previous
job, probably because my work involved people of every
kind and enabled me to visit them in their own homes.
There was also the social aspect, because I believed quite
genuinely that much of what I was doing was of help to
people; if nothing else, it made them think and plan for the
future.

With a steady income, therefore, and a secure profession,
complemented by the commission I earned both on new
business and renewals of existing policies, and with the
little bits of extra cash I could earn with my various side-
lines, such as the occasional motorcycle repair and sales of
wooden toys, I was giving serious consideration to the
purchase of a house. It was equally necessary, however, for
me to buy a car instead of using a motorbike. This was
becoming increasingly important both for business and
personal reasons – I could not transport both Evelyn and
Paul on the motorbike unless I had a sidecar fitted, and that

did not appeal to Evelyn at all! And, of course, there was the question of having the telephone installed, with its rental to be paid for out of my income. The question was – which should come first?

As we were heading towards the depth of my second winter, I must admit I did yearn for the comfort and additional safety of a car rather than the exposed, cold and often wet and dirty life aboard a motorcycle. The Premier would pay an allowance for use of the car in the course of my work, and from a domestic point of view I could use it to take Evelyn and Paul for outings at weekends. That would be a real treat for us all.

I knew that Evelyn wanted to learn to drive; not many women drove cars, but it would give her some independence and allow her to get into town for shopping expeditions. It might just be possible for me to keep the motorbike, too, which I could use for work on fine days, especially when Evelyn wanted to use the car. The thought of owning a car began to have more and more appeal, and although space was very limited in our cosy house, I began to think a car was perhaps more important than another house at that point. I could afford to buy a car, too – and I did not think I could afford to buy a house, even if the Premier offered very attractive mortgages.

Over the weeks, as I discussed things with Evelyn, my musings were gradually being hardened into a decision. There is no doubt that this was largely influenced by the discomfort and inconvenience of riding a motorbike while swathed in thick and dirty clothing in awful weather, but there was also the question of carrying objects such as my business papers, books and leaflets. That was not the easiest of matters aboard a motorbike, even if they did lodge in the panniers.

And, of course, there was the increasing number of things I took home with me after a day doing my rounds, such as goods bartered when people were short of cash. During the year, I'd taken home several rolls of wire netting, a pair of size five lady's riding boots with trees, a set of six ships' lanterns made from brass, umpteen pictures such as oils, water colours and prints, boxes of eggs, bags of apples or potatoes, lettuces and strawberries, a trumpet, violin and harmonica, two ships in bottles, a mantelpiece clock that didn't work, a Kodak box camera, an egg washing machine and a bird cage that would have accommodated a golden eagle. In some instances, I'd had to balance the objects on the petrol tank between my arms, which made steering rather difficult, and then, of course, there was the question of storage of such items once I got them home. The washhouse and lean-to shelter accommodated most of my treasures but as my collection of clutter (or saleable objects as I preferred to call them) increased, I was aware that a larger house, with plenty of sheds and outbuildings, would be a huge advantage.

I kept telling Evelyn that someone would buy these items in due course, that they were really investments, not rubbish, and that, as they had been accepted by me in lieu of premiums, I really must sell them if I wanted to capitalize upon their value. Because I'd accepted them in lieu of cash, their continued presence made me short of ready money, but I honestly thought they would eventually become antiques or collectors' items.

'You really should be more careful when you accept things in lieu of payment,' Evelyn would say each time I turned up with a peculiar object. 'I've told you before, I really do think people are using you to get rid of their useless junk, Matthew. I mean, who on earth around here will want that set of left-handed steel shafted golf clubs or those Italian linguaphone records, or even that Directory of Hampshire? And that saddle you brought home last week is for a narrow seat, and how many people do you know who could use that? I just hope no one offers you a live giraffe or an ex-army tank.'

'I did sell that egg washing machine for £2 10s,' I reminded her. 'I made a good profit on it, the premium I swapped it for was only £2, remember, so that kind of deal is worthwhile. That's what I mean when I say we could do with a bigger house, with more space to store things like that, and we need a garage for the car, but also if I take on repairs of motorbikes—'

'Matthew, you live in a dream world. How on earth can we afford to buy a bigger house, as well as buy a car, keep the motorbike and have the telephone installed? We've got to take things one step at a time.'

'Well, once I get known for selling good-quality objects, like those riding boots and golf clubs, we can get a bigger house with outbuildings, which will accommodate more high value objects like that. I could soon be running a useful sideline selling genuine antiques . . . and if I get a car I can fetch bigger things home, which means I can sell more and earn more, which would help us pay the mortgage when we get the house . . .'

'Remember what I said before? If we go for the car first, you will teach me to drive?'

'Yes, I said that, it was a promise. I've been thinking very hard about it all, and I think a car is vital to our plans, vital to everything else that follows.'

'All right. Forget the house for the time being. Concentrate on getting a car first. We have to start somewhere and a car is important now we've got Paul. It's all right me using the train when I go to Whitby or wherever, but the times can be very inconvenient and it's dreadful sitting in a cold waiting room or standing on windy platform, especially when Paul's tired and hungry.'

'Right, this all sounds fine by me.' I was pleased she was thinking in the same way as me.

'Forget the big house dream with sheds galore, Matthew; forget about your dream of being an antiques wizard. Just go out and get a car, but make sure it's reliable, make sure I can learn to drive it and that it's big enough to take the pushchair.'

'Yes, well, most cars are large enough for a family and they have good boots for luggage.'

'I think we should consider the telephone as well, and I mean now, as well as the car. Now that you're doing so well, with such good prospects, we should have one installed. It would be wonderful – I could ring my mum and friends and, let's face it, you must surely have discovered you can hardly run a business without one.'

Evelyn was extremely skilled at maintaining this kind of feminine pressure, especially when I turned up with things like a piano accordion, a set of chisels and a complete ten-year *Encyclopaedia Britannica* in twenty-five volumes, which I had to transport in relays because my pannier could only carry two at a time. But she was absolutely right. Definitely, a car was a high priority.

With a new sense of purpose, therefore, I visited all the garages in Delverdale as I made my rounds, and asked their owners to look out for a good used car, something suitable for my work and family, something reliable, cheap to buy and economical to run, bearing in mind the steep hills and narrow lanes on which it would be used. And it had to be large enough to take a growing family and all the accoutrements such as a pushchair and perhaps a carry cot.

It was early December when I called at the garage in Lexingthorpe to fill the tank of my Coventry Eagle, and the owner, Alex Whittaker, said, 'Ah, Matthew, did you ever get that car you were looking for?'

'No, not yet,' I told him. 'I thought I would have the pick of the bunch but there's not many around just now, not in my price bracket that is, I can't afford a new one.'

'Well,' he said with a smile, 'I've got one coming in next Saturday, part exchange for a three-year-old Hillman I'm selling. It might be just what you're looking for.'

'Go on, tell me!'

'It's an Austin 10,' he said. 'Nineteen thirty-six, but in real good fettle. It'll need taxing on December 31st, but it was fitted with a set of new tyres recently, and I replaced some new brake shoes five or six months ago, the plugs are new and I put a cylinder head gasket on myself when I did the brakes. The owner looks after it as if it's made of diamonds, and doesn't do a big mileage. It's a bargain, Matthew, in beautiful condition, and it's yours if you want it. First refusal.'

I asked the crucial question: 'How much?'

'To you, £45.' He smiled.

'Too much.' I shook my head. 'I can only afford £30 – that's what I've got saved up, but with tax and insurance even that's pushing things a bit!'

'You won't get much of a car for thirty quid!' he joked. 'More like a board with four wheels on it – one you'd really have to push!'

'I can do my own repairs and maintenance,' I said. 'If the body's in reasonable condition and I don't have to spend much on new tyres then I can cope. But £45? It must have gold-plated bumper bars for that Alex.'

'All right, £42 10s.

'£37 10s,' was my next bid in this battle whose progress we both recognized.

'Call it £40,' and he held out his hand, palm upwards, which I was supposed to smack with mine to signify acceptance.

'I haven't seen it yet,' I reminded him, without sealing the deal. 'How about taking my motorbike in part exchange?'

'No chance. You'll have to sell that yourself. Put an advert in the *Gazette*.'

'Hmm. Well, if it's in reasonable condition, £40 sounds realistic enough, Alex, with no part exchange. When can I see it?'

'It's coming in on Saturday morning, but if you want to see it before then it's at Castle Cottage, Ron Stockdale's place. He's coming in for the Hillman at half past ten, but remember you'll be seeing it in its raw state, Matthew. I'll give it a good service and a clean before it leaves here, change the oil and check over the brakes, points, plugs, fan belt and so on.'

'I'm due to call at the Stockdale's today,' I informed him. 'Their house insurance is due for renewal, and so is the car insurance, then Mrs Stockdale's been thinking about a life insurance for Ron. I might be able to do a bit of extra business there.'

'Well, can I be fairer than that, Matthew?' smiled Alex.

'The chance to see a car before it gets its beauty treatment from me.'

'Suppose I did a deal with Ron direct?' I countered. 'I'd get it cheaper, wouldn't I?'

'You would, Matthew, but it wouldn't have the benefit of a thorough mechanical check and a full service – and if I didn't take his car in, I'd have to charge Ron more for the Hillman, profit margins on both cars to consider, you see. So I think he'll settle for doing the deal through me – it'll cost him money not to.'

'I am a trained mechanic,' I reminded Alex. 'I could fix most things myself.'

'Forty quid it is, Matthew, if you get it through me, fully serviced. I know the car well, it's been around this village for years and years with hardly anything ever going wrong with it, except a bit of welding needed here and there, under the mudguards chiefly, and on the doors near the running boards. It's a real beauty, believe me.'

'I'll look at it while I'm at Stockdale's today,' I promised him. 'And I'll come back and see you afterwards.'

I was unable to discuss this development with Evelyn because I was too far up the dale to rush home – besides, she might have been out visiting friends or family. I wished I'd had a telephone at that point, but I had to make my decision now. I would go and see the car. It was early afternoon by the time I reached Castle Cottage, to find Ruth Stockdale in her garden, clearing away some dead vegetation from her borders. Ron was out, he'd gone to help a near neighbour erect a garden shed, and so she invited me in for a cup of tea and a scone with strawberry jam.

I dealt with the renewals – Ruth, a plump and jolly little woman with a head of thick fair hair, always dealt with the financial aspects of their domestic routine – and before I could broach the subject of the car she reminded me that she wanted to take out an insurance on her husband's life. Ron had been a sergeant major in the army, a career soldier rather than a conscript, and he'd retired at an early age with a good military pension.

He was now fifty-eight, she told me, and she felt she ought to take out some kind of life insurance. I pointed out the question of his age and the shortened lifespan of, say, an endowment policy, with its associated limitations, but told her such a policy was not impossible provided he passed an independent medical examination in addition to having a previous good health record and was prepared to pay the premiums, which could be substantially higher than those for, say, a man of thirty-five. I produced a proposal form, which I began to complete on her behalf, stressing that when it reached my District Office Ron would be contacted and asked to submit himself to a medical examination by a practitioner nominated by the Premier. She understood that and was happy for the arrangement to go ahead.

'Has Ron any illness that would affect something like a life insurance?' I put to her as I completed the form. 'If he has, Mrs Stockdale, you must declare it now and then one of the company's retained doctors will decide whether or not he is an acceptable risk.'

'No, he's as fit as he was when he was in his twenties,' she said. 'He never ails a thing . . . except he nods off to sleep in his chair at a moment's notice. One minute I'll be chatting to him, and the next he'll be fast asleep. Then he wakes up again and doesn't know he's nodded off.'

'A sign of advancing years.' I smiled. 'It happens to a lot of people.'

'Oh, it's nothing to do with his age, Mr Taylor, he's always been like that, that's why I want this insurance on his life.'

'You want him insured against falling asleep?' I smiled.

'When he goes fishing, yes,' she said in all seriousness.

'Fishing?'

'He goes fishing down on the Delver, Mr Taylor, he's in the Delverdale Angling Club, his main interest really, but when he sits down on his little canvas stool, watching his line and float, he's liable to go to sleep and fall off the stool. That wakes him up, of course, but my worry is that one of these days he'll pitch headfirst off his stool and land in the river to get drowned before he has a chance to wake up. I mean, there's some deep and nasty pools under those riverbanks, full of weeds and underwater roots. He could get tangled up and drown very easily. And if he goes I need some kind of assurance to see me through the rest of my life.'

'I'll pretend you haven't told me all this!' I told her. 'Look, to be fair, I think you should declare that your husband is liable to drop off to sleep without warning, and our medical experts will examine him to see if it is due to any kind of illness. Of course, we'll need his consent and signature to all this, but I don't think we should state on this form that he's liable to fall into a deep river. It's just as likely he might fall in front of a steamroller or drop off when he's driving – just say he falls asleep without notice.'

'Oh, well, whatever you say . . .'

And so I placed an endorsement on her proposal forms warning my District Office of Ron's unfortunate habit, and I knew they would ask their doctor to take that into consideration in deciding whether or not to accept him as a risk. Having explained all this, I turned the topic of conversation round to the car.

'Yes, he wants to get a more modern one, Mr Taylor. Whittaker's Garage will take the old one off his hands.'

'I'm thinking of buying it from Whittaker's,' I told her. 'I thought I might have a look at it before it goes in on Saturday – Alex has given me first refusal.'

'Oh, well it's been a very good little car, Mr Taylor, it's never been a moment's bother to us but Ron thought we'd better get something a bit more modern, now we're getting older.'

'That sounds very sensible to me.' I smiled.

'He has looked after it you know, all these years, polished it and cleaned it and kept things in very good working order.'

She led me to the garage at the side of the cottage and opened the door to reveal a gleaming Austin 10 in the customary black. It looked immaculate, with all its metal

197

polished, its chrome gleaming and its interior looking as splendid as brand new household furniture. The tyres were hardly worn and, as I wandered round it, I could not see a speck of rust, even if Alex Whittaker did think it needed attention.

'Start her if you want, Mr Taylor,' she invited with just a hint of emotion in her voice. 'The keys are hanging on that nail just inside the door.'

When I fired the engine, without even having to make use of the starting handle, it purred smoothly and beautifully; the exhaust showed no signs of being ready for replacement, and when she invited me to take it along the road to test the steering and brakes I found everything was perfectly adjusted and efficient.

There was no sign of wear on the steering, the brakes didn't pull to one side or the other and worked very efficiently, and neither the engine, gearbox or back axle had unusual noises coming from them. And although the bodywork seemed immaculate, Alex had been right – underneath there was just a hint of rust, which he would fix before it left the premises, but it was nothing to worry about. Here was a little gem of a car, one which had been lovingly kept for years and years.

'I'll be sorry to see her go,' said Mrs Stockdale after I had reversed into the garage following my run. 'But Ron feels he needs something that will mean a little less hard work. He's taken real care of Betsy, we've had her for fifteen years, you know, she's part of the family.'

'I am a trained mechanic,' I told her, hoping this would indicate that Betsy would have a good home if she came to live at our house. 'I would make sure she was well kept, looked after and loved – my wife will love her, I know that.'

'Does she drive?' asked Mrs Stockdale.

'No, but she's keen to learn,' I told her. 'I think it's useful for a woman, especially someone living in these remote areas, to know how to drive. We have a little boy, too, so we need something to carry him and his things around. I'll probably teach Evelyn myself. And I bet she calls the car Betsy, just as you have.'

'That would be nice,' smiled Mrs Stockdale. 'And maybe you would let me see her now and again?'

'Of course. I might come to your house in her most weeks, and you could come and pat her on the bonnet!'

'I would like that even though I never learned to drive,' she said in all sincerity. 'It was my job to polish her after Ron had washed her and leathered her. Ron always wanted me to learn, you know, he was quite ahead of his time for an RSM, but I'm far too nervous to handle something as powerful and fast as a car – give me a pedal cycle any time!'

I did not wish to start bargaining with this lady. Somehow, I felt it would be discourteous to start bidding for Betsy, reducing her to a mere commodity, and it would be difficult enough for Mrs Stockdale to say goodbye after all these years. I thanked her for her kindness and said I would tell my wife all about Betsy, and would then make the necessary arrangements with Whittaker's Garage.

Immediately upon leaving Mrs Stockdale I hurried to see Alex Whittaker and told him I would have the car.

'I thought you'd like it,' he said. 'You've got a real good one there, Matthew, make no mistake about it. Beautiful Betsy. See you Saturday then?'

'Forty pounds?' I confirmed, and held out my hand. He spat on his own right hand and slapped mine with it, the sign of an agreed deal.

At home, after posting Ruth Stockdale's proposal form for an insurance on her husband's life, I sat down with Evelyn and told her all about Betsy.

'Oh, it sounds lovely, Matthew. Aren't we lucky to find a car like that?'

'We are. It's nice when people consider us like that. I bet Mrs Stockdale cries when Betsy's gone,' I told her. 'But we'll have to cherish her, too, you know, and we've no garage.'

'There's one next door,' she said. 'It's empty, you can

use it. I spoke to Mr Browning only today and said we were thinking of getting a car, and he put the idea to me. He said he's never used his garage since he gave up driving, and he'd be happy for us to use it, Matthew, free.'

'I never thought of that!' I had to admit. 'I just assumed he had a garage full of something or other.'

'It's for the car!' Evelyn said with a flash in her eyes. 'Not that other stuff you keep bringing home! I don't want to do battle with a pile of junk every time we take the car out! And I don't want you using the garage for your trophies!'

'Fair enough, but I'd want to pay him something. It's only fair.'

'He insisted we don't pay him, and only asked that if he wanted any shopping getting and couldn't get up to the shop, we got it for him.'

'Well, that's no problem, we could do that anyway.'

'You can talk to him when you see him, Matthew, but he is very keen for us to make use of the garage, and I know his demands would never be a nuisance. I could easily get his groceries when I'm collecting mine.'

And so the deal was done. Because I wanted Evelyn to see the car and to be present at our purchase, we agreed to take the train to Lexingthorpe on Saturday morning, along with Paul in his pushchair, so that we could all experience the thrill of driving home in our new purchase. The car was taxed until the year end but I would write out a cover note and would insure it comprehensively for any driver so that Evelyn could learn to drive.

I also decided to take a small token of appreciation for Mrs Stockdale. I thought she might like to meet Evelyn and Paul, to see who would now be extending feminine care to her Betsy, but, in addition, I had a small model car that had been beautifully made by Eric Newton of Baysthorpe. It was an almost perfect replica of Besty, even down to the colour, and was small enough to stand on a bookshelf or mantelpiece. This would be our gift to Ruth Stockdale, and a permanent reminder of her beloved little vehicle.

On Saturday morning, as the train carried us along Delverdale towards Lexingthorpe, Paul played on the seat while Evelyn and I gazed at the wonderful scenery, marvelling that we were able to live and work in such beautiful surroundings and with such nice people. By twelve noon that day we had collected our car, paid for it in cash and given a tearful Mrs Stockdale her wooden replica. After this we took our first ride into the countryside, deciding to drive down to Whitby. We would find a nice café where we could have a celebratory meal.

That night, as we relived the joys of that day, Evelyn said, 'Matthew, I really think we should have the telephone installed, it would enhance your reputation as a successful local businessman, and it would be so useful for keeping in touch with people, like our parents and friends. It wouldn't be too expensive and the company would pay for some of the costs.'

'I've been thinking about it, too,' I said. 'I did think we should wait until we had a house of our own, but as we don't know when that will be perhaps we should do something straight away.'

'You'd save a lot on postage,' she told me. 'And it would stop a lot of running about, chasing people when they were out and so on, saving on your petrol ration. What's it cost in rental? Twelve pounds a year, a pound a month? It would enable you to earn more, and the rental's not a lot for a man with your earning potential . . .' and I saw the twinkle in her eye and knew she was referring to my hoard of unsold 'antiques'.

Within ten days we had a telephone installed, a large black instrument that sat on the sitting room window-ledge, and our number was Micklesfield 27. We rang all our friends and relations to announce our new acquisitions – a car and a telephone – and then I waited for the business calls to start arriving.

Nothing happened for a couple of days, and then one evening, around seven o'clock, the phone rang, its noise jerking Evelyn and me into instant activity, thinking perhaps our parents had had an accident or a friend had died.

But it wasn't anything like that. A deep male voice with a distinct local accent asked, 'Is that Matthew's insurance?'

Matthew's insurance! He'd asked for Matthew's insurance, not the Premier.

'Yes,' I replied with a certain pride in my voice. 'This is Matthew's insurance, how can I help you?'

'This is Featherstone fre' Lexingthorpe, thoo killed them pigs for us remember, well, Ah've just 'ad t' phone put in and thowt Ah'd better fettle some insurance, like Ah promised.'

'I'll see to it right away,' I assured him.